Albert Morris Bagby

Miss Träumerei

A Weimar Idyl

Albert Morris Bagby

Miss Träumerei
A Weimar Idyl

ISBN/EAN: 9783744797306

Printed in Europe, USA, Canada, Australia, Japan

Cover: Foto ©Andreas Hilbeck / pixelio.de

More available books at **www.hansebooks.com**

"Miss Träumerei"

A Weimar Idyl

By

Albert Morris Bagby

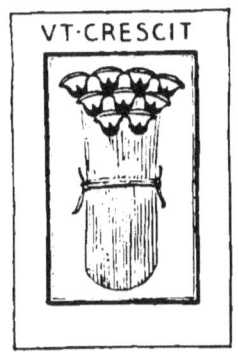

VT·CRESCIT

Boston
Lamson, Wolffe, and Company
6, Beacon Street
1895

"MISS TRÄUMEREI"

CHAPTER I.

Hidden away in a secluded oblong basin formed by the green hills of Thuringia nestles sleepy little Weimar. Its narrow, crooked streets, ill-paved and lined by plain two and three-story stucco-walled houses, are confined to the old town proper. Their monotonous irregularity is broken by the open, paved market and by the broadening of the way before the mediaeval city church, the theatre and post office, where an occasional bronze statue, public fountain or row of trees gives variety to the dreary stretch of stone and mortar.

Facing the incline a few paces to the left of the market, a proud, many-windowed palace with a great rectangular court and quaint detached tower—the principal landmark for the townsfolk—looms up on the left and lower bank of a brawling little stream dignified by the name of river. An ancient stone-arched bridge leads the approach to the military barracks, pleasure gardens and villas on the neighboring hill. Stretching upward from the palace, on both sides of the winding Ilm, the Grand Ducal Park, whose romantic nooks and seductive walks were planned by Duke Carl August and the immortal Goethe, terminates in the hamlet of Ober-Weimar. In the diametrically opposite quarter of the city broad, modern streets ascend gentle slopes to meet fields of waving grain, brilliant in summer with the crimson of the poppy and the deep blue of the cornflower. At the lower extremity of the old town a handsome new museum faces an imposing residence street which climbs the hill to the ornamental Empress Augusta Place before the railway station at the base of the lofty, forest-crowned Ettersberg. From the upper end of Weimar the magnificent Belvedere Allee, with its long line of stately villas facing the open park, leads to Belvedere, the summer home of the Grand Duke, on the hill a mile-and-a-half distant. Flanking the junction of the Allee with the city street, stand, like the pillars of a huge gateway, companion houses—square, thick-walled and singularly plain.

That on the left is noticeable as the former home of Franz Liszt. His apartments occupied the second, or top, floor. The lower rooms are still inhabited by the family of the court gardener. The royal garden, upon which the sole outer door of the house opens, is hedged from the public gaze by high dense foliage. It is reached by a narrow portal on the Allee at the corner of the residence and by a rustic gate at the end of a drive between long hot-houses, extending from the gravelled space about the entry door to the park. An old gabled tool-house with overhanging eaves, a clump of slender towering pines and a high latticed enclosure for poultry crowd close to the worn stone stoop at the further corner of the edifice, whose prison-like aspect is relieved by a sill full of gay scarlet geraniums in the dormer window under the low roof, and a row of tall exotics partially screening the neatly curtained windows of the ground floor. In this modest home the great Master Liszt received each summer up to the year of his death young pianists whose talents and accomplishments rendered them, in his judgment, worthy of his gratuitous instruction.

One June morning, not a great while previous to the date which deprived the world of this greatest piano-virtuoso of any time, Pauline, his faithful housekeeper and cook, sat, knitting, on the settle before the house. She was a comely, rich-complexioned brunette of forty odd years, with glossy hair, bright eyes and a tall, robust figure. Her feet rested on a low foot-stool; for no sun had appeared by ten o'clock to dry the earth, soaked with a heavy rain the previous night. As usual, at this hour, all was quiet about the Royal Gardens save the occasional rattling of a carriage over the stony, city approach to the Belvedere Allee, the low cooing of the pigeons on the roof of the tool-house or the shrill cackling from the hennery. The side gate clicked, and a tall spare form, with long flowing hair and broad-brimmed slouch hat, strode out from the cluster of bushy pot plants concealing the entrance.

"Good morning, Pauline."

"Good morning, Herr von Ilmstedt," responded the housekeeper in a pleasant voice.

"Has the Master risen?"

"No, he is still sleeping, but he has some important writing on hand and will receive no one this morning. He gave orders, in case any of the pupils called, to say that there would be a lesson this afternoon."

"Ach, so!" he exclaimed, with habitual celerity. At this familiar rejoinder Pauline drew down the corners of her mouth and professed such ignorance in answer to questions about the Master with which he plied her that he soon called over his shoulder, "Adieu!" and disappeared as he came.

"Of course," she muttered contemptuously, listening to his receding footsteps. "I knew he would be the first. Trust me to free this house of such bores! He imitates Herr Doctor in everything. I believe he would wear the coat of an Abbe, too, if he dared. Why, he has even begun to say 'Sapprement' when he is surprised at anything. Ha, ha, ha!"

"How is that, Frau Pauline?"

"Herr Je!" almost shouted the startled matron, jerking her face up to the light to meet a pair of glorious hazel eyes twinkling at her with amusement through a gap in the shrubbery on her right. "Du lieber Himmel!" she ejaculated impressively in further astonishment, at the same time dropping her knitting on the settle and rising in a stupefied fashion slowly to her feet. "Is it you, Miss Muriel?"

"See for yourself, Frau Pauline," laughed the pos-

sessor of the handsome eyes, stepping into full view
to receive a warm embrace and kiss for either
cheek.

Then Pauline, flushing with pleasure, held her off
at arm's length, exclaiming, "Mein Gott, how you
did frighten me, arriving in that ghostlike fashion;
but I am none the less delighted to see you!"

"I slipped in on tiptoe to avoid being seen by Ilmstedt. He came up the Allee just as I entered it from
the city."

"I sent him off in a hurry," added Pauline, with a
mocking grimace; "luckily, too, for now I can hear
something of you, while Herr Doctor finishes his
nap."

"How is the dear Master?" There was a touch
of tenderness and reverence in the inquiry which the
speaker's eyes reflected.

"Ach!" began Pauline, with a gesture more eloquent than words; "never in better health; but you
will see for yourself presently. Please be seated and
tell me everything." Lifting the half-knit stocking
from the settle, she placed herself in a listening attitude and resumed work.

"Very well, when you seat yourself," was the response; "you will take cold standing there on the
damp earth."

Pauline, flashing a grateful look, murmured
"Thanks!" and took the proffered seat on the further end of the settle.

Although long service and responsible position had
elevated her rank in the household, she never forgot

the restrictions imposed by caste, and tempered her familiar treatment of Liszt's divers pupils with proportionate deference. The few who addressed her respectfully as Frau Pauline, however, won her highest regard. Of these Muriel Holme, whom she called "Missey," ostensibly intending compliment to her nationality, but secretly as the easiest, most excusable word of endearment, was her prime favorite.

Indeed, nearly every one loved and admired Muriel Holme. Many another gentlewoman might have as shapely and graceful a figure and dress in as excellent taste, but few could compete with her in personal charm and magnetism. Though she was not handsome in the common acceptance of the term, the general contour of her features was refined and highbred, and her hazel eyes, not noticeable in moments of repose, the instant she spoke, darkened and gleamed with a quick intelligence which fascinated the beholder. She was of medium height, graceful and dignified in every movement. Her voice was agreeable and well modulated; in conversation it was not so much what she said as how she said it that held the attention of the listener. Her innate modesty caused her to undervalue her own attractiveness and tinged her utterances with a charity as delightful as it was rare. In her presence one knew instinctively the underlying strength and purity of her character. In brief, her personality was so marked that she drew to herself the instant sympathy of strangers without fully realizing herself to be the magnet. The ready tact which enabled her to deepen that first favorable impression was the key to her wide popularity.

"Well, when did you reach Weimar?" asked Pauline, knitting industriously, with her smiling eyes fixed on Muriel.

"Last night at nine o'clock."

"Again at Frau von Berwitz's? But of course," exclaimed Pauline, answering her own question, "you would never go elsewhere!"

"Never, unless Frau von Berwitz sent me away. It is the only place now where I feel at home, and she is like a mother to me. Ah, Frau Pauline," said Muriel impulsively, a sudden look of ecstasy illuminating her face, "I can't express the happiness I felt at once more opening my eyes in my dear, silent old gable room this morning; to see the pink and white roses hanging in great clusters about the windows, to inhale their sweet, fresh fragrance, to lie there and dream—waking—of nothing, only knowing peace, rest, contentment!"

Muriel's nature was a curious mixture of the artistic and practical. The inevitable result of yielding to the former tendency had influenced her early musical life. Therefore she sought now to gain a more tranquil mentality, and thereby a superior foundation for her own artistic growth, by a zealous and constant search for general knowledge. A noble, enlightened womanhood crowned her efforts; but, here, in the intensely musical atmosphere of Weimar, the luxury-craving side of her nature irresistibly demanded expression.

At so unusual an expression of feeling Pauline gave her a scrutinizing look, noticing for the first time a slight pallor in her face, from which the first deceptive flush of welcome was gradually fading.

"You have been overworking again, Missey," she said.

Muriel glanced up with all the old light in her eyes. "Oh, no," she exclaimed, in a convincing tone; "I never do that; I am always very well, ready for everything; but the heat and dust of Berlin have been intolerable the past fortnight. This place is a garden of enchantment in comparison." She dropped her head gently back into the rich foliage rising high behind the settle, and pressed the green leaves lovingly to her face. "I shall rest for a few days, if there is no present necessity for playing in the lessons. Are many of the pupils in town?"

"Very few."

"When is the first lesson?"

"This afternoon."

"Oh, then, I must begin work at once."

"Herr Doctor will not expect it if you need rest," said Pauline.

"He shall not know it, for, if he gives his time for the lessons, there must be some one to play. I intended being idle for a week. He wrote me from Aachen that he would not return before the twentieth of this month——"

"He surprised us all by coming back so soon," interposed Pauline, with a glance of inquiry at the upper windows.

"Ah, well, I can take my vacation later, when the class fills up."

"Herr Doctor has risen!" announced the house-keeper abruptly. "I hear him moving about."

Muriel's dreamy languor vanished instantly.

"Then I shall go up at once, before any one else comes," she said, rising with animation and readjusting her hat, which had been jostled by contact with the foliage. "Michael is there to let me in, is he not? Very well, then, I will see you when I come down."

CHAPTER II.

Mounting the four worn stone steps to the square entrance hall, Muriel crossed a threshold on the right and followed the winding stair to the landing before Liszt's apartments. The door of the music-room on the left, being unlocked for special occasions only, was, as usual, closed; the one before her stood open, revealing the length of the narrow ante-chamber where Michael, the Hungarian valet, faithfully guarded the venerable Master's privacy. At first glance he was not to be seen; but a strong odor of brandy, that sent her back apace, and a measured, rasping snore which made the walls of the little apartment tremble, told their own tale. A smile flitted over her bright expectant face at sight of a stout boot protruding from the green baize curtains concealing the couch at the end of the room. Hesitating an instant in uncertainty, whether to try to rouse the valet or to appeal to Pauline for assistance, she failed to hear the dining-room door swing noiselessly back. A voice, thick from sleep, startled her by calling, "Michael!" A snoring crescendo from within the curtains was the sole response, as the Master himself, following the tones of his voice, shuffled sluggishly into the room, glanced helplessly in the direction of the hidden couch, and then turned to retreat. He appeared very old at that moment, with his eyes still heavy from slumber. His thick mass of silky hair was dishevelled, and stood out from the grand rugged head in fluffy white cascades descending to his shoulders. Perspiration bedewed the broad, high forehead and deeply-lined, powerful face, now flushed from sleeping in a close room. His once tall, spare form was bowed with age and comfortably corpulent. His white-hosed feet were thrust into easy, heelless house slippers, and he wore a black suit with sack coat of velvet. A black silk neckerchief hung unknotted over a pleated shirt-front, which had been loosened at the throat. Muriel stood like a statue, fearing a breath would draw his attention to her. He glanced up, saw her, advanced a step and darted her a penetrating look, with a mien of severity which would have rebuffed a stranger. A glimmer of recognition ruffled the sombre expression of his face, and broke into a smile of pleasure as he extended his arms, exclaiming in accents still husky, "Is it possible! My dear Amerika!"

"Dear Master!" responded Muriel, affectionately, as he grasped both her hands, kissing her lightly on the forehead—his customary salute to ladies of good acquaintance. "I am indeed glad to see you once more."

"Ah, dear friend," he said, this time in German, "you are always very welcome; but step into the music-room a moment until I make myself more presentable. As you see, I am scarcely ready to receive a visit from a lady. I must be my own valet this morning," he added, motioning ruefully at Michael's boot. "Poor fellow! He is worn out. We came home late and he is just getting his sleep after

putting things to rights. But come!" Taking her
arm they entered the dining-room together, Muriel
asking if she should not summon Pauline to help him.

"If you will be so kind," he answered, disappearing
hastily through the bedchamber door opposite, as
if ashamed of his disorderly appearance. Muriel
turned into the music-room on her left—an oblong
apartment comprising the garden front of the house.
It was darkened, the atmosphere close and stifling.
The Master had been napping here, and the impress
of his head was visible on the white sofa-pillow at the
side of an inner door to his sleeping-room. Opening a window, Muriel called the housekeeper, after
which she rolled up the white blinds and spread
wide the other casements. Then beating the pillow
into shape, she gave a few hasty, necessary touches
to the general order of the salon to make it the more
attractive to the sharp-eyed host when he came in.
The Master was accustomed to these thoughtful attentions from Muriel, and never forgot to take verbal
notice. Consequently she had come to regard them
as her special privilege. It gratified her ambition;
gave her, in fact, inexpressible heart delight, for Liszt
had been not only the distant guiding star of her
earliest musical life, but now, in this new near rela-
tionship of teacher and friend, instead of falling from
his pedestal he had became an object of veneration
and love. Therefore she made a final survey of the
room with a satisfaction which she had frequently
craved since leaving it the previous autumn.

The general arrangement was the same as at her

first acquaintance. There, before the window over-
looking the Allee, stood the Master's broad, flat-
topped, well-equipped writing-desk, adorned with
conspicuous easel portraits of the Princess Wittgen-
stein and Hans von Bülow; a bronze dish of the favorite cigars—long, slender and strong; another for
collecting cigar tips, to be converted later into snuff
and the proceeds of the sale applied to orphan char-
ities—a common practice in Germany; a large, flat
shell for cigar ashes, and, on a sliding extension,
a cut glass decanter of cognac, a second one of water
and a half-filled tumbler of the mixture. A vermil-
ion silk handkerchief and a pair of spectacles lay beside a half-finished letter in the Master's unique chir-
ography. At the side of a comfortable leather chair,
there stood a spacious waste-basket, from which the
pupils culled, year after year, the choicest odds and
ends not already seized by the servants, who were,
however, quite willing to let them go again for a
financial consideration. A concert grand piano extended before the first two windows, and behind the
player's stool was a long sofa, on which new pupils
were prone to seat themselves in full view, after their
first performance, as on a judgment seat, and suffer
untold agonies of mind if they had not tact enough to
slip away. This clumsy piece of furniture and an
upright piano—used only to supply the orchestral
part to concertos—stood in line against the side wall.
Under the mantel, on the inner wall by the dining-
room door, stood a round card-table, where the pupils
deposited their music during the lesson; and a little

beyond, near the parti-colored portière, dividing the length of the salon, was another table laden with miscellaneous periodicals in various languages. Two handsome lamps ornamented the marble slab, upon which rested a gilt pier-glass at one side of the door to the bedchamber. Some bric-à-brac on a table in the further corner behind the writing desk, a pot of flowering begonias at its base, a few scattered prints and hanging casts along the white, gilt-corniced walls, a number of cherry-wood chairs, upholstered in maroon velvet, and a sober green carpet completed the furnishing of this room. The piano was stacked high with new music and books, mostly the gifts of authors, and to these Muriel had turned to read their written inscriptions and autographs, when the side door opened and the Master, now quite wide awake and spruce of appearance in a new black house-coat, stepped lightly into the salon.

"So you are again in the little nest Weimar for the summer! Not a bad place to come to, is it? I confess that I am heartily glad to be here once more myself." He spoke cheerily in his progress across the room, and as he put out his hands to give her a second welcome, Muriel said: "Indeed, dear Master, it would not be Weimar without you." He shook her hands warmly at this avowal, laughing in a jovial way, as if to imply: "I hear much of that sort of thing; but you, I know, are true, and I believe you."

If the spirit of the coquette were in Muriel she was quite clever enough to conceal it, for she impressed all alike with her sincerity. It was the secret of her strong hold upon the Master, surrounded, as he was, by a coterie of young artists, too many of whom tried to effect a way to his good graces by fawning servility. Her open-faced frankness and that rare dignity of character born of purity and self-respect, would have given her a first place in his esteem and affections had she been less gifted musically than she was.

"And while you are here," continued Muriel, smiling a response to his laugh, "it must be comfortable for you. There is too much draught in this room." Taking this opportunity to release her hands, she closed the first two windows before the Master, who had followed leisurely, could overtake her. "Thanks! Thanks!" he murmured, "but it is not necessary."

"Safer at any rate," Muriel replied, decisively, understanding him too thoroughly ever to question his preferences. "You are looking so much better than last year, dear Master, that I hope to see you remain so."

"I am better—I am better!" he exclaimed, hastily— the subject of his health never having become a favorite one with him, even under pain of the severest malady. "The visit to Aachen was most beneficial to me." At this admission he straightened up and walked briskly across to the reading-table.

"And a most enjoyable visit, too," he added, as an after-thought. "I met dear friends there whom I had not seen for many years. Here is the programme of a concert given by the local singing society." "In my honor," he might have added, but modesty forbade. "It was good—very good!" Lifting a gorgeously conceived fancy in white satin, with blue script, he held it up for Muriel's inspection. This began a recital of fresh reminiscences, which he pursued at length near the open window, glancing from time to time at the multi-colored glory of the garden against the verdant background of the park. The low cooing of the pigeons and the spasmodic music from the hennery, mellowed by distance, kept up a running accompaniment, which he seemed to follow with pleasure. Mild woodland breezes crept gently into the salon and faintly stirred the snowy locks of the venerable Master. Into his rugged, powerful face, so suggestive of the awe-inspiring gloom of mighty mountains, had crept a look of peaceful repose, which Muriel had not seen there since their earliest acquaintance. He had chosen this tranquil home for old age, and in her heart she hoped that he might live many more years to enjoy it. She was noting the Master's robust appearance as a subject of congratulation, not only to himself, but to the pupils who had borne the brunt of his irritability, aggravated by disease during the past two seasons, when the clicking of the Allee gate and the disjointed murmur of familiar, masculine voices below the window interrupted fugitive meditations. The Master heard the sound also, and, resting both hands on the stone sill, leaned forward to greet the young men, whose impending visit gave him apparent pleasure. "Ho, ho, August—Arthur—Holland!"

"Good-morning, Master!" rose in trio from below. There was a little peal of laughter at this sudden and unexpected appearance of the Master, to which he responded with a chuckle of amusement.

"May we come up?"

"Certainly, certainly!"

At this abrupt termination of their tête-à-tête, and foreseeing a series of visits for that morning, Muriel signified her intent to depart. "Play something this afternoon in the class. Anything that you will!" the Master said, accompanying her to the exit and giving her a parting kiss on the forehead. "So, aufwiedersehen, dear—Ah, ha, ha, ha!" The young men had rushed eagerly up the stairway, and their appearance at the salon door was the signal for a jovial reception by the Master. Muriel exchanged civilities with two of them, and departed unperceived in the midst of their animated chatter. She found their delinquent companion in the ante-room holding back the bed curtains with one hand and tickling Michael's nose with the forefinger of the other. The valet brushed his face with his arm, groaning dismally.

"Let him alone, Herr Arthur," said Muriel, involuntarily sharing his mirth. "The poor fellow is worn out."

"Ach, Fräulein! I am heartily glad to see you again!" exclaimed the impulsive tormentor, springing forward to greet her, and forgetting his victim for the moment. When Muriel started downstairs, Arthur entered the salon and left Michael snoring with renewed vigor behind the green baize curtains, serenely unconscious of the entertainment he had furnished.

CHAPTER III.

At exactly half-past three o'clock Michael, once more restored to his bowing and smiling alertness, stood in his little guard-room, ushering the first arrival for the lesson into the dining-room to await the Master's waking. He was a tall, heavily-built Hungarian of thirty odd summers, with a shrewd, determined face and authoritative manner. He could be disagreeable when occasion demanded, but to-day he was apparently as happy to see a renewal of the old life at the Royal Gardens as Pauline herself, whose cheery voice floated up faintly from her station at the house-door, whither she had taken her knitting in order to engage her favorites in a brief chat before they entered. Ten young people of both sexes straggled in, singly or in pairs, deposited hats and sunshades on a low chest of drawers and the valet's trunk, and disappeared through the side door. They were grouped about the dining-room, conversing in subdued tones, whenever Michael appeared at short intervals to softly open the salon door, take a surreptitious peep within and retreat with a shake of his head at the score of inquiring eyes turned upon him.

"He is oversleeping," said Ilmstedt, yawning and looking at his watch. "It is four, already." A slight noise from the other room reached his ear. He hurried out for the valet, who dashed precipitately through to the salon with noise enough to rouse the

Master, had he still been sleeping. Again all was silent; and Ilmstedt once more consulted his timepiece and yawned before Michael threw back the door with a flourish to permit the aged Master to advance to the threshold, smiling and extending his hands in a general greeting. The pupils pressed forward, each of the ladies receiving a kiss of welcome on the forehead as she slowly entered the salon. Standing by the grand piano, the Master then gave the gentlemen his hand, and some of them he drew forward to kiss his cheek. He had a cordial word and smile of welcome for each. Michael closed the procession, which filed past him out into the room, and, leaning over him, whispered in his ear.

"Ask him in!" was the audible response. A moment later, a tall youth with a white, scared face entered and neared the group at the piano. Having averted his head to speak to some one on his right, the Master failed to see the stranger trembling before him. Muriel noticed him sitting before the house as she came in, and surmised his transatlantic origin at a glance. Pauline said he was the bearer of letters to the Master, which he had delivered, without getting an audience, that morning. With compassion for her scared countryman, Muriel touched the Master's arm to gain his attention. In turning, he saw the new-comer.

"Ah!" he exclaimed, graciously extending his hand, "Bonjour!"

The American made a profound obeisance, and then, too embarrassed to speak, stood as if rooted to

the spot.   A voice whispered to him in English:
"Now is your chance.   Ask him if you may attend
the lessons.   Make haste!" it added, as the youth
parted his colorless lips in an ineffectual effort to articulate a sound.

"May I ask permission to——" he began with a
spasmodic gasp.

"Pardon me!" exclaimed Liszt, stopping the renewed conversation. to smile benignly at him and
turn a listening ear.

"May I ask the privilege of——" He could get no
further.   A sudden and awful silence reigned in the
room.   He could hear his own voice uttering the
most execrable German he had ever spoken ; he
could see before him Liszt—the Liszt whom he had
worshipped from afar as a supreme being—and sur-
rounding him a half-dozen celebrated young concert pianists all watching him.   The faces multi-
plied a hundredfold.   The room danced up and down
before his eyes.   His brain was in a whirl.   It was
the space of an instant, though it seemed to him an
hour, when the same friendly voice whispered softly,
this time in German, "—— of attending the lessons?"

"—— of attending the lessons?" he repeated mechanically.

"You may play something presently," said the
Master in a non-committal sort of way, and maybe
just to have a little innocent fun with the youth; for
he had, doubtless, summed up his good points at a
glance, being an extraordinary judge of men.

The bewildered petitioner felt himself swallowed

up in the ensuing hum of voices. Relieved to escape at any price, he found refuge in the corner, where he stood, unobserved, mopping the great beads of perspiration from his brow, and wondering who his unseen benefactor could be.

"Well," said Liszt, after a little, "Miss Muriel shall open the lesson, for she was the first to welcome me home this morning."

At this information Herr von Ilmstedt was violently attacked by his chronic complaint: insane jealousy of the Master's favors or attentions. However, he rarely spoke at such times; so no one gave the least heed to his sulky bearing. He was reserving his grievances for a more opportune outlet; consoling himself meantime with a cat-like glance at Muriel, as she accepted the Master's gallantly proffered arm and walked to the piano. Aside from this one blemish on his career in Weimar, Ilmstedt was a thoroughly good fellow, and his colleagues had many pleasant things to relate of him amidst other surroundings.

His adoration of Liszt dominated his entire being. Not content with the small personal notice accorded, he sought to ingratiate himself by cringing servility. Failing dismally. in that, he had bethought himself, the previous season, of the earlier, and in many instances forgotten, piano transcriptions of Liszt's. The leading music-publishing houses of Europe were searched, and the result provided Ilmstedt with a formidable list of compositions with which to wage war against the Master's indifference. He had the satisfaction of hearing many an exclamation of surprise, and

sometimes pleasure, from the gratified composer
when he played one of these in the lesson. At such
times his face grew radiant; but, did the Master venture to say a word of approval or offer his cheek for a
kiss, his joy knew no bounds. Could his bliss have
induced unconsciousness until the awarding of further favors, all would have been well; but, alas, it was
too evident that the Master cherished a warmer regard for certain other pupils. The visible proof was
anguish to him. Hence the puerile intrigues which
spiced the serenity of social intercourse in the Liszt
clique, though they were rarely of lasting harm to
others than Ilmstedt himself.

Muriel noticed the expression of his face as she
took her place at the keyboard; and as she recalled
the incident of the morning, related by Pauline, she
mentally calculated the extent of the harm brewing
for her in Ilmstedt's prejudiced imagination. The
thought was of short duration, for the Master, who occupied the chair at her right side, interrupted her by
asking her what she purposed playing.

"The three nocturnes, 'Dreams of Love,'" she responded, hastily placing the music on the rack.

"Ach, so!" he exclaimed, adjusting his eyeglasses
to examine a set of his own compositions, and turning the leaves slowly, as if to refresh memory with
forgotten harmonies. Then, leaning back in his
chair, he turned his face to Muriel, saying, with a
smile, which displaced his eyeglasses and sent them
dangling over his shirt front, "Well?"

Only those who had overcome in great part or

entirely the technical difficulties of the pianoforte were supposed to apply to Liszt for instruction. To have attempted a piece beyond one's powers would have meant banishment from the class. Failure was due rather to nervous fright than incompetency, for no pupil dared risk a performance without the most careful preparation. Therefore Liszt concerned himself with the artistic touches only. His remarks, though brief, were revelations to a pianist, and his illustrations at the keyboard of incalculable worth. The pupils stood about the piano, carefully noting every suggestion.

Accordingly, when the keys responded to Muriel's touch, there was an instantaneous hush in the room. She was not allowed to proceed far. The Master placed his hands on hers. "Not so," he said, "but this way." He repeated the fragment without changing his position. Muriel began anew. "Good—good!" he muttered encouragingly. In like manner they worked through the three pieces, sometimes slowly, again pushing rapidly forward.

Muriel was an individual player, having some original ideas regarding interpretation. The Master did not venture to repress them, unless radically wrong, though differing somewhat from his own conception of the compositions. He followed her with earnest attention, using the blue pencil freely in altering certain passages. Only once—it was in the first nocturne—did he take her place at the keyboard. Two of the oldest pupils, conversing in low tones at the opposite end of the room, instantly recognized the magic touch, and noiselessly joined the group of listeners. The Master was in one of his rare moods. He had slept well and was, moreover, happy to be again the centre of his beloved circle. It was home and family to him, and absorbed the tender affections of his declining years.

Liszt had the power of a necromancer, with the keyboard under his fingers. He could sway his audience with the emotion which inspired him. If it were his will to-day to witness an ethereal tenderness steal into the faces of those behind him, he succeeded. All thought of the fingers that produced such strains seemed to have fled their minds.

The softly murmuring undulations of the accompaniment became the tonal embodiment of man's complex inner self; the divine sweetness and beauty of the beseeching, caressing melody, the true voice of that ideal love which dominates and purifies life. In that moment every nature, however small and tarnished, translated beyond the worldly atmosphere of actual being, drank the pure ether of the over-soul. Each passed an exalted moment with his nobler self; but only a moment, for a sudden cessation of sound cut short loftier flights.

"There!" exclaimed the Master, rising abruptly, as if sufficiently convinced of his own unimpaired power to require no further test.

Ten transfigured faces grew blank. It was a rude shock to be suddenly precipitated from such empyrean heights. A dull look of disappointment settled in every eye. No one spoke as Muriel reluctantly resumed her place. Presently an impetuous youth of vigorous speech whispered to his neighbor: "I am in despair at such ill luck! I have heard him play an entire piece but twice in as many years!" But no one dared to request the Master to continue to the end, and the lesson went on.

"Bravo, bravo! you have played well—very well!" Still under the influence of the emotions awakened by her performance, Muriel responded, with true artistic sensitiveness, in an almost inaudible voice, "Thank you, dear Master," and quietly folded her music together.

A smooth-faced young fellow, standing on the outer edge of the circle, neared the piano. "Oh, ho, August!" ejaculated the Master, rising and folding him to his breast, "Why so late to-day?" The pupils fell aside to let them cross the room arm in arm. One of the younger girls grasped Liszt's hand in passing and raised it to her lips. A shadow, so slight that few detected it, darkened his face for an instant as he turned to see who it was. "Ah, Mariechen," he said, leaving with her the recollection of a kindly smile. Another step, and some one else had him by the hand. This time he held it closely to his side. Ilmstedt, his hair falling loosely over his forearm, was struggling to get his head on a level with their clasped hands. With a quick movement Liszt patted him on the shoulder, for he was in a good humor and did not wish to appear entirely unresponsive. Ilmstedt, lifting his head, gave it a sideward twist and smacked his lips at space. The hand that had lingered upon his shoulder was gone. Two other demonstrative pupils took warning at this and permitted their venerable host to promenade unmolested. Such scenes were frequent. None but the participants gave them heed.

CHAPTER IV.

"Amerika seems to have the floor to-day; suppose you play us something." Liszt stood before the young stranger in the corner, regarding him closely from under his heavy, protruding brows. "Did you bring anything?"

The words sent a chill to the heart of the American. Every nerve was paralyzed by the shock. His spirit seemed to have left its body for the time being. He heard his own voice reply calmly, "Yes, Master," and noted with grim amusement its hollow, far-away sound. Mechanically he unfastened his coat and drew a folded piece of music from the inner pocket. He had placed it there hoping to escape an invitation to play at the first lesson, if he came without notes.

"What!" exclaimed Liszt, in amused surprise, "have you brought such trash that you must needs conceal it?" The youth felt as if he were playing a part in a comedy when he heard himself respond diplomatically, "Nothing from the Master could be called trash!" He held the title page up for perusal as he spoke. Leaning forward at the same moment the Master recognized his own "Faust Fantaisie." Wild gusts of laughter caught him with electrical rapidity and shook him until his countenance assumed an apoplectic hue. The hilarity became general; Ilmstedt having the most uproarious attack, out of policy. This diversion brought the American to himself. Hot and cold waves tortured his body from head to foot. With the sensitiveness to ridicule common to mortals, he resented the situation; but there being no time for soliloquy, he made a ghastly effort to smile instead.

The composer was not displeased, it was evident, when he had recovered sufficiently to speak. "Well, that is trash! I played it myself, a quarter of a century ago, but now, every boarding school girl attempts it. It has not been heard in this room for many a day; but——" he pointed to the piano and elevated his shoulders slightly as he laughingly forsook the spot, "I am willing—play it!"

For various reasons, Liszt declined hearing certain compositions in the lessons. An unpleasant association with a too frequent or a notably bad performance of a piece, would often occasion its protracted exile. The pupils, therefore, were surprised at this concession to a stranger, and thought it an extraordinary mark of favor. Instinctively, Ilmstedt stationed himself at his side to turn the leaves. The Master gave the signal for the music to begin; and, forthwith, joined a small group at the extreme end of the room. He usually made the initial performance by a novice a rigorous test of ability, which decided whether the aspirant should go or stay. To-day he turned his back to the instrument to relate an amusing incident, called to memory by the foregoing scene —apparently deaf to other sounds. It seemed for a time as if the newcomer were to be accepted solely on the strength of the fun he had furnished, when Liszt, who, as usual, had not lost a note, made a wry face and uttered an exclamation of displeasure.

"He is nervous and terribly frightened, Master," said Muriel, hoping to get her countryman safely through.

"Oh, not that," he replied, with less asperity, "not that—he plays quite well—it is the piece. Trashy stuff—trashy stuff!" He approached the piano and motioned the youth to rise. "Well played," he said, lightly touching his shoulder, "well played. Now listen." Dropping into the chair, he burlesqued two pages of the piece and stopped. "That is too trivial," he said, tapping the notes here and there with his blue pencil; "that also—and that!"

"Ah!" he finally said, shutting the composition with derisive vigor, "no more of that! You played quite well," he added, looking up reassuringly at the embarrassed American, "but bring something else next lesson."

"May I, then, play the Beethoven Sonata, Op. 78?"

The Master did not hear the low-spoken inquiry as he turned to glance at the music which the pupils had deposited on the round table. Muriel answered for him in English: "I am sure he will hear that; but, if you will permit me—this is my third year here —I will suggest one of his own compositions." Her voice fell to a whisper, and she gave the youth a kindly look which he understood.

"How good of you!" he exclaimed, flushing with grateful enthusiasm and grasping her hand. "I am doubly indebted to you, for now I know who befriended me when I entered the room. I was terribly embarrassed. I didn't know just what was expected of me."

"Naturally. But you will feel differently when you learn the singular etiquette of the house. Then he is easy to approach, and a delightful companion. Every one loves him; but the majority also fear him, because they do not understand him."

"You think, then, he will let me stay?"

"Of course! Did he not tell you to play next lesson?"

"Yes—but——"

"Never fear," said Muriel, with smiling assurance; "you will not have to suffer another examination. You may congratulate yourself on having escaped so lightly. He will work with you next time."

"I have just brushed up his A major concerto," the youth said, reflectively; "will he hear that?"

"You couldn't make a better choice! The sonata will do for the following lesson. Let me introduce you to Arthur,"—Muriel indicated a beardless young fellow near by, whose resemblance to Liszt was universally remarked—"he made a tremendous success with the concerto on his last tour."

"Ah, yes; I read of it," murmured the youth, his constrained expression rapidly relaxing into one of genial surprise at this timely, disinterested assistance from an unknown and charming woman, a splendid artist as he had heard, possibly a famous one.

"Perhaps he will play the second piano part for you."

"Pardon me—I do not yet know your name."

"Rivington," he answered; "Walter Rivington."

Another hour passed pleasantly, the assembly proving more of a reunion—being the first of the season —than a lesson. A little Hollander, a great favorite with all, played in fine style a Chopin sonata which Liszt had selected from the table.

After repeated efforts to attract his notice to a certain transcription, and, finally, being forced to tell the Master that he had obtained it under peculiarly trying circumstances, Ilmstedt secured the last place on the programme. He received but brief instruction—one or two hints and a reminiscent remark. However, he was overjoyed to be even so short a time the object of attention, and rose from the piano with a proud flash of the eye at the scattered groups.

"We have not had much of a lesson," said the Master, beginning to show signs of weariness, "but it will do for to-day. Come again on Thursday. Adieu, dear Norway."

It was the same as at coming. A hand pressure, a courtly kiss on the forehead, an embrace—all proportionate to his regard for the pupil—and a hearty word for each.

"Aufwiedersehen, Amerika." The native country or city of a pupil sufficed for Liszt, when he forgot the family name. However, as they came to him from every civilized portion of the globe—sometimes with unpronounceable patronymics—such an omission was quite pardonable. "Something else on Thursday."

"Will you hear the A major concerto, Master?" inquired. Rivington, having by this time recovered something of his usual ease of manner.

"With pleasure."

"Thank you, Master."

"So," he repeated, extending his hand a second time, "the concerto on Thursday. Aufwiedersehen, Amerika!"

This evidence of goodwill might have rendered so emotional a creature as Rivington utterly speechless but for his gradual revolution of feeling since entering the salon. He made a hasty exit, seeming to tread thin air in his headstrong desire to reach an indefinite some one to whom he could open his heart. Outside the door he faltered. Naturally, his first thought had been of Muriel, and she was within. For a musical artist, he was as modest and unselfish as it was possible to be, attributing his good fortune entirely to her aid. To whom else, then, could he, alone and a stranger in Weimar, look for sympathy? Impulsively, he decided to wait until she came from the salon. Being a well-bred youth, he fancied she looked faintly surprised to see him standing, hat in hand, before her; and then, with exaggerated feeling, conscious of the audacity of his act after such brief acquaintance, he stammered:

"I beg your pardon for waiting here; but I—I——"

Seeing his confusion, and surmising the cause, Muriel said, in a manner to put him instantly at ease: "Why so? We are all like one family—a very numerous one later in the season—and it pleases the Master." They stopped in the ante-chamber for her hat and sunshade, but when they joined the other pupils on the stairway, Rivington needed nothing to arouse his eloquence. His cheeks were glowing, his eyes sparkling, when Pauline, who stood in the kitchen door watching them, interrupted his recital with this inopportune announcement: "The young Count has been waiting out in front this half hour, Missey!"

"Ah!" exclaimed Murial suavely. Rivington could not tell whether she was glad or not. She stopped to bid the housekeeper a hurried farewell; and then, he had barely time to say a final word of thanks, before they reached the outer door. "It gave me pleasure," she said, extending her hand to him as they halted on the stoop. "I cannot witness in others such suffering as I experienced at my first lesson in that room, if I can ease it in any way."

"You are never nervous now when you play?"

"Always! We fear each other; not the Master. But then," she said, looking naively down upon him, a step lower, "each must bear his turn."

"I am detaining you," he exclaimed, noticing her smile a recognition over his shoulder. "Good-by."

"Aufwiedersehen!" Muriel gave him a quick hand pressure and descended the short flight before him. Facing about, he saw a tall and handsome blonde-moustached lieutenant of infantry, his hand raised in military salute, striding, with ringing clank of sword, rapidly towards her. He was superbly uniformed in black, with scarlet coat facings, and burnished buttons, and a cap of the two colors. A phrenologist would have called his head the ideal type. Certainly there was the reverse of a warlike gleam in his clear blue eyes as they rested on Muriel's face.

Seeing the young couple move off towards the park, Rivington held the Allee gate slightly ajar to watch their stately tread; for Muriel walked noticeably well, even in comparison with the military gait of her companion.

He relaxed his hand; the lock sprang with a click. A feeling of unutterable loneliness came over him. With the image of the bepadded, richly apparelled nobleman in his eye, his gaze fell involuntarily upon his own gaunt undeveloped figure, in sober civilian's dress. Hastily averting his head, he saw the reflection of his dark, boyish locks in a closed side window of the house. With a flash of guilty consciousness, he sharply scanned the windows on the opposite side of the street. No one was in sight, and he turned ruefully toward the city.

CHAPTER V.

Facing one of the narrow crooked streets of the old city, whose notoriously bad pavement is here the roughest, an ancient, gloomy house towers conspicuously above the neighboring gables and tile roofs. The façade, with its round arched doorway at the left-hand corner, its first three rows of windows and the intervening patches of fruit and flowers in stucco, is of mediaeval origin, the high mansard roof having been added within this century. Many generations ago it was one of the grand residences of the little ducal capital. Even yet it retains an air of genteel respectability in this district of cheap shops and taverns. At one side of the great entrance, beneath the depending bell-wire which induces such a jangling within, is a low stone column.

Gretchen, the pretty, black-eyed maid-of-all-work to Frau von Berwitz, the mistress of the mansion, sits here on summer evenings after the tea things are put by, to exchange the news of the day with the neighborhood gossips, or—what is far dearer to her heart—to listen to the wooing of her blue-bloused lover Hans. With the stroke of ten from the clock in the castle tower she rises and says good-night—in the shadow of the arch, if to Hans, and with a pardonably greater show of feeling than to Frau Schwartz. The right wing of the heavy door opens and shuts to the discordant music of a tell-tale bell;

the key turns noisily in the rusty lock, and is not touched again until Gretchen appears bright and early next morning, with a huge wooden contrivance strapped to her back, to fetch drinking water from the neighboring public fountain. She hastens her footsteps; for before she serves the simple breakfast of coffee and rolls, many flowers must be sprinkled from the tall old-fashioned pump, standing, like a one-armed giant, with a cannon ball in his hand, at a corner of the open, paved inner court.

With the exception of the second story back, Frau von Berwitz occupies the entire four sides of the large parallelogram about which her ancestral home is built. The end and side wings, topped by high steep roofs with low overhanging eaves, have but two floors, the first being divided into storage and work-rooms. The doors and windows mark the only breaks in the rich growth of purple clematis which climbs to the open gallery on the front and left, and to the long row of tiny-paned windows on the right, humorously dubbed by Muriel the "Cloister." The rear end of the court is architecturally plain, save a low, round tower, with a spiral stairway, in the corner at the end of the gallery. At the end of this, an open passage, closed by a great iron door at night, leads under the "Cloister" to the private garden, a rectangular area at the side of the mansion and in the rear of a broad adjoining building. To the left, and on a line with this entrance, is the "Garden Salon," the cosy corner room of the ancient pile, with double glass doors, accessible from the court also, and beyond which a high stone wall encloses one side of the garden. On the side opposite the wall a row of bushy trees overhangs an old paling fence and obscures the view from neighboring private grounds. Along a box-bordered central walk roses of every hue bloom in luxuriant profusion; they shadow, on the one hand, neat little kitchen-garden beds, and, on the other, solid patches of pansies, pinks, marigold and mignonette. A gravelled terrace, lower by three steps and terminating a dozen feet above the back street, is strewn with tables, chairs, and settles in the protecting shade of some small trees at one side of a stone summer house occupying two-thirds of this level. By the iron railing surmounting the street wall, a dark flight of worn stone steps descends to the cellar of the building, which has an exit on the street.

The summer-house is supposed to be a portion of the ancient city wall, and more than seven hundred years old. Between two large deep-set windows, a broad arched entrance with double iron doors—its massive, oddly-shaped key a delight to antiquarians —faces the central walk. Without, rows of lemon, orange and fig trees, and clambering grape-vines partially conceal the time-stained walls. Within, the large square room is inviting and homelike. Pretty, light stuff curtains are held back from the entrance and windows; rugs cover the brick floor; comfortable wicker chairs surround a large, polished centre table; a superannuated grand piano, a capacious sofa, ottomans, and curious tables stand in relief against the tinted walls; and high up, terra-cotta brackets support busts of Carl August, Marie Palowna, and the present Grand Duke and Duchess Carl Alexander of Saxe-Weimar. Antiques of interest adorn the mantel and niches in the wall. Opposite the garden door a square opening in the inner wall communicates with a narrow corridor which runs across the street front of the house and·is lighted by small, old-fashioned windows. An easy couch is the only practical piece of furniture, the place being stored with the childish toys of other days.

It had been a sort of play-room since time unknown. There was a period when it saddened the mistress of the mansion to enter here. Years have passed since then. Now she selects it for a quiet after-dinner nap, before joining the few intimate friends who usually drop in about four o'clock for a cup of coffee in the large, cool room, with its inviting outlook on the garden. In all Weimar no more secluded, restful spot can be found. This deep-cut, deserted back street rarely resounds to the rumble of wheels. An occasional footfall on the cobble stones seems to rebound and lodge somewhere under the eaves and on the high stone walls. At such times a servant in a lordly modern residence which fronts the cross street, peers down curiously from her second-floor kitchen opposite the old garden. This constant surveillance was annoying to the frequenters of the terrace until Frau von Berwitz set up a movable canvas screen. In acknowledgment, the servants continued their observations less offensively, though every whit as industriously as heretofore, by stealthy peeps irom behind the neat muslin curtains.

Lounging near the open window, long after the mid-day dinner, the cook was apparently oblivious to the doings of her neighbors. She was careful not to turn her head when a trim little woman, whose face was shadowed by a plain brown chip hat, tripped daintily along in the shadow of the wall; but, she said aloud "Only Fräulein Panzer!" Stopping at the summer-house door, Fräulien Panzer produced a key from a black satin reticule on her arm and let herself in. A moment later she came scrambling out on the terrace, the soft little white curls quivering about her face as she looked furtively over her shoulder down the dark stairway. The cook, drawing back, laughed immoderately and beckoned to the butler.

Finding herself safe out of the dungeon, Fräulein Panzer proceeded serenely around the corner of the stone house, without having spied the cackling pair over the way. The little lady's clear blue eyes opened in astonishment when she saw the curtains drawn at the portal. "Nah!" she exclaimed under her breath, standing still with one foot on the step, and looking over her shoulder at the mansion.

It was a sleepy afternoon; a tardy sun had just broken the rain-clouds, and nature had scarcely begun to awake from her two days' lethargy. The steep gable was covered by green vines to the comb of the roof. Heavy shrubbery concealed the entrance to the garden salon; but at the open windows of Muriel's apartment, soft white curtains, in their picturesque setting of pink and white rose clusters, were gently stirred by the breeze. The place was silent, and apparently deserted: not a sound from the street penetrated the stillness.

Some trees by the side wall threw long shadows before the summer house where Fräulein Panzer irresolutely stood. A deep-drawn sigh from within made her suddenly chirp like a startled bird and face about. Lightly springing up the step to the threshold, she thrust aside the hangings and began to laugh gaily, thereby rousing a matron in sober black who had been sleeping soundly in an easy-chair by the centre table. Slowly lifting her face, the matron regarded her visitor through half-opened lids, and said drowsily, "Ah, Clara, I thought it was you."

Fräulein Panzer continued to laugh without explaining the reason, as she looped the curtains back and let a flood of light into the room.

In her circle of intimates Fräulein Panzer was known as the "Canary Bird." Her voice was mellow and flute-like; and her quick sideward twist of the head, her light tripping step, her merry sprightly ways, made the name seem very appropriate.

These two women, the closest of friends since childhood, and differing only three months in age, were direct opposites physically and mentally. Frau von Berwitz, the elder, had an erect, full figure, just escaping corpulency, brown eyes, snow-white hair, drawn in rippling wavelets gently back from a broad, high forehead, and an agreeable contralto voice. In her youth she had been a famous beauty, and, until the end of her brief married life, a reigning belle at the Grand Ducal Court, where her husband filled high office. They had spent money so freely that his death left her in possession of only a very limited income in addition to the home which she had inherited. Thenceforward, she confined herself to the education of an only child, a girl of five, revisiting the scene of her former triumphs twice, at most, during a winter. With Teutonic foresight, she took into her family, to learn German, one or two young foreigners who could afford to pay liberally for so rare a privilege. Thus she was enabled to provide the requisite dower, without depleting her own little hoard, when her daughter, at twenty years of age, became the wife of an army officer stationed at Berlin. Through acquaintance with the latter, Muriel found a home at the old mansion on first coming to Weimar.

Frau von Berwitz was still comely to behold. Like her friend, her step was elastic, her eye undimmed, and her smooth firm skin tinged with the hue of health. A passing glimpse of these two, just entering on the final decade of life, inspired pity for the unhappy Ponce de Leon in his fruitless quest for the fountain of youth. They certainly had learned the secret of its source. Frau von Berwitz looked like a middle-aged Juno as she slowly rose from her chair and gazed from her stately height on the merry little woman flitting to and fro in the doorway. As she noticed the long shadows in the garden, her drowsiness vanished in a twinkling. "Can it be so late?" she exclaimed, in surprise. "It seems but a moment since Muriel went out.

Having inquired the latter's whereabouts, Fräulein Panzer tossed her hat upon the piano, and ensconcing herself in an easy-chair opposite her hostess, began work on a half-knit brown stocking. She was of a type seldom met, who entertain others merely by their presence. One followed her movements as one follows those of a bird, with lively, sympathetic interest, for their vivacious spontaneity was more eloquent than words. She conversed well. She knew also when to keep quiet, though that in no wise accounted for her present silence. Her laughing eyes were directed to the long, slender needles swiftly alternating in the woolen loop; and an occasional twitch at the supply-thread, which caused the ball to flounce madly in the reticule on her arm, seemed to accentuate her unvoiced amusement.

"The last I remember, Muriel called 'good-by,'" Frau von Berwitz was saying, as she settled herself in her chair and took up some fine needlework. "Gretchen must have found me nodding when she came to remove the coffee service, and have drawn the curtains to protect my eyes from the light. Why do you laugh?" she inquired, glancing askance from her embroidery, which she held very near her face.

"To find it you, and not the ghost."

"What ghost?" queried the dowager, glancing amusedly down at her own ample proportions. "Wherein lies the resemblance?"

"Have you forgotten," said the other, "the tale old
Johann told about this house to frighten us children
from the garden when we annoyed him?" And together they laughingly recalled the dialect used by
the old gardener in recounting the legend of a former occupant of the citadel, a mediaeval knight,
whose gnädige Frau, in retaliation for his cruelty during her lifetime, was wont to moan at midnight behind the portière of his sleeping-room. Finally, one
morning, he was discovered sitting upright in bed,
his eyes bulging out of his head in a cold and glassy
stare—dead!

"Served him right," said Frau von Berwitz, drying
the tears of merriment which trickled down her
cheeks. "It's a duty every maltreated wife owes her
sex. So you thought me the returned spirit of that
unhappy woman! No; had I departed before my
dear, lamented Heinrich, it would have been unnecessary. Never did better husband live!"

"True," murmured Fräulein Panzer, resuming her
knitting, with the mental addendum: "An early death
would save many an otherwise lost reputation."

"No wonder I was restless in my sleep," continued
Frau von Berwitz more soberly, also taking up her
work; "we didn't have half enough last night. Muriel
and I sat chatting until—well, no matter the hour. It
was wrong of me, too, for the dear child seems far
from well."

Forthwith the Canary Bird dropped a favorite and
sweetly ringing note of interrogation: "Nah! What
is it?"

"Overwork, of course. Constitutionally she is strong enough."

"Overwork! Humph!"

"But, you know, Clara, her——"

"Oh, yes, I know. She is quite right. Every girl should, as she preaches, be taught some one thing well. But she is a great artist already. It seems to me that, with her princely income, she might take life a trifle less seriously."

"Precisely; but a woman of five-and-twenty is her own mistress; and if she will not, why——" an expressive uplifting of the shoulders completed the sentence. "I remonstrated about the lessons for this week, but——"

"I wonder if Fritz von Hohenfels could induce a change of tactics?" Fräulein Panzer covertly studied the effect of her words as her companion raised her head to respond.

"I am sure not! What an unconscionable time he has been about it, anyway!"

"You were not quite so positive when we last discussed it, my dear." In the delicate flush that swept over her face the speaker betrayed a personal interest in the subject which her words strove to conceal. However, she bent lower over her work, and the other failed to see her confusion.

"Nor was I, until last night."

"How so?"

"It came about in this way," began Frau von Berwitz, in that subdued, impressive tone which makes the hearer feel that, but for this opportune outlet, the pent-up news would explode the narrator; and Fräulein Panzer, duly convinced of it, rested on her knitting-needles—to borrow a nautical form of expression—in order to lose none of it.

"Muriel was laughing about a penniless nobleman in Berlin, who last week inquired of her banker the size of her letter of credit, and immediately threw himself at her feet with the wildest protestations of adoration. She is reticent concerning herself, as you know; so, seeing my chance, I cautiously referred to Count von Hohenfels as a possible suitor for her hand. What do you suppose she said?" Fräulein Panzer could scarcely repress her impatience, in her eager excitement to hear faster than could be told, when Frau von Berwitz hesitated before giving the reply: "Sufficient unto the day is the evil thereof!"

"Oh!" chirped the little Canary Bird sharply, startled and wounded by this unlooked-for thrust at her beloved godson; she straightened portentously in her chair, only to relax her features again and utter a mollified "Ah!" at Frau von Berwitz's concluding sentence.

" 'But I hope he won't spoil our friendship by any such nonsense,' she went on, not alluding to him after, and declaring it her purpose never to marry."

Fräulein Panzer's brows expressed incredulity; her eyes, hope.

Observing this, Frau von Berwitz hastened to explain. "Ah, but she meant it! Listen! It was just five years ago yesterday that she was to have married her brother's law partner, a young man ten years her senior. A fortnight before, they went with a party of friends for an afternoon's yachting. The vessel capsized. Of twelve souls aboard, eight were lost. He was one. She was picked up as dead by a rescuing boat. Fearful of the shock to her mind, her friends hurried her off to Europe for a change. In course of time she found consolation in music; so they left her here, and she has never returned home. There is, I believe, a compact that some one of them shall visit her annually during her absence. Both parents are dead; the brother and sisters are married, and have families of their own. They all offer her a home, and beg her to come; but—you know how it is."

"That I do! She is wise!" ejaculated the spinster, with fervency inspired by a momentary vision of a cosy home near by, where she constituted the family. "And?"

"In short, her heart is buried; she will never marry."

With a sympathetic moistening of the eye, Fräulein Panzer requested the details of the tragedy which had darkened the recent years of Muriel's life, accompanying the recital with a broken, low-voiced plaint like the distant song of a nightingale. "Oh, pshaw!" she interjected, suddenly recovering her buoyant spirits and resonant upper notes with the air of having parted company with a leaden ballast; "she will get over it, my dear. Never fear! I have studied her closely; and did I not recognize the growing want which prompts it, I should be inclined to laugh at her vague notions about spending her time and money for the

good of her country-people; or—for aught I know—
the entire human race, when she shall have completed her musical studies here."

"At any rate, Clara, she is terribly in earnest."

"True; but she is drifting like a ship without an
anchor, and must find a mooring sooner or later. Her
love has had a backset, and at her age, with her crav-
ing for affection, it will revive some day, in overwhelming intensity. Then the entire human race will
have to abdicate for one man."

"Candidates are persistent enough already."

"Better say fortune-hunters! Some sincere man
will win her heart, though, before she knows it; and
then she will frankly admit her present delusions."

"Maybe!" remarked Frau von Berwitz skeptically,
"but only a more powerful will than her own could
accomplish that."

"Surely Fritz von Hohenfels has given us proof of
——"

"Ah, well," Fräulein Panzer began anew at an indication of a demurrer from the hostess, "where is there
another like him? He bears one of the proudest
names in the Empire, has a fine property, no vices, a
kindly disposition, is devoted to music; he is blessed
with rare good looks, and is, moreover, madly in love
with——"

"Sh! There is some one coming," came the warning from Frau von Berwitz, and none too soon, indeed, for a moment later Muriel Holme and Count
von Hohenfels appeared before them.

CHAPTER VI.

Count Friedrich von Hohenfels was consecrated—body to the army, and soul to music. The former very much against his own will, and the latter expressly against that of a stern parent. In his early youth he had been bold enough to petition his unloving and unloved paternal relative's consent to an artistic career. To crush this plebeian desire, young Fritz was promptly hurried into a military training school and forced to swear eternal allegiance to an army life on penalty of his birthright. But defeat, instead of smothering the flame of his ruling passion, only fanned it to a brighter inward glow. Its outward gleam, however, was sternly repressed as incompatible with the bold, combative spirit of a soldier. With a morose purpose to fulfill to the last degree the letter of his agreement, he even avoided prominence in the simple musical relaxations of his own circle. He maintained a reputation for good comradeship only by spending an evening or two each week with his convivial military brethren, listening to the regimental band at Werther's garden or at the Armbrust. None of them knew of the rapt hours he spent at his piano in his own secluded apartments in an unfrequented street, voicing in music the changeful, turbulent emotions of his intense nature. The longing for sympathetic, human response became, at times, almost unbearable.

Living in this way, within himself, without inti-

mates, he met Muriel Holme at coffee at Fräulein
Panzer's one afternoon, early in the first summer
of her stay in Weimar. On that memorable
occasion, while he listened wearily to platitudes, the
hostess carelessly informed him that Miss Holme
was one of that brilliant circle which he longed to
cultivate and dared not—the Lisztianer! Hohenfels
felt his heart give one sudden thump, and instantly
the young gentlewoman before him appeared as if
invested with Pandora's charms. She, on the contrary, placidly and almost immediately, took her
leave, as if it were the most natural thing in the world
to be a Lisztianer.

After a decent interval of two days he paid Frau
von Berwitz, a friend of his mother's since childhood,
a long-delayed visit. The summer grew and waned
like a dream, to him at least; and when Muriel
Holme had departed for Berlin, he awoke to the
knowledge that her presence was necessary to his
happiness. Never before had a woman's face come
between him and his piano. Hitherto he had
thought of marriage in a vague, disinterested sort
of way, as something ultimate and not relevant to
the present. As day followed day, and the old
routine of life forced itself upon him, the sense of
his loss fell like a pall over his soul. He missed
the musical afternoons and evenings in Muriel's practice room in the old rose-garden; and, above all, he
felt the absence of her refined companionship.

He had said at parting, "I shall miss you terribly!"
without realizing the full import of his words.

His hatred of the parade-ground had been temporarily subdued by a happy summer, but now it came back with redoubled force. He was convinced that his hitherto unendurable lot would be endurable with her near. This fact he communicated to his father. As was to be expected, the latter thought otherwise, and threatened to disinherit, him should he marry an American. His cousin, the heiress to a rich estate joining his own lands, the last of an ancient and noble line, was just coming of age. Overlook such an alliance? Never! Fritz was obdurate. His father thereupon promptly curtailed his allowance, which had never been generous—the pay of a lieutenant in the German army is a mere pittance— to a sum barely sufficient to keep him clear of debt, until he should accede to the demand. Under this iron rule he was powerless to swerve from the prescribed groove.

Another summer, and with it to Weimar came Muriel Holme. Again he knew happiness; living in the present, blind to the future; never speaking to her of, love, only hoping, fearing, praying, he shrank from wording his thoughts.

Reward came unexpectedly. Three weeks previous to the opening of this story the tyrannical father died suddenly of apoplexy. Fritz passed a fortnight at Hohenfels administering the estate. The terms of the will exacted of him but one distasteful condition—a military life. At last he was free to woo the wife of his choice, but not in Berlin, for duty called him imperatively to Weimar. Muriel had a

short note from him announcing his bereavement; in
his impatience of delay he would have written then
and there of marriage, had his mother not dissuaded
him. "She would rather hear it from your own lips,
if she loves you," she had said; and, after deliberation,
he thought so too. The next day Fräulein Panzer
received a long letter from the Countess, the contents of which she kept secret. Her reply was a
telegram of three words, "She comes to-night," sent
to Castle Hohenfels the day of Muriel's return to
Weimar.

When the Count met Muriel after the lesson at
Liszt's, it was with difficulty that he curbed a strong
impulse to hold her to his breast and whisper a tender "at last!"

"How did you learn of my arrival?" she asked as
they neared the rustic gate.

"Bernsdorf told me on the parade-ground—had
seen you passing the guard-house. The minutes
seemed hours until I was free to come to——"

Muriel's music slipped from her grasp, and the
Count was compelled to lift it. "I will carry it," he
said, as she extended her hand.

"Not in that uniform," she replied, with appreciation of German military customs, and carrying
her point. He stopped once more to open the gate,
and as they passed into the park, a boy of twelve, going in the same direction, overtook them. "Ah,
Hermann," said Muriel, pressing his hand cordially,
"is it possible to grow so tall in one year!" She prat-
tled with him in this strain through the park, across

the town to the very door of the old garden house. Hohenfels' face was scarlet with ill-concealed vexation as they bade the child adieu and ascended to the terrace. Then he observed the prying eyes across the way, and, turning the corner of the summer-house, heard voices within. Another moment, and they stood before Frau von Berwitz and Fräulein Panzer. The latter saw his discomfiture at a glance, and gave, by her infectious laughter, such a happy tone to the hum of general greetings that the cloud faded from his face. Muriel declined to be seated, saying she wished the Count to try her new piano, one of American make, which had been set up in her music-room —the garden salon—that morning, and she asked the others to join them there. It was her ruse to avoid a conversation, for she was more fatigued from the excitement of the afternoon than she would have admitted, in face of Frau von Berwitz's opposition to her playing in the lesson. Moreover, she did not purpose giving him an opportunity of voicing the sentiment which his eyes had expressed as they left the Royal Gardens.

"Presently, my dear, presently!" said Fräulein Panzer in response to Muriel's bidding, which the Count had heard with annoyance; but his face brightened as she subjoined, "we old women have something of importance to settle before we can come. Ah, yes, Fritz, I came near forgetting. Can you come to me about eleven to-morrow morning?"

"Yes," replied the Count, after a moment's reflection, "with pleasure."

Frau von Berwitz at once extended to both guests an invitation for tea, to celebrate Muriel's return. "Now run along, children, to your music." Fräulein Panzer recklessly flourished her knitting in the direction of the garden salon, and promptly resumed work.

Feeling that he had a powerful ally in his jolly little godmother, the Count sauntered up the garden walk at Muriel's side to a long rose arch, where a short path led at right angles to the broad open doorway of the music-room. It was a large square apartment, with a painted floor; gayly colored rugs dotting it here and there, like so many islets. There was a suggestion of the eighteenth century about the room; a suggestion due to the antique furniture in cherry and gilt, the wall decorations and two mirrors and some early Italian landscapes in quaint frames. The light was admitted through double glass doors in cool weather; the single side window, on a back alley, being curtained with brightly-flowered crétonne, like that which formed the portière. A new concert grand piano, enveloped, all but the legs, in a drab waterproof, occupied the centre of the room. "I detest those things," said Muriel, snatching the covering from the instrument with one impatient sweep, rolling it into a ball and tossing it upon a closet shelf.

"I never knew a pianist that did not," observed Hohenfels softly, as he raised the lid.

"Gretchen is more practical than aesthetic in her taste," she continued, unmindful of his words,

"Superb!" exclaimed the Count ecstatically, running his fingers lightly over the keys, then dropping into a simple, sustained melody, and ending the short extemporization with a tumultuous crescendo of powerful chords.

"Magnificent!"

"I like it," said Muriel, who had hung her hat on a peg in the closet, and was drawing an easy chair before the door, where she could look out on the wanton display of roses and inhale their exquisite perfume. "To my mind it surpasses any European piano."

The Count had risen and was coming towards her.

"Play me something," she said hastily, sinking into her chair; "it rests me when I am tired."

He stopped, hesitated an instant, but there was no disregarding the tone and look, and he reluctantly returned to the instrument. He thought she had fallen asleep, for her head leaned back and her eyelids were closed. He saw that every vestige of color had left her face, as unobserved he watched her delicate profile lined against the light, while his fingers wandered gently over the keys.

"Don't stop," she said, opening her eyes when the final notes died tenderly away under his touch; "nor feel obliged to play so gently on my account. Suit your own fancy, be it lively or subdued."

"H'm," the little Canary Bird was saying to herself, with some vexation, out in the summer-house, when Frau von Berwitz left her a few minutes to give an order about tea, "if Fritz wins here it will be through the medium of that piano. The boy must be crazy!"

Commenting thus, she gave the yarn an angry jerk, violently agitating the ball in the reticule, and, with compressed lips, did a deal of thinking before her hostess reappeared.

"Come, Clara," said Frau von Berwitz, starting to close one of the heavy iron doors; "they are expecting us."

"Maybe; but they don't want us."

"Think so?"

Fräulein Panzer burst into one of her inimitably musical laughs for reply. Frau von Berwitz, willing to be convinced, swung the massive door back again and took up her embroidery.

Gretchen found the two sitting here when she came a half-hour later to announce tea. She lingered a moment to close and lock the double doors, while the ladies went to summon the young people from the garden salon. The Count was still at the piano, and Muriel resting with closed eyes in her former position. After a second futile attempt to approach her he had been forced to yield to her wishes out of consideration for her obvious need of repose. Thus withheld, he sought by his art to express the sentiments which he might not utter in word; but the means were sadly inadequate, and Fritz had as yet received no response from the dear, pale face, which it had been his joy to scan steadfastly during the past hour.

Muriel looked up as the two ladies approached the rose bower. "Aren't you coming?" she inquired in surprise.

"We heard perfectly in the summer-house," said Frau von Berwitz. Muriel instinctively felt the answer to be a subterfuge, the cause of which she easily divined.

Upon leaving the room Muriel and the Count sought the stone court through a small brick entry, overtaking the two elderly ladies in the further corner by the great pump. Entering a dark corridor through an open arch three steps higher, they came to a triple-jointed stairway, on the second landing of which a glass door communicated with the Cloister; on the third landing two more doors gave access to living apartments of the household, and to the open gallery. Near one of the doors a porcelain handle, attached to a depending bell wire, bore "Von Berwitz" in black letters.

The faithful Gretchen unlocked the door with an oddly-shaped little key, which was strung like a locket on her neck, and admitted the quartette to a large, square vestibule, containing a long pier glass, several pieces of antique rosewood furniture, and a bewildering array of blue and drab Rhine pottery in various ornamental designs. The door to the drawing-room, the centre of the three family rooms across the front of the house, stood open, revealing a polished floor strewn with rugs; and, in marked contrast to the general appearance of the vestibule and garden apartments, modern appointments were visible everywhere.

It was a homelike suite, with the library on the left and the dining-room on the right, both visible beyond the graceful folds of heavy portières. Indeed, it could not have been otherwise than homelike under the artistic and practiced eye of Frau von Berwitz. Her large round tea-table, its spotless linen contrasting with a broad, low centre decoration of deep red roses, fairly glistened with its array of handsome china, cut glass and old family silver. As they all listened with bowed heads to a simple grace from the hostess, Hohenfels was hoping with the fervor of a hungry heart that Muriel might soon preside at his table—it should be just such an one—and thinking how fondly he would look into her eyes, lean forward and—the "Amen" came none too soon, for he could scarce restrain an impulse to slip his hand under the table and give hers a stealthy pressure.

At the sound of voices, a yellow canary, hanging in his gilt cage between the soft white curtains of the single window and just above a broad casement of scarlet geraniums, began to chirp pleadingly. He stood at the limit of his perch, his little head turning from right to left, gazing wistfully from his bead-like eyes on the silent company.

"Sweet—sweet?" answered Fräulein Panzer, in a voice as dulcet as his own, and so close upon the low-spoken "Amen" that everybody smiled. The little fellow puffed out his downy throat and broke into an overjoyous warble at this greeting, for it was the season of long twilights, and the quieting influence of slowly coming night had not yet subdued his spirit.

"Take him into the drawing-room, Gretchen," said

Frau von Berwitz, "or we shall not be able to hear a word."

A large, glossy black cat, looking very much like a fluffy silken ball, lay sleeping on a chair. As the maid lifted the cage over his head he opened a pair of topaz eyes, which gleamed with an eger, wicked light at sight of the tiny songster. With a noiseless bound he was on the floor, head up, every muscle alert, treading stealthily near the gilded prison. The bird fluttered uneasily against the bars, and Gretchen, hearing a frightened chirp, quickly raised the cage. "Sh!" came sharply from between her teeth, with a menace at the cat. The animal shrank back, but when Muriel cried out to him, "Come, Mime! Come my Mimechen," he needed no second bidding to spring into his mistress's lap and sit there blinking and purring loudly. As the meal progressed and attention was diverted from him, he slyly reached towards her plate, caught a piece of cold tongue in his claws and slipped to the floor.

Hohenfels, absorbed in the scene and envying the cat Muriel's caresses, was aroused by Frau von Berwitz's voice. She had finished pouring the tea from a little silver urn, surmounted by Lohengrin's swan, and was opening a sealed envelope which lay on her plate.

"With your permission," she said. "I have been anxiously awaiting this."

· Lifting her eyeglasses, she hastily read the letter, a look of glad surprise growing in her face.

"Carl will be here at one o'clock to-night," she said,

addressing Fräulein Panzer. Then turning to the others, "Mr. Stanford, an American whom I brought up is coming for a visit. He was only six and his sister eight when their father, a captain in the United States Navy, brought them to me. Their mother requested it on her deathbed. She was English, and had been educated here in Weimar. To be brief, they stayed with me twelve years, and, truly, I love them as my own. Helen was married to a physician in New York a year or so after their return. Carl went to Harvard College and became a lawyer. He spent a part of every summer with me until three years ago. This is his first trip to Europe since then. He reached London a fortnight ago on business of such a pressing nature that he was doubtful of visiting Weimar; but now he really is coming, and, I hope, for a long stay. I am sure——" Wishing them to like him, Frau von Berwitz checked the words of adulation on her lips.

Muriel and Hohenfels were both secretly vexed to hear of the approaching visit, though from widely different causes. In the first place, Liszt's early return to Weimar had frustrated the plan of recreation which her health demanded. Accepting that, then, as inevitable, she had resolved to avoid all social intercourse until such a time as the independent semi-open-air life at the old mansion should restore her to her normal physical condition. How would that be possible after the advent of a stranger? As a member of the household she would have to exert herself to be affable, and she was under too severe a strain already. What she needed was freedom, and apparently she had had the last of it. To-morrow would come this man, in whom she felt no interest. To be sure she had heard Frau von Berwitz mention his name occasionally, and there was a photograph of him in the library, which had not impressed her more than the picture of any other young man, though it was said to be a poor reproduction. At any rate he was coming at the wrong time; he would always be sitting in the garden, where, after a long practice, she liked to walk the central path, with her arms crossed behind her to expand her lungs. She was not especially opposed to his, but to any one's entering the household. She knew it would hamper her movements in every way. Her features, however, gave no indication of what was passing in her mind.

Presently the meal was over, and she was left alone with Frau von Berwitz. They sat a few moments conversing in the drawing-room; then, saying "good-night," Muriel started wearily down the Cloister. A long line of ancestral portraits on her right seemed so many living images pressing towards her in the dim light from without. Drawing herself together with a faint shudder, she tripped airily enough the rest of the way to her rose-embowered suite at the end of the corridor, just above the garden salon.

The moon was not yet up as she took a last look at the starry night. The garden below lay partially obscured in shadow, but its sweet, fresh fragrance filled the air. "To-morrow—ah, me——" she sighed, "it will be changed!"

CHAPTER VII.

The rising sun, streaming in at the open window, stole athwart Muriel's face by half-past six, and broke her deep slumber. She was invigorated by a long, undisturbed rest, and the first fresh breath of the early morning, freighted with the aromatic perfumes of the garden, acted as a stimulant to her senses. Impulsively she sprang up and went about a hasty toilet. Walking had ever been her favorite form of outdoor exercise, and was, in fact, the only one feasible at present. Thinking pleasurably of the walled garden where in the past she had roamed at will, secure from intrusion, she suddenly remembered the American who was to have come in the night. With a revulsion of feeling, she determined to go far over the hills beyond the river, rather than run the risk of meeting him in her private domain; but no, the barracks were up there, and she might meet Hohenfels, who was always out early. There was the Belvedere Allee though, lovely at all times, but never more so than at early morning, with the birds singing in the patriarchal trees overhead, the fresh, sweet odors rising from the flowering shrubs in the park, and the sunbeams stealing through the interstices of the foliage and dancing across the white, still promenade.

She slipped quietly out of the house, through the court to the garden. In a distant corner she espied Gretchen, who, watering-pot in hand, was closely followed by two little flaxen-haired, pale-eyed sisters who lived on the second floor back. Unsuspected, Muriel approached the trio.

"Mariechen," she called; "Mariechen, have you forgotten me?"

The younger of the two children, a baby of three, turned so quickly at hearing her name that she sat down in the gravel path. Elsa, the elder by six years, tugged vigorously and vainly at her hand to help her to her feet. "Get up!" she cried; but Mariechen only became the more abject, sinking her head lower and running her thumb further into her mouth.

"Mariechen!" remonstrated Gretchen, "shame! shame! The black man will get you if you act so. This is the kind Fräulein who has given you so many pretty things. Where did you get 'Schneeweiss and Röschen'? Ah, ha! And the big picture book?"

Muriel had gathered up the little maid and imprinted a kiss on the single clean spot on her tear-besmeared face, a mark of attention which made her kick and sniffle plaintively.

"Look! There comes the black man!" cried Gretchen.

Mariechen broke into a terrified howl, and squirmed so vigorously that Muriel, fearful of dropping her, had to put her down. The child clutched convulsively at Elsa's short frock and buried her head in its skimp folds, her chubby body trembling from tip to toe with nervous fright. Muriel delivered to the servant a mild lecture on the evils of false representation; and, after a second ineffectual attempt to win Mariechen's confidence, left the garden by the rear exit.

More than an hour had elapsed when she returned to find the breakfast-table spread under the protecting boughs of two bushy plum-trees just outside the music-room door; and, facing each other across the spotless cloth, her hostess and the gray-clad figure of a broad-shouldered man. Her first impulse was to turn back, go round the block, and come in by the front entrance. It would give her a chance to take a reassuring look in the mirror before meeting her countryman.

But it was too late to retreat. Frau von Berwitz had seen her; and nodded a greeting from the distance. What difference did it make, after all, she reflected, coming up the path. He was nothing to her and never would be. In fact, she wished him well out of the way for a fortnight at least. Was it, though, right of her to cherish resentment when it made dear, good Frau von Berwitz so blissful to have her foster-son there? Putting aside personal considerations for the moment, she gave herself a mental shake and stopped at the table.

"Muriel, this is Mr. Stanford. Miss Holme, Carl."

The young man quickly proved his six feet of stature, and Muriel, acknowledging the introduction, became aware of a blonde head and moustache, and two large gray eyes nearing the line of her vision. With no further notice of him, she sat down beside Frau von Berwitz and began to remove her gloves.

The abrupt silence, following the animated conversation which her advent had checked, gave her an uncomfortable sensation. Instinctively she turned to her hostess, who was regarding her bright color and quicker glance with a quiet smile of approval, unmindful of the embarrassing pause.

At Muriel's look Frau von Berwitz said kindly: "We were just speaking of you, my dear, as you came up."

"I don't wonder, when I was delaying breakfast so long."

"Not for that reason, Miss Holme," said Stanford, speaking for the first time; "Tante Anna was relating some very pleasant things of you which——"

"——Have prepared you to hate me, of course," she quickly, though pleasantly, interposed, giving him a bright look. "So much the better," she observed mentally, with a return of the old antagonism; "now he will leave the garden to me."

Something in the quality of his voice had given her a peculiar thrill. She only remarked its clear, ringing tones and admirable modulation, thinking he ought to sing well. So he did! Frau von Berwitz had once said so. She would bear it in mind. All this flashed through her brain as she lifted her eyes to his face.

"No," he replied, in firm, sonorous accents, a pure enunciation giving special significance to each word, "my mental digestion was too slow; your arrival is— 'pportune!" An affable smile parted his lips, barely revealing two rows of perfect teeth.

"His features are all perfect," she thought, regarding him with wonder. He is equal to any masterpiece of the sculptor's art. What a pity he is so handsome. I am always suspicious of handsome men. Fortunately his eyes and mouth protect him from any imputation of weakness. Probably there is some wickedness, though, lurking under the surface somewhere. Probably, too, he has plenty of conceit. But supposing he has; any self-respecting man must place a value on himself; even if it is too high, it must improve him."

But Muriel's spoken thought was only: "Ah, that restores my appetite."

"Then you have found one at last?" questioned Frau von Berwitz, taking her at her word and turning to Stanford. "Miss Holme has subsisted on music since her arrival. A good thing in its way; but not conducive to physical growth. Now, Muriel, I hope you purpose being reasonable by repeating that walk daily."

"I do," she said, reflecting in secret amusement on the cause of the pilgrimage, "since it resulted so agreeably."

"Where did you go?"

"Toward Belvedere! I met the Master coming from early mass as I turned into the Allee by his house. 'I will not detain you,' he said to Ilmstedt, who was with him. We were just at the gate. Poor Ilmstedt! It is such a pity the Master dislikes him! Off he went, looking miserably dejected, trying to smile an 'adieu' as he saw us start up the promenade. Pauline says he is at the house by half-past five, every morning, to escort Liszt to six o'clock mass. His devo-

tion is touching. The Master is too kindly to resent
it; but as Ilmstedt disappeared he said, 'A good fellow; but——" Muriel shrugged her shoulders, spread
her palms, and put out her under lip in imitation of
the Master.

"Meister went only a few steps further, saying he
had to work before breakfast—he rises by four, at
latest," she explained to Stanford—"so I returned
with him to the house door and then went my way."

"Had he anything special to say?" queried Frau
von Berwitz.

"Yes. Xaver Scharwenka is coming to-morrow for
a short visit."

"Ah? We must invite him here."

"Of course," assented Muriel; "I told the Master so.
He dines there at half-past one. I will send him a
note asking him to tea."

"Miss Holme has studied with him in Berlin for
five years," said Frau von Berwitz, addressing Stanford.

"Yes; as I went to take leave of the Master after
my first summer here, I requested him to recommend
a Berlin teacher for the ensuing winter; and he named
Xaver Scharwenka. I had been with him three years
already, though he did not know it, for he never asks
with whom we have studied, possibly fearing it may
have been in a conservatory," she subjoined with a
smile. "He hates them. Here, Gretchen," said Muriel to the maid, who was approaching the hostess
with a heavily laden tray; "let me serve the coffee.
I am not quite ready for breakfast."

Whilst Gretchen transferred her burden to the table, Stanford joined in the conversation.

"Is it not delightful, Miss Holme, this German custom of breakfasting in the open air?"

"Dear children," interposed Frau von Berwitz, with an impulsive gesture, "do speak your mother tongue! Don't let my presence deter you. I understand it quite well."

"Always unselfish, little aunt!" said Stanford, with a look of filial affection. The good woman raised her hands in mute protest; but he continued, "I like to speak German." His eyes appealed to Muriel for a similar avowal. She was filling a cup from a rare old Dresden china coffee-pot, and did not look up. "The happiest recollections of my life are in that language."

She suddenly caught his glance, which had strayed to Frau von Berwitz. "One is said to like best the language in which one has learned to speak love," she observed sweetly.

The other two laughed abruptly, and Stanford's face flushed slightly.

"Then I confess a preference for German," he admitted candidly. "I never knew the meaning of love before coming to Weimar. Father was always at sea; and my mother, who rarely saw us, was a nervous invalid until her death. We were left to an old colored nurse's care. Tante Anna is the only mother I ever knew. My heart was developed here in this house and garden. Nicht wahr, Tante Anna?"

"One or two?" inquired Grace, in an aside,

holding a block of sugar in the tiny silver sugar tongs.

"One, please," he answered, appreciatively recognizing another interpretation of her question.

Frau Von Berwitz's brown eyes were luminous with feeling as she said gently: "You were always like a son, Carl. I never knew any difference."

The adroit construction which Stanford had given Muriel's statement touched her readily responsive nature. As she looked from one to the other she realized for the first time the close bond of feeling uniting the two—for Frau von Berwitz was a woman of sense, who never paraded her heart's interests. All irritation at his coming suddenly disappeared under new compunctions of conscience. She saw herself, and not Stanford, the interloper. He had a prior and stronger claim on the place; and far be it from her to encroach.

With a determination to atone in manner for any wrong she may have done him at heart, Muriel was now all unselfish attention. The conversation drifted aimlessly for a time. Stanford declared the bread of Saxony, and of Weimar in particular, the best under the sun; and the wild strawberries, to which Muriel presently helped him, superior in flavor to all others. Frau von Berwitz laughingly attributed all this to his partiality for the old home; but Muriel stoutly supported his assertions, to the no small delight of the hostess.

A glimpse of Mariechen's tow-head appearing at the entrance for a stolen peep, induced a chance reference to the early training of the young. From this the conversation branched into the common school system and the duties of citizenship, and they soon found themselves deep in a discussion of American politics. Muriel surprised Stanford by her familiarity with affairs at home, after so long a residence abroad, and by her intelligent understanding of them. He responded with quick interest, and her eyes gleamed with enthusiasm as he gave expression to tastes and modes of thought similar to her own. It was an experience so rare that her whole being thrilled with the novelty of the emotion, and her calm, self-contained expression changed to one of spontaneous sympathy.

Frau von Berwitz, a silent spectator, had always recognized something beyond mere beauty in Muriel's face; she had seen it in all its changes; but now, for the first time, she was forced to acknowledge it enthrallingly handsome. Satisfied as to their congeniality, she smiled vaguely on the young people, without heeding a word spoken, mentally absorbed in the details of her housekeeping.

Stanford logically reverted to the foundation of things in each argument; following it systematically and comprehensively to the end; invariably gaining his point by a statement of undeniable facts.

Acknowledging, at length, his superior grasp of the subjects discussed, Muriel was content to listen and learn. She observed the delicacy with which he reverted to her incomplete arguments, presenting them anew with a lucidity and force which drew from her the oft-repeated comment: "He puts into words that which I feel, and cannot express." Clearly he was a man given to serious thought; one to work out the involved problems of life for himself.

A sense of her own crude mentality suddenly shadowed her happy unconsciousness of self. "Was he the kind of man to think this crudeness of hers due to any limitation of sex?" This thought was sufficient to set in motion the troubled undercurrent of her easily excited imagination, colliding at every turn with his.

Noticing her expression, Stanford abruptly terminated his discourse.

"But I weary you with all this talk, Miss Holme."

"Weary me?" she said, in a tone of puzzled surprise that she should have betrayed her wandering thoughts by changing countenance. "No; but an oppressive sense of my own ignorance does!"

She had unconsciously spoken with a noticeable shade of bitterness, and the next instant was all repentance to see him flash a look of understanding and half reproach.

Before he could reply, she hurried on, an apology in her tone: "Music takes all my time. It leaves me no strength for other serious study; and what little knowledge I gather, here and there, only helps me to realize my deplorable superficiality."

She was now thoroughly uncomfortable at the tone she had given their conversation. To her it seemed childish, as it must to him. She was dimly conscious that it was due to her overwrought nerves. Any wo̅ man might have spoken as she did. But by nature she was too candid to seek for a covert thrust in a courteous exchange of opinion.

Muriel was eminently combative. She was like adamant to the least unjust resistance; but she declined to conquer by strategy. Positive evidence of right was her only weapon of warfare. If she fancied her sex depreciated by Stanford, she was certain to set to work to undermine the supports of his belief, until convinced of her victory or her error. She needed no greater incentive to show her strength. Intuition, rather than reason, seemed to guide her at such times. At present, her first impulse was toward conciliation. Therefore, she was gratified to have Stanford meet her half way in his reply.

"But you know one thing—music—eminently well! That gives you a pedestal above the many. That assured——"

"A momentary assurance!" interposed Muriel, with a mollified laugh. "It is like the ballet-dancer standing on one toe. Let her neglect daily practice in the art, and she falls on her head. Ah, well," she continued, not caring to confide in him at their initial meeting. her plans for the future, "some people can subsist on hope. I shall try to gain some of their comfort."

"If it isn't Sophie von Hohenfels!" exclaimed Frau von Berwitz in amazement, breaking abruptly into their conversation; and rising to her feet she started down the path to meet Fräulein Panzer with a tall slender, elderly woman, in widow's weeds.

This interruption prevented any further discussion;
and Muriel was well pleased, for she felt that their
congenial footing was well established, though she
was still smarting under the humiliating opinion of
her sex which an indefinable something in Stanford's
voice or manner led her to suspect him of holding.

CHAPTER VIII.

Muriel took a stealthy peep at her watch, and saw to her surprise that it was half-past nine o'clock. One hour late for practicing! No matter. She had learned something by staying; most of all, that women were of inferior mental calibre to men, she reflected with grim humor. She didn't believe it; but, were it so, it was not pleasant to be told it.

She looked up. It was not possible to meet Stanford's honest, kindly eyes and harbor such thoughts. A delicious warmth suffused her entire being. How delightful the garden seemed this morning. Were the roses ever more beautiful or their perfume more intoxicating. See how the sheltering foliage traces delicate, flitting shadows over the immaculate cloth. One could almost taste the soft sunlit air, such a day as this.

Muriel had completely forgotten the danger which threatened her enjoyment of the place at rising-time. She leaned back heavily against the trunk of the tree and gave way to unalloyed contentment, as if to make the most of the minute or two left before the advancing trio joined them. Then she must excuse herself and go to work.

"Oh, vexation! That must be the Count's mother. It will never do to go running off the minute she arrives. My practicing, my practicing! I wonder how soon I can excuse myself? That is like unto the reception of the Prodigal Son. A cheerful greeting for a newly-made widow. I suppose Frau von Berwitz is congratulating her, if, as reported, she was being tyrannized to death by the old Count. Why, that is the way they used to call the cows at Pembroke Farm!" Muriel smiled faintly at the remembrance.

These last reflections were induced by the gyrations and vociferations of the hostess, who had flung her arms about the Countess with a laugh of welcome, and thereupon began hallooing in her right ear. Fräulein Panzer was dancing about them in a nervous, delighted way, excitedly shouting detached phrases in a high-pitched voice, so that neither of the women could be understood by Muriel and Stanford.

"I suppose I ought to toss up my hat and cheer lustily to make the reception complete," observed the latter, looking over his shoulder in humorous appreciation of the scene.

Fräulein Panzer, catching his eye, suddenly ceased her lively movements.

"Mr. Stanford!" she shrieked in the same high voice. "Herr Je! I had entirely forgotten that you were to be here in the excitement of the Countess' coming:" but she darted forward to meet him with a manner which amply atoned for the candid indifference of her words.

"It is worth the trouble of a journey just to have a German welcome one home," Muriel was thinking, as she watched the genuine heartiness of the reception so distinctively national; and she forthwith

marked one more to the score of her affectionate regard for the people whose hospitable country had so
long been her shelter.

Fräulein Panzer suddenly lowered her voice with
a little laugh as Muriel rose to greet her. "It proves
the slavery of habit," she apologized; "my friend is
painfully deaf, and we have been conversing for two
hours. I had to invent some excuse to get my
maid out of the house, as I didn't care to take her
into our confidence." And the little woman won-
dered what Muriel would have said, had she known
the theme of their discussion.

The latter innocently remarked upon the unan-
nounced arrival of the Countess.

"It was a surprise planned for Fritz and Frau von
Berwitz, my dear. The boy will know nothing of
it until he comes to me at eleven o'clock."

"My American children!" hallooed the hostess,
coming opposite with a flourish of her unoccupied
arm. Miss Holme—Mr. Stanford."

As Fräulein Panzer's nervous laugh increased the
confusion of tones, Muriel lost the Countess' low-
spoken words; their significance, however, was in-
terpreted by the warm hand-pressure and the cordial.
smile illuminating her refined features—so like her
son's, Muriel thought—as both lingered a moment,
standing. Muriel felt herself in sympathy with the
Countess and wished to see her eyes, concealed by
a pair of smoked spectacles. Her voice, too, was
agreeable, when given a chance to be heard in the
general conversation which followed.

"But you will join our party at Tiefurt this afternoon, will you not?" inquired Fräulein Panzer in a high key. "Of course, you'll go, Anna; and you," she added, with a smile at Stanford. "Fritz will, doubtless, come, tco, later."

"I fear it——"

"Nonsense, Muriel!" exclaimed Frau von Berwitz, interrupting her, "if you don't amuse yourself more I myself will go to Meister Liszt and tell him how you work at the expense of your health!"

"Very well, then," rejoined Muriel, with a yielding smile, "but I can't leave here until after four. I will walk out, Tante Anna, so make your plans accordingly; I prefer the exercise."

"So do I," said Stanford, hastily; "you will permit me to accompany you, will you not, Miss Holme?"

"How stupid of me," thought Muriel. "Now he will think I did that purposely." She darted a nervous glance at the three ladies as she said: "Don't think of it! I am accustomed to go everywhere alone about here. Thank you, but——"

"Certainly, it is just the thing——" ejaculated Fräulein Panzer. "And we old ladies will drive out." The next instant she would have been glad to frustrate that very plan, as Fritz came into her mind; but it was too late. Frau von Berwitz was saying, "Quite right, we will arrange the details at dinner."

"Muriel looked helplessly at Stanford and felt herself flush slightly as she said "Aufwiedersehen" to the company, and turned towards the mansion.

CHAPTER IX.

"Boom—boom!" pealed out the first octaves of Liszt's E flat major concerto, which, as a special dispensation, the composer had consented to hear the following day, saying, as he did so, "Its strains have long been silent at the Royal Gardens"; and, though Muriel had been careful to close the doors of her music-room, the roar of the ensuing crescendo passage made conversation with the Countess impracticable. Having, like the majority of pianists, an antipathy to being overheard at practice, Muriel was gratified to have Frau von Berwitz push open the double doors and say, "We are going to the front," as she led her guests away.

After two hours of concentration upon her work Muriel stood hatless in the bright, warm sunshine without, too absorbed still to divert her train of thought. Though wearied by countless repetitions of the many difficult passages of the concerto, she nevertheless rubbed and stretched her moist hands with an exquisite sense of joy in the feeling of mastery assured by their firm, supple grasp. The chime in the castle tower abruptly silenced the faint indefinable murmur rising from the little city. Muriel glanced at the painted table under the plum-trees. It was flooded with sunshine, and a last fragment of shadow cooled the broad threshhold of her music-room door. With a quickened gleam of the eye, as she thought of the breakfast party, she moved toward the central walk.

When she resumed practicing a half-hour later, Muriel was not conscious of having devoted the entire interval to thought of Stanford, nor that the combative spirit aroused in her and stimulating her weary muscles, was a mere desire to gain his homage.

Gretchen came at half-past one to announce dinner.

As Muriel crossed the inner court, she experienced a strange commingling of emotions, now that she was again to meet Stanford. The magnetism of his presence attracted her; his possible undervaluation of the female intellect made her dread to face him again, and the fact that she must conceal her own thoughts in bright conversation fell like a new burden on her weary shoulders. Her spirit shed tears of vexation. Whilst ascending the rambling stairway she acknowledged to herself, for the first time, that overwork had unnerved her. In a state of agitated uncertainty, ready to respond with either a genial smile or an easy indifference to Stanford's greeting, she entered the drawing-room.

He was alone, reading by an open window; but he immediately dropped his paper and rose to receive her, saying, "Your industry, Miss Holme, deserves the reward of a good appetite."

Something in his voice or his presence seemed to give her strength. Self was forgotten in the frank return of his genial look. "Thank you," she responded, with equal affability, "I think it must be the atmosphere of that charming garden. I can truly say, I always welcome Gretchen's summons to dinner."

"You are fortunate in having that ideal retreat for your work."

"Doubly so!" said Muriel. "You know the statute which regulates practicing?"

"I do not recall it."

"The city authorities have prohibited, under penalty of the law, the playing of any musical instrument in a room with doors or windows open on the street."

"Which makes music a hot-house growth in Weimar," suggested Stanford, offering Muriel a chair and resuming his former seat.

"Practically!" was the animated response, "for it is the summer time which draws so many pianists here. With the addition of players of every sort from the Orchestral School, every block in town would otherwise be rendered uninhabitable. It is hard, though, for the poor workers, who have to swelter through the midsummer heat. Only one restriction is placed on me in my garden salon. Owing to the proximity of the church, no music is permitted in our neighborhood during the hours of service, Sunday morning, from half-past nine to eleven o'clock. I knew nothing of this until one Sunday morning last summer, when a loud clapping of hands interrupted my practice, and through the back window of an adjacent house stentorian lungs proclaimed the law covering my offense."

"What! speaking German together?" Frau von Berwitz stood in the dining-room arch, fastening the portières in place as she spoke.

"I was not aware of it," replied Muriel simply; and she remembered having said to Stanford at breakfast: "One prefers the language in which one has learned to speak love. How silly!" she thought, with annoyance at the suggestion.

"Dinner, my children. Come!" Frau von Berwitz smiled at Muriel without speaking, as Stanford leaned over the table to put aside an exquisite centrepiece of freshly-cut roses, and trace, with his finger, the outlines of a faded figure which had been woven into the immaculate linen.

"The Fall of Babylon," said he finally, looking up with a smile of interest at Muriel. "My first and most lasting lessons in Biblical history were gained from Tante Anna's various tablecloths. They would make a regular picture gallery if put on exhibition. Tante Anna explained each to me as it chanced to appear."

"A biennial event!" interposed Frau von Berwitz. "To see my storerooms, one would think me descended from generations of weavers. I was left little else than products of the loom! Regardless of how it has been accumulating in the family, each bride brought with her bed and table-linen enough for her lifetime. Consequently my largest possession to-day is so much dead capital."

"And here is the date of its foundation," said Stanford, who had taken his place with the others at the table and was deciphering the dim figure "1710," which had originally been hand-embroidered in blue silk above a heraldic device in the corner of his napkin. "That is the oldest. Then comes the next generation, 'seventeen hundred twenty-eight'——"

"Seventeen forty-eight," continued Muriel, beginning to name them off on her fingers, "seventeen sixty-sev——"

"Quite right!" laughed Stanford, "I see you know them, too."

"And the pictures also," responded she. "We had 'Abraham offering up Jacob' at breakfast."

"Isaac, my dear!" exclaimed Frau von Berwitz, "not Jacob."

Muriel subsided with a merry laugh.

"Ah! That one I shall never forget," began Stanford, jocosely, "though I didn't notice it this morning. One of my earliest recollections is letting an overripe strawberry fall on Isaac. As table deportment was a feature of Tante Anna's discipline, I gathered it up, mashing it the more, of course, and then pushed my saucer over the stain. 'So Abraham did actually sacrifice his son, Carl?' inquired Tante Anna, promptly uncovering the spot with a significant look at me. I never forgave Isaac the harm I had done him!"

"I hope time has exonerated me, my son," laughed Frau von Berwitz.

"Judge of that yourself, Tante," said Stanford, lifting her hand to his lips.

In this genial atmosphere Muriel became lighthearted, and felt increasing satisfaction with her young countryman. Their acquaintance had progressed considerably, when Frau von Berwitz pushed back

her chair after dessert, and said: "Now, Carl, we
will leave you to your cigar; or, if Muriel does not
object to the smoke, you may come into the drawing-
room."

"Not in the least!" interposed Muriel, hastily, "I
rather enjoy the fumes of a good cigar."

"Thank you very much, ladies, but I have not
smoked for a year, and shall not begin again to-day."

"How so?" said Frau von Berwitz in surprise.

"I am trying an experiment," replied Stanford,
following them into the next room.   "I hope to at-
tain my greatest working capacity, and, therefore,
deny myself everything which might prove a hin-
drance.   I have not touched wine or liquor of any
sort for a twelvemonth, and take coffee for breakfast only.   Perhaps I shall have to change my rule
somewhat while in Europe, but only when courtesy
demands it."

As he did not dwell on the subject Muriel believed
him, and she unconsciously dropped out of the conversation in thinking how few men had the courage
and strength to live up to their better convictions.
It was some little time before Muriel recovered herself with a scarcely perceptible start, to rise abruptly
and say she must practice.   She was going, without
a reference to the projected excursion, when Stanford asked where they should meet to walk out and
join the others.

"In this room," she said, "at four:" and she passed
out thinking ruefully of the short time left for her
work.

CHAPTER X.

The extensive and beautiful royal park of Tiefurt, once the favorite residence of the Duchess Amalia, and now, through the grace of her grandson—the venerable Grand Duke Carl Alexander—free of access to the public, lies distant from Weimar about a mile and a half down the valley of the Ilm. It was here, on the greensward and in the shadow of grand old forest trees, that the plays of Goethe and Schiller were first enacted, near the end of the last century, in the presence of the assembled ducal court.

The ancient building, called by courtesy the "Castle," has degenerated into an abode for the small restaurateur who furnishes simple refreshment to the wayfarer, under the spreading boughs of a group of trees on the other side of the drive, and opposite the worn stone entrance.

As the first arrivals of the afternoon, Frau von Berwitz, Fräulein Panzer and the Countess dismissed their conveyance and settled themselves at the longest table available; Muriel and Stanford passed over the new stone bridge which faces the Ilm's falling waters below the palace in Weimar, and ascended a slight elevation to a fork in the road. The main branch, which turns and leads on up the hill, is soon merged in the splendid Tiefurter Chaussee which skirts, on the left, the "Webicht," a heavily wooded pheasant-preserve occupying almost the entire plateau. The other, a narrow carriageway, plunges abruptly into a lesser thicket and follows the river course through the low-lands.

"Which way?" asked Stanford, halting to look down the shadowy vista, and then at the canopy of fleckless blue above.

"The lower," said Muriel, divining his preference, and moving on.

"You are not afraid of the dampness?"

"Not in the least."

Her heart lightened by a feeling of security in his companionship, Muriel's spirits rose at the vision of the broadening grasslands, dashed with the varie-gated tints of a myriad flowers, whose delicate per-fume a day's sun had drawn from moist petals into the rain-clarified air.

"Isn't it delicious!" she exclaimed, fervently, turn-ing her face to the sun and closing her eyes as a boundless caress of all nature welled up from a heart full of thanksgiving to the great Unknown. She won-dered at her happiness; why had the world never be-fore seemed so beautiful to her? She had taken this path many a time. She knew every depression and turn in it; the enclosing hills were her friends.

"It's Weimar," she said aloud, answering her own silent questioning; "dear Weimar!"

Stanford watched her with a smile on his handsome face and began plucking the blue cornflowers peep-ing out the long grass. "Kaiser-Blumen," the Ger-man likes to call them, for they were the favored of the beloved old Emperor William I,

Muriel pulled her hat further over her face and looked down.

"I sometimes feel that it must hurt," she mused, watching him snap the stems.

"But it does not withhold you from wearing them?"

"No, thank you," she laughingly added, taking the proffered flowers and fastening them in her dress. "I am cruel enough for that."

They passed beneath the lofty, handsome railroad bridge of stone, and following a short cut across the meadows to the right, came into the hard white Tiefurter Chaussee where it descends between long rows of cherry-trees to the valley. On a terrace above the street, a popular inn and embowered garden, the "Felsenkeller," looked across the fields to its vine-enshrouded rival, "The Rosenkranz," planted on the perpendicular further bank of the Ilm, where the waters are lashed into foam as they leap noisily over the milldam in the shadow of Tiefurt.

The Chaussee bridges the stream where its turbulent flight has sobered down into a dignified gait; and, just beyond lies the defunct-looking hamlet.

There is a great stone wall, interrupted by a broad entrance with massive gates thrown back; but, instead of the green turf, gorgeous flowers, and patriarchal trees of the grand old park, an ancient farmyard unfolds its paved length.

As Muriel and Stanford cautiously sought a footing between the opposing lines of oddly-fashioned hayracks, carts, and tall milk-cans outlying the quaint low buildings, a pea-hen, promenading the tall inner wall alongside the second gateway, called attention to her brilliant plumage by prolonged and discordant vociferations.

"Ach, that terrible fowl!" cried a high-pitched musical voice in the distance. "I would rather hear a fog-horn."

"Fräulein Panzer!" said Muriel, with a hearty laugh; and as they confronted the beauteous vista opening up before them, the little spinster raised her head to shout again in the ear of the Countess, who sat between her and Frau von Berwitz, and espied them coming down the broad drive.

"Ah! Welcome, my friends!" she cried, with a sincerity which her oversight in aiding the two young people to come together italicized. "Now I have them under my eye," she reflected. "Use diplomacy, Clara!" Resigning her seat by the Countess to Muriel, she took a place next to Stanford, on the opposite side of the table.

At the sound of new voices a ponderous waiting-woman waddled forth across the drive to take the order.

"That is the charm of life in Germany," exclaimed Fräulein Panzer, glancing over her shoulder at the stolid visage. "Coffee for five—in a hurry—Hanchen, dear!—you can always get refreshment of some sort, everywhere. Last summer I had such an experience up in Christiania!" The little woman paused in her knitting to raise her hands and roll her eyes at the overhanging boughs. "I had stopped there two or three days with my brother and his wife on our way to the North Cape. One morning, after breakfast, a gentleman to whom we had a letter of introduction invited us to accompany him up a hill celebrated for its view. The way was endless, and my brother almost a ton in weight, so we stopped often to rest and chat. About ten o'clock I began to get hungry, but thinking we would soon reach an inn, I said nothing about it. After a time, I grew actually faint. Again I consoled myself with a vision of an imminent refreshment stand, for the hill was a popular resort. We plodded on and up. When I was ready to drop with fatigue, we caught sight of a Greek-looking house on the summit of the eminence. 'Almighty Father!' I gasped, stopping short in the path, 'I thank Thee from the depths of my—heart for that restaurant!'"

"'Restaurant? Where?' Our guide looked naively up hill and down.

"'There!' I whispered, breathlessly.

"'That is not a restaurant,' said the Swede, 'it is merely a lookout built for the comfort of pedestrians.'

"'What! a lookout? A lookout? Oh, I see,' said I, calming my fears somewhat by the thought, 'the restaurant is close behind it.'

"'No,' answered he, quite indifferently, 'there is nothing of the kind on this hill.' Well," resumed Fräulein Panzer, after a bit of ludicrous by-play, "we went without food until we reached our hotel again at two o'clock! Ah, the coffee!"

With the steaming beverage in hand, and followed by a dull-faced maid bearing a tray of cups and saucers, Hanchen was powdering the gravel under her spreading feet. Frau von Berwitz prepared to do the honors by producing a paper parcel of homemade cake from her embroidered bag and arranging it on a plate. "A necessary precaution," she explained, "one can't depend upon getting it here."

Groups of women and children, who had walked out from Weimar, enlivened the scene at intervals, and then disappeared amongst the foliage. Suddenly a score or more boarding school misses, with two elderly teachers following the buzz of their voices, came from the park.

Making a concerted swoop on the scattered chairs, they gathered about some long tables which they had joined in line. The combined efforts of the two attendants proved unavailing in this emergency. Accordingly, five or six hungry pupils had a merry time racing to the castle and back with earthen jars of sweet milk or bonnie-clabber, which was ladled out by one of the teachers.

In the midst of this hurry and scurry, a trio of erect, brilliantly uniformed young officers marched with clank of sabre and spur out through the great gateway and towards Frau von Berwitz's table. Fräulein Panzer, who had been expecting them, sprang up with a cry of welcome, and, after they had greeted the other ladies, she introduced Stanford to Count von Hohenfels, Lieutenant von Jahn, and Lieutenant von Bernsdorf.

"Just enough to discourage general conversation," she reflected gleefully, as von Hohenfels seized the vacant chair beside Muriel at the further end of the table. "Bernsdorf has a voice like a calliope. Anna must give him her place next the Countess and sit at the other end; then I think I can manage things." This arrangement relieved Muriel. The sustained effort attending a prolonged conversation on rambling topics with the Countess had taken from her cheeks all the bloom which the walk from Weimar had given; therefore, von Hohenfels found an appreciative listener to his animated flow of words.

Stanford was discussing Goethe with Herr von Jahn, who dabbled somewhat in literature as a recreation from military life, when he sprang suddenly to his feet and threw up his arms with a shout of warning.

"Halt, man!" he cried, darting at an aged workman who had come out of a side path concealed by the shrubbery, and was pushing a wheelbarrow before him. The laborer stood still in utter bewilderment. Stanford bent over and lifted a tiny object out of a rut, almost from under the wheel of the barrow.

"There," he said quietly, in a tone of relief. "Of course you couldn't see it. All right!" He passed a small coin to the man, who tipped his cap and moved wonderingly on without speaking.

"What is it, Carl?" inquired Frau von Berwitz, relaxing an anxious countenance.

"A young bird. See the little fellow. He is just from the nest, and doesn't quite know what to make of it all." And Stanford tenderly stroked the ugly little creature, who, finding himself subjected to such unusual attentions, began to show signs of uneasiness.

"All right, little one; try your wings, if you like," said he, watching the bird as it fluttered away to an adjacent shrub and sat there panting from fright and exertion.

Stanford's spontaneous act had removed any possible constraint following from a first introduction, and a more genial warmth pervaded the entire company.

Muriel was a smiling observer of the general awakening, though until she heard his voice again she gave no heed to what was being said, for her mind was occupied with Stanford's tender consideration of the brute creation.

"That workman recalls a character study, the portrait of a wrinkled, dried-up old man which I saw a year or so ago in America. The original was said to be the former night watchman in this hamlet."

"He lives here still," interjected Lieutenant von Jahn, with sudden interest, "and is regarded as quite a historical personage. The frequenters of this place often send for him to come over."

"Then let us do so," exclaimed Muriel: and she turned to question the obese hostess, who had taken her station near the table, with speculative intent to serve those carrying the longest purses.

"He works on the roads, gracious Fräulein, and will not be at leisure until after seven o'clock. If you are disposed to await the hour, I will send my maid to his cottage to summon him."

"Very well; and I invite you all to stay and take

with me the best supper Hanchen can provide.. The old man can perform for us afterwards, and——"

"We can walk home by moonlight," interposed Fräulein Panzer, at once delighted with the scheme, and foreseeing an opportunity for her godson. Indeed, her vigilance never once relaxed, and when Muriel turned from giving some orders about the supper, before joining the party for a stroll in the park, it was Count von Hohenfels who stood waiting for her.

Fräulein Panzer, looking back over her shoulder, immediately hastened her steps with Lieutenant von Bernsdorf to overtake the others, who had disappeared on the way to a long, shady promenade at the rear of the castle.

With an instinct quickened by the Count's ardent manner, and the knowledge of his new-born independence, as well as by the friendly approaches of his mother, Muriel divined their pre-arranged scheme at a glance. She could not be displeased; he had known her long enough and well enough to declare himself were it his will; but just because of her decided, unaffected liking for him, and a premonition that he never could be anything more to her, the prospect of a change in their agreeable relations made her unhappy.

At that moment an indefinable impulse to command the situation possessed her. Almost any other man would have profited by her agitated bearing to request a word with her alone; but Hohenfels was the weaker nature of the two, and felt the force of her mood sufficiently to yield and follow almost submissively as she moved swiftly away. Fully aware that she read his present mind aright, he looked upon her action as a rebuff. Wounded and too bewildered to collect himself, he strode silently at her side, listening to her now steady voice as they came up with the others. He could not help attributing some of his misfortune to the arrival of Stanford. He had first heard his rival's name with a foreboding which pursued him until the hour of meeting; and at the table he regarded Stanford's every expression with a jealous thought of its possible influence on Muriel.

"Why will a woman show her first admiration for a man so unmistakably?" he mused, in recalling her glance at Stanford as he caressed the young bird. "She is hard enough to read when she is on her guard and he really wants to know her mind." He could hear the American's clean-cut, melodious utterances as he courteously guided the dim-eyed Countess in advance of the party: and at this attention to his parent von Hohenfels conceived a special hatred for Stanford. He had seen Muriel too often in the society of his comrades and her other acquaintances in Weimar to exalt any one above himself in her regard. Stanford was the first man, therefore, to arouse his jealousy.

Under the safeguard of other eyes, Muriel resumed her accustomed manner with Hohenfels, and by the time a circuitous route again brought them out before the castle, the gloom had lifted from his face.

With the certainty of a good fee in prospect, Hanchen had been so skillful in the arrangement of the

rose-bedecked table that Muriel, as hostess, was left
without a care. But again the Count's proximity—
for he had been quick to secure a place beside her—
and his unrelaxing devotion, created in her a growing
protest. Though she was not conscious of pre-con·
ceived intent, yet, when, in an opportune moment, she
made the conversation general, and knew that he was
alternately steeped in ecstasy and devoured by jealousy,
she did not desist from tantalizing him to the utmost.
She knew she was appearing at her best; therefore,
how could she refrain from attacking Stanford's sus-
ceptibilities, as the memory of her slight grievance
towards him flamed brighter.

It was this random bestowal of notice on the
American that maddened Hohenfels, for Muriel's
quick intelligence made eloquent each word and
glance. Her charm dominated the entire company.
Each hung on her speech and spontaneously answered her magnetic appeals.

She observed the dancing light in Frau von Berwitz's eyes, which had caught the reflection of her
own, flicker dubiously as she turned to the Countess,
who, in trying to understand, had rested an elbow on
the table and placed her hand behind her ear. The
good woman merely wondered if her afflicted friend
could hear; but it occurred to Muriel that these conventional German matrons might be critical witnesses of her—a young, unmarried woman's too animated bearing in gentlemen's society—and with a
sharp twinge of conscience, she abruptly inquired
for the old night watchman.

"He is in the house, gracious Fräulein," responded Hanchen, starting in an elephantine trot for the castle. She returned with a tall, shaded lamp, which illuminated the table and cast long black stripes across the graying driveway as twilight vanished in night; and when she stepped aside, the ancient Tiefurter stood, cap in hand, bowing a hoarse "Goodevening to the gracious company."

He was tall, spare, and very much bent, and clad in coarse working-clothes. Keen eyes looked eagerly forth from a beardless countenance, seared and seamed with years and exposure to all sorts of weather. As he awaited orders, he drew the back of one horny hand across his nervously-twitching mouth and scraped his foot restlessly on the gravel.

"Where are your paraphernalia?" asked Muriel, looking him over in surprise. The man didn't seem to understand, and opened his mouth to speak, when Lieutenant von Jahn explained to him in simple language that he was desired to appear in his old costume of night watchman.

"My home is near; I can fetch them in a hurry," answered the old fellow briskly, and, with an obeisance to the company, he trotted stiffly away.

The manner of his return was worthy the wit of a Thespian.

Muriel's party sat alone in the vast silence of the park. Their voices rose, fell, died away and rose again. Hanchen stood near to do their bidding. The castle was as still as the night itself. A large bat darted through the lengthening rays of the lamp, and

the light for an instant fought madly with great
black shadows in the drive. The swelling monotone
of a lusty horn rolled over the tree-tops into space.
From knoll and grove a thousand faint notes floated
back in response.

"The great hobgoblin summoning his clan," whispered Fräulein Panzer. "Look!"

In the dim light of the gateway he stood, a quaint,
bent figure enveloped in an ample circular cloak, and
wearing a high round-peaked hat; and as he rested
on his weapon of defense and attack, a long, halberd-
like spear, he raised aloft a short horn and quavered
in sometimes cracked, though not unmelodious, tones
a semi-incoherent stanza. Between frequent repetitions of the name of the Deity could be distinguished
an announcement to "Ye good people all" that the
clock had "struck nine." Advancing a few steps, his
horn again woke the echoes, and he repeated his
stanza to proclaim the stroke of "ten." Thus, by easy
approaches, the Lord was praised at each hour of the
night until broad daylight, for having permitted the
simple folk of Tiefurt to live so long.

"The sun is a bit late to-day," observed Fräulein
Panzer facetiously, as the old man stopped for breath;
but he could no more than pucker his wrinkled visage into the semblance of a smile.

"Bravo! bravo! Good-morning, old friend!"
shouted Stanford.

"Bravo! bravo! Good-morning!" the company
sang at him in gleeful chorus.

"Sit here," said Muriel, resigning her place at the

end of the table that he might be seen by all, and taking a seat which Bernsdorf provided for her by the Countess.

"Fetch him something he will like, Hanchen!"

"He don't want nothin' better 'an beer," remarked the woman, ambling off.

The foaming liquid unloosed the old watchman's tongue. "To a long life for the gracious company," he mumbled, holding his glass before his eyes; then, draining it at one draught, he handed it over to be refilled.

Stanford referred to his well-preserved lung power and unimpaired intonation in a way that the old man comprehended, and when each of the party added a word of praise, the octogenarian scarcely knew how to express his delight. A fresh glass of beer, however, gave him opportunity to drink again "to the health and longevity of the assembled gracious company," and then he settled down in his chair to be catechised.

"Did you know Goethe personally?" began Muriel.

"I had not the honor, gracious lady; but in my childhood I frequently saw him here in Tiefurt, and, indeed, on this very spot."

When asked to tell something of the great poet's appearance, the man seemed stupefied, but he vouch-safed, finally: "My third wife—now dead, God save her—had been for five or six years in her youth a housemaid in his service, and she related me much of him." What that information was, however, no amount of questioning could elicit.

Stanford asked him if he remembered being sketched by an artist.

"Yes," he answered vacantly.

"I have seen that portrait of you very far from here; the other side of the broad ocean, in America."

A vague stare was the only response, and he eagerly sought refuge in the third glass of beer and an enticing sandwich prepared by Frau von Berwitz. When he was ready to go Muriel slipped a gold piece into his rough hand. With a delighted angular bow, much scraping of the gravel, and a "God's blessing on the gracious company," the grotesque figure hobbled away towards the castle.

Notwithstanding Fräulein Panzer's manoeuvres, Muriel's plan for Hohenfels to escort his mother, and Stanford Frau von Berwitz, came about quite naturally, as they left the park with Hanchen calling a "fine good-night!" after them.

The rising moon had already whitened the broad, smooth Chaussee beyond the Ilm, and the cooling night air came over the lowland meadows in waves of delicious perfume.

What a long, but, on the whole, what a pleasant day it had been, thought Muriel, as she leisurely ascended the hill with Lieutenant von Jahn. At the entrance to the gloomy Webicht, Stanford smilingly offered her his left arm, and Hohenfels, looking over his shoulder, saw them walking four abreast. Once, in helping her lightly over a damp stretch in the road, Stanford held her hand so close under his arm that she felt the beating of his heart, and after that, she observed with pleasure that he bestowed upon her the same protecting attention that he bestowed upon Frau von Berwitz.

Just beyond the lower bridge at Weimar, in the deep shadow of the old palace, hasty "good-nights" were said.

Muriel had barely time to remark the feverish touch of the Count's hand, before they again passed into the moonlight, as the clock in the tower struck eleven.

CHAPTER XI.

The sound of childish prattle, rising from the garden to her open windows, awoke Muriel the next morning at six o'clock. The events of the preceding day recurred to her with such force that a return to slumber was impossible. Moreover, the prospect of playing in the lesson at Liszt's that afternoon was incentive enough to forthwith bestir herself for an hour's practice before breakfast.

Gretchen had temporarily abandoned her watering-pot to do some weeding about the door of the garden salon. Elsa's little fingers were busied with knitting a stocking for herself. Mariechen had become unusually loquacious, and, forgetting her wonted timidity, she gave vent to a rippling peal of laughter.

"Sh!" Gretchen gave her a warning look. "You will disturb the Fräulein, Mariechen; she is still sleeping—up there."

As she pointed to the upper window, an exclamation of surprise escaped her. Muriel was smiling at them from amidst the rich mass of pink and white bloom.

"Ach, Fräulein! Good-morning! Now, Mariechen, see what you have done by making such a noise. The gracious Fräulein could not sleep." Mariechen's chubby face fell. Her head sank forward on her breast and she thrust one thumb into her mouth— the personification of abject woe.

"Poor little thing. Really, Gretchen, you are too hard on her. She didn't mean to do it, and it is high time I was up. I love to hear her laugh. Good morning, Elsa. Look up, Mariechen. Here!" Muriel plucked a rose and dropped it at the tiny maiden's feet.

"Thank the Fräulein, stupid!" admonished the elder sister, sticking the flower into the baby's clinched fist. "Ach, fie, fie! what will mother say?". It was of no avail. The child timidly raised her head enough to roll her eyes at Muriel, and as quickly lowered them.

"Never mind, Mariechen, I will soon be down, and then we will talk about it." And Muriel drew back into the room to complete her toilet.

As she was about to descend, she was attracted to the window by the mingling of a man's laugh with a quick chuckle of mirth from Mariechen. Stanford was standing by the rose-arbor tossing the child above his head. Mariechen alternately caught her breath and screamed with delight, while Gretchen stood with her arms akimbo, the muddy palms of her hands turned out and a broad smile coaxing the corners of her mouth towards her ears. Elsa had ceased knitting to gape in speechless admiration.

"Well, little one, how do you like it?" cried Stanford merrily.

Mariechen responded by an irrepressible chuckle, as she clutched his shoulders with her two fat little hands, and turned her clear, laughing blue eyes on his moustache.

"What is your name? Can you tell me? No?"

"Tell the gentleman your name, Mariechen," said Elsa reprovingly.

"Mariechen, is it? Now, then, Mariechen, what say you to a canter on my shoulder?" With a quick movement he pitched her into place, and never waiting for an answer, he started down the central walk. The child's merry shouts started Stanford's spontaneous laughter.

"Now, tell me, little girl, who are you? Where do you live?"

"They live one flight up, sir, at the rear end of the court, next to our Fräulein's rooms," volunteered Gretchen, who had already begun to linger over any task which brought her into Stanford's charmed proximity.

"Neighbors! Then we shall meet often. Eh, Mariechen? You won't forget me?"

"Indeed, she won't, sir," piped in Elsa.

"So! Aufwiedersehen, little girl."

"No—no!" screamed the little one, in her childish treble, running with outstretched arms in pursuit. Stanford whirled about and saved her a bruised nose, as she tripped on the gravel and headed downwards. Catching her to his breast, he caressed the little tow head nestling against his cheek, as the child flung her arms about his neck in close embrace. A tender smile lit up his face, and he stood a moment as if lost in reverie. With a preoccupied expression Muriel drew back from the rose-blooms, and descended to the music-room. When she threw open the doors he was gone, and Mariechen was sniffing audibly, her head buried in the scanty folds of Elsa's skirt. All verbal attempts failing to pacify the child, Muriel resorted to stratagem, by suddenly winding a long blue ribbon about Elsa. In self-interest Mariechen whirled about and demurely stood still to have her arms bound close to her body in like manner.

"So I must appeal to your vanity to win you over, little lady?" Muriel shook her finger in mock reproval. Mariechen blinked away the tears and smiled sheepishly.

"Is it a bargain, coquette? We are friends?" No resistance being offered, she stooped and kissed the child affectionately on both cheeks. "The very spots which his lips touched!" Muriel remembered, with a rush of blood to her face. She arose almost brusquely, and, with a hasty farewell, started for the music-room.

"What am I coming to!" she reflected, feeling the beatings of her heart. "This is utter nonsense!" She wrinkled her brow into a frown of determination, began to hum aimlessly, and was astonished to find herself lapsing into Schumann's lovely song, "Du meine Seele, Du meine Herzen."

She raised the lid of her piano with a bang and plunged recklessly into the introduction of the Liszt concerto. Nevertheless, an indefinable memory seemed to keep warm the region of her heart, and spread, like a lingering caress, to her throat and brow; and when she caught herself at intervals dwelling with admiration on Stanford's unfolding character, she frightened herself back to mental concentration on her work by picturing the horrors of a fiasco in the afternoon lesson.

It seemed two hours, instead of one, before Gretchen summoned her to breakfast under the plum-trees. With a vague sentiment that she had something to resist, Muriel preserved an easy repose throughout the meal, saying little and listening to Stanford's animated account of a rapid walk amongst the old haunts in the park.

In remembrance of an early-learned duty, after breakfast he picked up the daily paper and read aloud the most interesting bits of news. Muriel lounged back, forgetful of her nervousness about the lesson, and listened in luxurious indolence while the sun line crept nearer and nearer the table. A paragraph referring to Liszt brought her to a realization of the hour.

"Oh!" she ejaculated, with a start; and instantly the benumbing fear which always accompanied her to a performance at the Royal Gardens, possessed her every nerve. "The concerto! Excuse me, please."

"What is there so dreadful about those lessons?" queried Frau von Berwitz.

"One's self, sometimes," laughed Muriel, retreating without further parley.

CHAPTER XII.

"What a life!" sighed Muriel, after two consecutive hours' practice. "I recover only to work again, and so on throughout the day, until those days become weeks, months, years, a lifetime! How must it feel to sleep long, to lie in a hammock without a care, to drift aimlessly through an existence. That's it exactly, 'an existence,' not life! We prefer ours, don't we, dear heart?" and Muriel rested her moist cheek lovingly on the silent piano, as if it, too, understood. "No! Rather the delight which we only can know. It is worth all the back-aches in Christendom." Straightening herself laboriously, Muriel sought the outer air, and, with the rapidity peculiar to one of her temperament, regained her wonted strength and buoyancy after a few turns in the long walk.

Her thoughts had gone a-calling with Frau von Berwitz and Stanford, when she tripped restlessly down the steps to the lower terrace, and came face to face with her young countryman, who was quietly reading a paper-covered volume in the shade of a sturdy young tree.

"I beg pardon," she said in surprise, and stopping short she turned to retreat. "I thought you had gone with Tante Anna to make some visits."

"We have postponed them. Fräulein Panzer sent a note as we were leaving, to say that she and the Countess would be here before noon."

"Then I will not!" observed Muriel emphatically to herself, pondering on the scheme meant to entrap her. "There is a law in this household as to the disposition of callers during practice hours."

"Pray, don't go! I haven't a monopoly of this terrace," continued Stanford.

"But you are reading—and—I am walking." Muriel smiled brilliantly, every trace of weariness in her expression gone, and moved on towards the stairs.

"What is that?" queried Stanford, listening, with an evident disposition to detain her.

The regular tramp, tramp, tramp of many feet filled the air. It grew louder, and so near that Stanford glanced questioningly towards the back street.

"Yes, they sometimes come this way," said Muriel, and she walked with him to the iron railing and leaned over. At that instant there came into the street from the first turn at the left, an officer on a handsome bay charger, followed by a solid body of soldiers, with glittering bayonets and helmets.

"The troops returning from target practice at the Ettersberg," she added. A peculiar light flashed from her eye and she quickly averted her face. "Count von Hohenfels told me last night that they were to leave the barracks at six o'clock this morning. Poor man,"—she was closely eyeing the soldiers,—"how he does dislike military life! The discipline is, undoubtedly, wholesome for one of his temperament, but his heart and thoughts are engaged elsewhere."

Stanford gave her a curious sideward glance, which she did not see; but as she spoke quite indifferently, he transferred his scrutiny to the superb-looking regimental band, whose burnished horns were ordered into requisition as they came under the garden wall.

Almost deafening was the sudden blare of brass; then the inspiring music of a well-played military march slowly receded. The ranks followed with pomp and dazzling glitter. The three officers of the Tiefurt party were recognized in turn, though only Count von Hohenfels lifted his eyes as he approached the terrace wall. Above him stood the woman he loved, and at her side her handsome, stalwart young countryman. He smiled a response to their friendly greeting, as a suffocating sensation crept into his breast, and blackness descended like a veil between his eyes and the bright sunlight.

"He makes a fine-looking officer," observed Stanford, with a motion at Hohenfels.

"Very," said Muriel, still watching him. "He once told me that he invariably pulled on his uniform with a bad grace, as being the outward semblance of war, a thing which he abhors as a relic of barbarism and wholly unworthy our nineteenth-century enlightenment."

"True," said Stanford, with the indifferent air of a thinking man enjoying his vacation too much to enter into protracted discussion; "if a thing isn't right, it's wrong. Courts decide the question for individuals, why shouldn't representatives of all nations meet in conclave; in other words, form an international court to settle disputes arising between countries?"

"They will, some day, if more of our young men will give themselves up to serious thought. The future of our country is dependent upon its young men!" exclaimed Muriel, feeling that she had not said a very original thing, yet unable to repress a certain patriotic enthusiasm, which a growing acquaintance with Stanford's manner of thought had revived.

"Is 'our country' Germany or America?"

Muriel turned sharply. She could see nothing in this attempt at facetiousness beyond a disinclination for serious conversation with a woman. They were both lounging on the iron baluster, and he was watching her with a mysterious twinkle in his eye.

"America," she said, and looked back at the last soldiers vacating the street. "If I am a good German, I am a still better American."

"When in foreign lands, possibly?"

"By no means," affirmed Muriel stoutly; "I love my home. I would be there now, were it not for the Master. I feel as if I must make the most of the present opportunity, for he is a very old man."

"So America will profit by the result after all?"

"I suppose all earnest workers do some good, no matter how humble their attainments," said Muriel modestly; "but I don't mean to use my music in a professional sense. I dream of a time when routine in my art will have strengthened me to take my daily recreation in the pursuance of other studies. As yet, music masters me, and I succumb to sheer idleness when I get up from the piano."

"Then, in time, you will have to find a relief from

'recreation,' as I am doing now," said Stanford with a genial smile, which made Muriel again think that perhaps she had, after all, misinterpreted his motive for avoiding serious conversation with her. With a plausible excuse for lingering on the terrace, she had willingly ignored the curious eyes across the street for a few enjoyable moments, but the sudden appearance of Fräulein Panzer and the Countess von Hohenfels, coming arm in arm down the slope from the palace, warned her to withdraw.

"Complete relaxation," continued Stanford, who had not seen them, as he accompanied her towards the garden, "is the best cure for an overworked brain. This is my first vacation in three years. See how I pass it!" He laughingly indicated the book in his hand—one of the latest ephemeral novels. "As a rule I have neither time nor inclination for such things, but I have concluded to free my mind absolutely of business and 'recreation' worries, and be lazy awhile, as an experiment!"

Muriel thought she knew what he meant by 'recreation' worries. Frau von Berwitz had referred to his political activity, and from what Muriel herself had seen, she invested him with the loftiest ideals and the noblest endeavors in carrying them out. What higher aim in life could a man have? Especially in America, where, it seemed to her, men were ruled by party spirit and the prospect of personal gain rather than by a desire to protect the united interests of the land. Stanford took on the outlines of a hero in her eyes as she pictured him denouncing corruption and demanding absolute honesty in public offices. She foresaw the day when men would no longer refuse to associate their names with politics for fear of the resulting stigma; and at the head of this reformation stood Stanford. She wondered if there were others in America as brave and able as he. Certainly she had known no other like him. Those whom she had met abroad seemed either indifferent to the national good or lacking the courage of their convictions. Workers, not grumblers, were needed.

Muriel was beginning to get so much inspiration out of Stanford's society and her own curiosity about him, that the nearing click, click, click, click of two pairs of heels in the echoing street fell untimely on her ears.

"It is my hour for rest," she said, halting reluctantly on the ascending steps.

"Then you do rest sometimes?" Stanford gave her an incredulous smile, as he forebore to follow.

"Always—the day of a lesson—for an hour or more before dinner. Pianists, as a rule, don't practice at all the day of a public appearance, and this is much more trying, I assure you," added Muriel, with a nervous shrug of the shoulders; "but—my playing to-day was rather unexpected, and—I didn't feel quite —'in finger,' as the Master sometimes says. Aufwiedersehen!"

He was still looking after her as she turned away, as if he were not quite ready to terminate the interview. It was the first frank, trustful glance—in which there is no reserve—of a friend. In the in-

timacy of life in a united household, it had taken little
more than twenty-four hours to dissipate the newness
and formality of early acquaintance.

To Muriel the last memory of his blond head, as
he bared it for a sunbath, was as that of one out of the
"long ago," who had reappeared after having dropped
entirely away from her life. "Of course he didn't
mean it! But I should really like to know what he
thinks," she was saying to herself at the entrance to
the Court. "It was my own freaky imagination. I
must have a vacation soon, when more of the pupils
are in, or I shall be a wreck. So, good-by, Resentment! Ah, Gretchen! Should any one inquire for
me, say I play this afternoon at Liszt's, and am sleeping."

CHAPTER XIII.

It had been a busy day up at the great, factory-like barracks on the hill. The troops were undergoing the annual extra drill which precedes the autumn manoeuvres. The few unmarried officers whose incomes enabled them to habitually assemble at the mid-day table d'hote in the "Hotel zum Erbprinzen," had been compelled to take soldier's fare in the mess-room. All the afternoon a cloud of dust hung over the vast exercise ground, as bugle-calls and stern commands arose in obligato above the dull thunder of many descending feet. Hohenfels led his men through their evolutions with a gusto that astonished them. He was painfully in earnest, had they but known it. The advent of Stanford in the household of Frau von Berwitz had suddenly developed in the Count a combativeness which his long military training had failed to incite. Moreover, under the penetrating rays of a scorching sun, the physical discomfort of thickly-padded shoulders and a heavy helmet intensified his irritability.

The army of the enemy stood before his mind's eye concentrated in the person of Stanford; and ere he gave order to break ranks, the American had fallen a thousand times under his fierce onslaught.

Hohenfels took abrupt leave of his comrades and hurried diagonally across a corner of the parade ground to the verdurous arch shading the way to the old stone bridge by the palace. After her first meeting with Muriel, his mother had given him her full sanction to their union. What, then, but his own cowardly heart prevented his asking her to become his wife? The memory of opportunities lost within the twenty-four hours brought an angry flush to his face, and all the more because of the newly-arisen peril menacing his suit.

Why had he submitted to Muriel's elusive impulses? As they ante-dated the arrival of Stanford, an utter stranger to her, what did they signify? Was it a woman's way in such a crisis; and did she wish to be won by storm? Did she, then, lay more stress on his manner of offering himself than on the sincerity of the act itself?

Was his ignorance of feminine foibles to mar his future happiness. Did not a true woman value the first pure love of a man? Could she not accept him, unsophisticated as she found him, or would she have him as artful as "Tannhäuser" in the "Venusberg"? If Muriel cared even the half for him that he did for her, why couldn't she say so without reserve? And supposing she did not. He had had unshaken faith in the ultimate winning power of his all-absorbing love. Now, with imprecations on Stanford, he questioned it.

The worldly advantages of wealth and social rank, weighing in his favor, had never occurred to Hohenfels as a possible temptation to Muriel, for he was one of those who exalt talent, such as hers, above a mere empty title; and as for riches, she had an abundance. Therefore, he resolved upon a bold stroke to still the tortures of suspense. Could he but reach Liszt's by the close of the lesson, he would ask Muriel for a stroll in the park. It was his only chance to interview her, unattended, before the half-past seven o'clock supper to which Frau von Berwitz had bidden him with his mother and Fräulein Panzer. Scharwenka was to be there also, and, of course, the ubiquitous Stanford.

The severe discipline to which mind and body had been subjected fortified him as he started down the hill. He felt as if he could overthrow mountains in his boundless strength. For a moment only he halted on the old bridge to listen to the falling water. He loved its music; it rested his fevered brain.

He hastened onward. A soft breeze was sweeping over the lowlands. It cooled his flushed cheeks and touched the leafy boughs overhanging the serpentine way through the open park. The moving shadows about his feet, it now occurred to him with despair, reflected the inner workings of his heart. His spirit faltered with each step which brought him nearer the Royal Gardens. Had he hearkened too long to the Ilm? Was the curse of the Lorelei in its entrancing song? Did his courage belong to the hill alone? Doubts and fears assailed him like so many invisible demons tugging at the cords tightened about his heart. He felt that he would rather lead Bernsdorf's easy-minded, phlegmatic existence than to purchase heavenly raptures at such a price.

At the rustic gate a great fear overcame him. How could his asinine manner secure him else than a refusal? "Be a man!" he muttered between his teeth; and aware of curious eyes watching him from the house, he strode resolutely up the walk. Some pupils had just straggled out into the door-yard. Hohenfels gave the military salute, and inquired for Miss Holme.

"She is still above," said one of them, pointing at the upper windows.

Hohenfels sprang upon the stoop and pulled the bell. Other pupils were coming out. He stood aside to let them pass, and because of his conspicuous uniform, he stepped into the dim vestibule, and ran face to face with a man who had likewise an evident purpose in loitering there. It was Stanford.

"Good afternoon, Count." He had come forward and proffered his hand. Hohenfels accepted it and made a mighty effort not to think, in order to be perfectly conventional.

"Good afternoon," he responded, in a dull tone. Instinctively he drew back into deeper shadow.

"You are late for the lesson."

"Yes——. That is—I am not a pupil. I sometimes come to—to——"

"You are seeking the young Fräulein, are you not, Herr Lieutenant?" inquired the housekeeper, appearing in the kitchen door. "She has not yet come down."

"Yes, she has, Frau Pauline."

Following the tones of her voice around the final

turn in the descent, Muriel stopped on the open threshold at the foot of the stairway. She was evidently very nervous. Her cheeks were flaming with color, and her restless eyes seemed to emit fiery darts from their darkening depths. It was apparent to the two young men that she was not thinking of them.

"You have just played?" said Stanford, after an interchange of greetings.

"My concerto had the last place," she answered, with a pathetic little smile.

Stanford divined the rest. He had amused himself, back in the shadow, studying the pupils as they came down the stairs. They were much of a type—pale, earnest youths and maidens with eyes which were roving and intelligent in speaking, and dreamy or introspective in repose; abnormally sensitive, and pursuing life at a nervous tension which unfitted them for associations outside their own mental workshops. He pictured to himself Muriel waiting throughout the long lesson in a spiritual atmosphere created by these high-strung natures and intensified by the magnetic intellectuality of Franz Liszt, waiting to submit herself as the objective point of rigid discipline in all that critical throng; and he ceased wondering at her pallor and quiet, preoccupied expression during dinner, and, later, at three o'clock "coffee" in the summer house.

Out of regard to her obvious desire for solitude, he had desisted from offering his escort to Liszt's; but when Frau von Berwitz reminded her that after the lesson she must call on the Countess, he had asked

Muriel if he might not join her at the Royal Gardens
and go with her. In view of her unqualified assent,
he suspected that the coming of Hohenfels was
equally a surprise to her. Therefore, as he had no
desire to withdraw, courtesy certainly did not demand
it of him; and, for the rest—the Count would doubtless survive it.

From the transformation in Muriel's countenance,
Stanford surmised something of her success; but not
all. Liszt had encouraged her as never before, and
those of the pupils who ever acknowledged anything
agreeable of a colleague went away pronouncing her
performance the greatest thus far of the season.
Even she herself was faintly surprised at her display
of unknown power. However, her strength seemed
to go with the last note of the concerto. In her bewilderment at the measure of praise bestowed, she remembered Stanford's promise to await her below.
Buoyed up by a momentary consciousness of triumph, she hastened to depart; but Liszt had not finished expressing pleasure at her interpretation of his
concerto. He slowly accompanied her to the head of
the stairs, and stood there, smiling to call, "Aufwiedersehen."

The unexpected appearance and all too plain confusion of Hohenfels gave her an uncomfortable sensation. An effort was required to overcome the awkward situation. She stood irresolutely in the doorway, quite ready to prolong the conversation.

"Herr Scharwenka, who dined here," she said, "had
gone to the city with some of the gentlemen. As I

had studied the concerto with him, I told the Master I knew he would play the orchestral part at the second piano, if I waited. He came late, and is now in the salon."

Muriel stood aside as some one started down the stairs. It was Rivington, whom she stopped to introduce to the others.

"I am sorry to have been the cause of your not playing," she said in English. "The Master said he could not stand more than one of his concertos in an afternoon. Whether he meant it," she continued, with an amused laugh, "I don't know; but he promised he would hear you play the 'A major' next lesson."

"I have to thank you for much," said Rivington, who had exhausted his encomiums on her playing, in the salon.

Muriel raised her hand in protest, and then said quietly to Hohenfels, as they all passed into the dooryard: "You are just in time to go with us to call on your mother."

"Will you not come in this evening informally?" she added in English to Rivington, who had evinced considerable timidity, during the lesson, about approaching his fellow-students. She felt sorry for the boy in his loneliness, and considered it a duty to give her young countryman, as far as practicable, the benefit of her experience. "I live at —— Strasse, number ten, one flight up. Mr. Stanford has promised to sing, and—I hope Count von Hohenfels will play for us?"

Hohenfels avowed, in very broken, though fluent English, his readiness to do anything Miss Holme desired.

It was a happy thought of Muriel's to continue conversation in her mother tongue, as the three bade Rivington "Aufwiedersehen" and started for the park; for the mercurial Hohenfels found speedily relief from his disappointment in the construction of his English sentences, and still further in the fact that she firmly refused to let Stanford carry her music-roll. And Hohenfels staid with his mother, when Muriel, after a formal call, went home on the plea of needing rest. She had forgotten her plea, however, when they reached the old rose-garden, and she sat talking with Stanford on the lower terrace, until twilight shadows crept around them.

CHAPTER XIV.

The genial wit and brilliant conversational gifts of the Berlin pianist and composer gave the final touch of success to Frau von Berwitz's supper party. Under the sway of his magnetic personality selfish considerations were forgotten. Nor did they again spring up to disturb the serenity of the little company until after Herr Scharwenka's early departure for the Russischer Hof to join a party of Lisztianer, as the pupils of the old Master were called in Weimar.

Rivington came in, and immediately Fräulein Panzer began to speak of Liszt. Everywhere in the little capital his name was used as a wedge to open conversation with a new-comer. Already the lad had begun to think of the Weimaraner as of two factions —those who knew Liszt and those who did not. The former related reminiscences of him; and the latter, the freshest gossip of the Royal Gardens. Fräulein Panzer was doing both. She had known the Master for five-and-thirty years, and now reverted to their first meeting.

Muriel had begun to feel bored; she had heard the story until she knew every word of it by heart. She was in a mood for enjoyment, and so determined to frustrate the narrator.

Hohenfels was listening to Fräulein Panzer with an attentive, downcast expression. "Poor fellow," thought Muriel, with a single throb of compassion; and she forthwith made a cat's-paw of him in her impatience to hear Stanford sing.

"Count," she said in an undertone, "will you play something now?"

"Certainly," he cried, springing up with alertness and totally confusing his astonished godmother.

. "I think we will go to the music-room," said Muriel, rising also. "Count von Hohenfels, who has consented to play, is partial to the other piano. Please remember your songs, Mr. Stanford."

The latter was making a martyr of himself by supporting Frau von Berwitz in a conversation with the deaf Countess. Although Muriel thought that he might have been more attentive to her, she none the less admired his devotion to the elderly ladies. His kindness to her pet "Mime," however, would have atoned for more serious shortcomings. With selfish feline instinct the cat had claimed and rebelliously maintained a position upon Stanford's knees.

"Come, Mimechen," he said in English, tossing the fluffy black creature up to his shoulder, "don't despise the Caucasian. You see, ladies, he has no race prejudice."

They all found it pleasanter in the music-room. The broad, open doorway gave them the additional enjoyment of the night. They gathered there to watch the distant stars twinkling in the interspaces of the leafy framework, and to inhale the sweetness of the June roses. A tall lamp stood on the table by the piano, and a thick red shade focused the tinted light cn the keyboard. The room was full of shadow; the profiles of the silent listeners showed darkly to Count von Hohenfels, as he let his fingers wander dreamily over the keys.

The time seemed made for rhapsodizing. It was a night such as Thuringia sometimes cedes to the brains and hearts of her lover-poets. It spoke its mystic spell to the player in the first mellow-toned response of the vibrating wires. The day and its trials were gone. His spirit had grown light with hope, and only the sympathetic appeal in his touch gave echo to his recent emotions. The language whose utterance was denied to his lips, sought expression through the medium of his fingers, and he knew that Muriel alone would understand him.

Hohenfels was fond of extemporizing, and he had found amusement in Muriel's verbal interpretation of his ideas thus expressed. This form of communication had, the previous summer, become their favorite pastime. Indeed, aided by her knowledge of his temperament and trend of thought, she had become so proficient that he, in his ignorance of woman's wit, invested her with miraculous powers.

"I cannot grasp it!" he exclaimed one day, after she had repeated to him what he believed to be the actual words of his thoughts. "How do you do it?"

"I do not know."

"Play for me!" he cried, springing up from the piano; I too will try it."

"No," said Muriel, "I do not improvise well. I have little or no creative power in music. Mine is solely interpretative. Your gift is inborn. Let us continue as we have begun."

But her elucidations were given only when alone with him in the music-room. In truth she approved of pianoforte improvisations for chosen occasions only. She had been too often bored by the hour-long impromptu fantasies of pianists much more distinguished than the Count—professional men of genius, who gave such reminiscent settings to occasional inspired measures that the whole was simply an infliction. Liszt was the only improvisator she had ever heard with pleasure in an assembly after passing her novitiate, and that pleaure she ascribed in part to his tactful brevity. Hohenfels, on the contrary, loving his piano blindly, made no note of time Muriel therefore heard his preluding with apprehension.

"What will you play, Count?" she asked, hoping that he would change his purpose out of consideration for the musical culture of his guests.

He looked at her an instant without speaking. "A drama," he repeated in a low voice.

"A what?" called Fräulein Panzer, sharply, raising her eyeglasses to scrutinize the face of her embarrassed godson. "It's the wine," she added in a jocular way, and turned aside to study the stars.

"No, Tante Clara! Before Heaven, no! A veritable drama in tone."

"From whom?"

"From God or the Devil! I wish I knew which," he muttered, as he let his fingers again wander over the keys. "I don't know," he said aloud.

"You are too modest, Fritz. Claim it openly. He composes exceedingly well," she said, lowering her voice. "Does he not, Miss Holme?"

"Very," replied Muriel, trying to conceal her displeasure at Hohenfels' decision. He was eyeing her uneasily, but her expression was lost to him in the gloom.

The dialogue had aroused the curiosity of the group at the door. With misgivings as to his purpose, Muriel anxiously noted the intentness with which they listened to the first notes of Hohenfels' tonal "drama" floating out on the quiet night. Only a few measures were needed to confirm her fears. His recital was a history of their acquaintance, and so vividly expressed that none could fail to understand. Once she detected a significant look passing between Fräulein Panzer and Frau von Berwitz; and, later on, Rivington raised his questioning eyes to her face.

Muriel was mortified at her old friend's lack of delicacy in thus openly parading his feelings. He began to recall strains from favorite compositions with which they had beguiled the previous summer, whilst the underflow of passionate emotion grew even wilder and bolder, threatening, at last, to break its bonds and pour triumphantly forth.

Again the spell of the music spoke to the perturbed spirit of the player, and led him into such a maze of soulful harmonies that, carried beyond himself, he abandoned his fancy to the eloquence of his overmastering love. It found reflection in his face and held the listeners in breathless expectation of a stirring climax. Muriel knew better, and waited with a throbbing heart for a brief diminuendo and pause.

Then with a single phrase—the inevitable question, so full of beseeching tenderness—he gazed steadily at Muriel a moment and rose from the piano. A general look of surprise followed him.

"Come, Fritz, this is too abrupt," exclaimed Fräulein Panzer, who was the first to recover herself. Like the others, having merely comprehended the general drift of his improvisation, she did not sufficiently appreciate the unhappy position of Muriel, who had with each moment grown more painfully self-conscious. Fräulein Panzer, indeed, had been not a little amused by the incident, as something novel and quite clear to herself only. As it occurred to her that timely assistance might be desirable, she added slyly: "Give the satisfactory solution of your harmonies."

"Perhaps Miss Holme will do that?" responded Hohenfels, rising.

For the moment Muriel was too stunned by his audacity to speak. Pride, however, over-ruled her outraged sensibilities. Though Hohenfels had behaved foolishly, he was an old and faithful friend, and her pending answer would determine their future relations. As a woman of tact she could not do else than make light of so trying a situation. Whatever the facts of the case, the witnesses would regard his attitude as one of weak sentimentality; and so would he with a return of reason. However, in that

brief interval of thought Muriel had laid more stress
on the manner than on the wording of her reply.

"I could not do that better," she began, with an
assumption of merriment, rising briskly to her feet,
"than by playing Mr. Stanford's accompaniments."

She stopped aghast at the insinuation in her statement. "I have done enough solo work for one day,"
she added so hastily that none could mistake her own
interpretation of the words.

That Hohenfels was wounded by the unintentional
blow was natural. In her heart she felt it a deserved
and wholesome lesson for him. However, she had
a part to play until matters adjusted themselves, and
she looked into his blanched face without a pang of
regret.

"I have memorized the Mephisto waltzes, if you
care to take them to-night," she said, indicating some
sheet music on the piano, and resuming her usual
tone with him. "Meister has promised to hear the
first one the next time I play for him. Perhaps you
can give me some new ideas after looking it over.
It is always a pleasure to hear Liszt praise an interpretation which differs from his own."

Muriel was but faintly conscious of what she said.
Her only desire was to dispose of Hohenfels without
further friction, and when she saw him, at last,
quietly take a seat on the doorstep and turn his face
to the stars, she looked round for Stanford. He had
selected a volume from a collection which he had

brought with him and placed it on the music-rest.

"It is very good of you to play for me," he said; "I make a frightful bungle of my accompaniments."

"You should never have to play them to sing well," she added, as she read the composer's name·on the cover of the book with a brightening countenance.

"Then you like Schubert?" He spoke softly,· as his glance met her uplifted eyes.

"He satisfies me as no other writer of pure song who has ever lived."

"He is my favorite also.. What shall it be?" He leaned over her to open the book.

"Wait!" exclaimed Muriel, taking it from him. "I have a fancy to see where it will fall open. Then I shall know what you have been singing to yourself." Balancing the bound edge on the palm of her hand, she watched the pages flutter apart and stop at "Am Meer."

"It was my choice, too!" cried Muriel, forgetting the listening group at the door in her elation at having an unvoiced wish come true.

While putting the book into place, she was momentarily conscious of Hohenfels' penetrating glance, without being disturbed by it. She was thinking of "Am Meer." "What if he does not sing well, or is only a weak lyric tenor? I would rather never hear him!" It would be so horribly out of keeping with the man himself."

Muriel felt her cheeks burning. "They will think it the color from the shade," she reassured herself.

I do hope I shall not be disappointed. I don't look for a great artistic treat from an amateur; only let it be in accord with his intelligence and nobility of character." What she did expect she hardly knew. A vague unrest had seized her. She was in sudden terror of having an ideal spoiled. Surely, though, Stanford was not the man to make himself ridiculous by an ignoble exhibition of weak vanity. The thought gave her comfort. "Of course he won't!" she kept repeating to herself. "Of course he won't! But why should I work myself up so about Mr. Stanford?" Muriel was somewhat abashed by the reflection. "My deplorable nervousness again!"

The sensuous charm of her excellent performance in the lesson, was still in the tips of Muriel's fingers, as they sought the introductory chords with that tender caress which true pianists intuitively give those harmonies most in touch with their own nature. It was like a sympathetic, spoken appeal to Stanford. He gave her a quick look of response, but she was intent upon the keyboard, and when she glanced up at him, as a signal for concerted action, he had receded a step and was gazing beyond the silent listeners into the night.

Music is an intoxicant for certain temperaments. After the first measures of "Am Meer" Muriel was conscious only of an ecstatic thrill, which ravished her senses and dispelled doubts, fears and even reason. Swayed by the power of the singer, her fingers moved over the keys as in a dream. A rich, sonorous voice, breathed forth so naturally as to conceal the art which guided it, was singing lines beloved and already engraved upon her memory:

Das Meer erglänzte weit hinaus
Im letzten Abendscheine,
Wir sassen am einsamen Fischerhaus,
Wir sassen stumm und alleine.

The absolute sweetness and purity of intonation in that dying cadence:

Wir sassen stumm und alleine,

melted into Muriel's heart. The music of her own fingers fell as tenderly on the ear. Voice and piano blended as one. With the words

Der Nebel stieg, das Wasser schwoll,
Die Möwe flog hin und wieder

a dramatic fibre vibrated in the swelling notes of the singer. Muriel's whole consciousness seemed uplifted in the crescendo of the music; her body swayed lightly to the rhythm, and when the lines sank into quieter measure:

Aus deinen Augen liebevoll
Fielen die Thränen nieder,

real tears crowded into her eyes. She played on, unmindful of the blurred page before her. The notes were rising from her heart in response to each utterance of the singer.

Muriel was already in that realm of fancy where she spent half her waking hours and found her truest happiness. Had it ever before revealed to her such bliss, such transport? Was not the present a reality? Did not the mists surround them? Was not that the North Sea breaking in foaming billows on the broad sands at their feet, the low caves of the fisher's hut above them, limitless space about them, and they two alone in that vast universe. He was at her side; she could feel his presence, hear his inspired voice. Listen! it is no dream. These are his words:

> Ich sah sie fallen auf deine Hand,
> Und bin auf's knie gesunken ;
> Ich hab' sie aus deiner weissen Hand,
> Die Thränen fort getrunken.
>
> Seit jener Stunde verzehrt sich mein Leib,
> Die Seele stirbt von Sehnen ;
> Mich hat das unglückselg'e Weib,
> Vergiftet mit ihren Thränen.

Muriel's heart was ready to break with the sweet sadness of that lingering, softly-dying strain. A great sob welled up in her throat, and then the murmuring accompaniment, too, was gone. A deathlike stillness oppressed her. She opened her eyes with a start. They were moist, and she could dimly discern the far-reaching shadows beyond the mellow light thrown over the white keys of her piano. Suddenly it all came back to her where she was, and that her acquaintance of two days, Tante Anna's foster son Carl, was standing at her side, and had been singing. And then a great warmth enveloped her and made her brain reel. What was it? The fleeting magic of his song—or himself? Her heart answered with a rush of hot blood, "Both." What madness! And yet— why not? It must have been meant so from the beginning. Yes, it was her fate. It had been ordained thus, and she had nothing to do with it. She had not desired it. She had rebelled at his coming. And here he was at her side. What had he become in those thirty-six hours? Her world! Her all! For the instant she could think of nothing else! She loved—and how? The beating of her heart resounded in her ears; and as she strove to calm herself, the ticking of the little clock on the wall was the only sound that broke the silence of the room.

A sudden rush of maidenly shame possessed her. "No one must know," she said tumultuously to herself. "How horrible if they did!" Muriel threw her head proudly back, and slowly closed and opened her eyes in the effort to dry them without calling attention to her emotion. As a pretext for not speaking, she turned to the index of songs and ran her finger down the list. She had missed it. She could not see distinctly, and began again.

"What is it?" said Stanford, softly, with the tenderness of Schubert's inspired melody still in his voice.

"The 'Serenade,'" she murmured. She had to turn her face in profile to make him hear. His head was almost touching hers, and she felt his penetrating glance. A tear still glistened on her eyelash.

"He saw it," she repeated helplessly to herself. To hide her confusion, she began a pianissimo modulation from C major to the key of the "Serenade"—D minor. "Perhaps he will only wonder what significance 'Am Meer' has had in my past life that it should call forth the tears. Certainly, he could not surmise anything from my manner."

"I defy any one to take me unawares now," she added, as a final support to herself.

When she began the simple prelude to the "Serenade," the insidious charm in her first touch of the white keys stole over her own senses like a celestial balm. The book on the music-rest screened the spell-bound group at the door. Not a soul had so much as stirred. A word would have been to them a sacrilege. Muriel thought of them no more. The red light behind her shoulder seemed flaming from her brain, and, as it grew brighter and brighter, she felt herself wafted into space on billowy rose-scented clouds. A thrilling presence, which she did not see, was near. Sweet, tender strains lured them on together; and then his voice, so mellow and free, that it seemed to penetrate and fill limitless space with its glory, rose above all like a benediction of love.

A strange, deep sadness breathed through the song. Memory was travelling backward to America—her early home—and her mother. Her dear voice, now silent forever, had sung these self-same words. It was a translation into the English which had long since passed from Muriel's mind. Had the dead past risen to sanctify her love as something sacred, a thing from above, which divine Providence had foreordained? "Thus it was intended and always shall be." Her life, with its strivings and its sorrows, had been simply a preparation for this new, great joy just come to her. Everything else faded before it. The thought was sufficient answer to every question that might arise; and in the security of that belief she yielded to the present rapture, for that, too, like all things of this world, must end.

She drank in his words until her brain seemed be-

numbed as with wine, and when the final tone died
slowly, as a vapor vanishes in the heavens, she
remembered only the impassioned appeal in that last
line:

> And my heart for thee is yearning,
> Bid it, love, be still.

It voiced in its concentrated intensity the lifelong,
pent-up yearnings of a loving heart.   Was it art—or
was it real?   Muriel's heart throbbed madly as she
strove to reason; but the music had ceased; once
more she opened her eyes to actual being.

It all came back to her quickly enough—the large
room, with its deep shadows where the listeners sat,
and the screen of the friendly book which she had not
once seen from the beginning.   Nor had he, so it
seemed, for the page had not been turned.   The
music had come from both their hearts; and, yes,
she fancied she saw a tremor pass over Stanford
where he stood, this time at her side, while his hand,
which rested on the piano, certainly did shake perceptibly.   At his show of emotion, Muriel felt herself so
uplifted in spirit that she was enabled to look
up at him with that calm peace in her eyes which be-
trays nothing that passes within.

"Thank you," she said, softly, and she gradually
raised her voice that the others might hear.   "I am
glad to find that particular translation again.   I was
trying to recall it only the other day; but I had not
heard it since my early childhood, and it had gone,
all but the first few lines."

Stanford was regarding her with searching intensity, and as she spoke she observed the eloquence of his dilating pupils changing—fading, as if forced swiftly back out of sight in waves of lightening color until the last flame flickered—went out—and once more he wore merely the frank, kindly expression which seemed a reflection of the man's great, sunny nature.

"I will write them down for you," he said, in a low, husky voice, so unlike that of the inspired singer who had held them entranced, that Fräulein Panzer's quick ear remarked the change.

"You have wearied your voice," she said, with a sympathetic, maternal sort of interest.

Stanford gave a peculiar smile, Muriel thought, and his voice was as firm and as clear as a bell in his evasive reply: "I have not sung before since leaving America."

"Write the translation down for me," she repeated to herself. "Every word of that song is inscribed on my heart!"

Rivington had pushed his chair back to make room for Stanford, who advanced as if to join the group, and Muriel observed that it would give him a view of her profile as she sat at the piano.

"No more music, then, to-night," she reflected, with resignation, and she rose from the instrument. It was growing late for early-to-bed Weimar, and the guests prepared to go. Muriel followed them into the garden, for, as Gretchen had brought wraps and hats from the front of the house, they were to take the nearer way home by the rear exit.

"Good-night," said Hohenfels, in his best officer's manner, but he held Muriel's hand as in a last farewell.

"Good-night," she answered, startled out of herself. A wave of compassion for her lover-friend mingled with the memory of her old regard for him. "Good-night," she repeated, with the friendly intonation which he knew so well, and, looking up in the darkness with an animated smile, she gave him a warm, quick hand pressure and spoke again of the "Mephisto" waltz.

CHAPTER XV.

After their guests had reached the street, Frau von Berwitz and Muriel stood by the iron railing to call a final "good-night," and to wait for Stanford, who had gone down to lock the door behind them. Rejoining the ladies on the terrace, he exclaimed impulsively:

"It is not bedtime, is it, Tante Anna?"

"Why no, my child, if you do not wish it. There!" The matron threw one arm about his neck and drew his head down to kiss him, with a loud smack, first on one cheek and then on the other.

"And there! That, dear boy, is for those two songs. They went to my heart. Shall we sit here?"

"Do you know, Mr. Stanford," said Muriel musingly, as the three sat down on some settles under the trees, "since hearing you, I have been wondering how you could have resisted the temptations to an operatic career."

"Possibly because they came too late," replied Stanford, without a trace of regret at what might have been. "The debates in our college societies had fostered my taste for speechifying, and I did not begin the cultivation of my singing voice until after I graduated."

"But were you never tempted to make it your vocation in life?"

"No—it was hardly a temptation; perhaps a mere pleasurable thought of what I might do, if I would.

I love to sing for—my friends and—myself, and I am sufficiently desirous of doing it well to give all the time I can to study and practice."

"I am surprised, though, that some enterprising impresario has not persuaded you," said Muriel, tentatively.

"I have had offers," continued Stanford, "but not till I was already more deeply interested in other work."

"But only think of the mission of music to humanity—of the sermon in a song—when one is gifted with a voice," persevered Muriel, inwardly delighted with his statements.

"Very true; but while I might move some few hearts to better deeds by my music, I find more inspiration in haranguing an audience. It is more exhilarating to watch a sea of faces change expression, sway to your will, and to feel that it is all so much towards the advancement of a cause which men of all time and every country have held first in their hearts; and, then, afterwards—afterwards—they don't treat one like a tenor."

"The women, you mean? I suppose there is no reason why a tenor should not have intellect," said Muriel, creating a laugh by her seriousness; "but they certainly do not treat him as if he had one."

"It is precisely that which makes a manly man shrink from singing professionally," interjected Stanford, warmly. "He too often feels the truth of your statement."

Muriel felt a benumbing chill creeping over her.

Though convinced that no one had read her secret, still his last remark struck with pain to her heart.

"There never is but one woman who can see all that is good in a man, and that one ought to be his wife," she remarked to herself, philosophically. "The world seldom sees him through her eyes, but I believe she is happier when it may."

Again a warm flush spread to her temples, and dreams of conquest for him in her narrow circle in Weimar began to occupy her mind. Before all, he must meet the Master; and then be guided to the various haunts of the jovial Lisztianer. "He will think the more of me for it," she thought, "and how it will unite our interests."

Her purpose found unexpected introduction through Frau von Berwitz. "Surely," said the matron, nodding in the direction of the Court Gardens, "no tenor ever received the homage tendered by both men and women to our own Liszt."

"Do you know the Master?" Muriel asked Stanford, with sudden animation.

"Not personally, though I once had some conversation with him," he replied, with a reminiscent smile. "It was long ago, when I first came to Weimar. Liszt one day visited our school. He stopped me as I was passing him and asked my name. 'Charles Roland Stanford,' I said, looking him fearlessly in the face. I was a wee bit of a chap then—not over seven or eight—and he tall, straight, and at the zenith of his fame.

"'Ah! a little Englishman,' he replied, patting my shoulder.

"'No, Meister; an American,' I said, loud enough to be heard all over the room.

"'And you have come so far over the great ocean?' he exclaimed, opening his eyes very wide to impress me with the distance.

"'Yes, Meister. Papa brought me to Tante Anna von Berwitz because Mamma is dead.' Don't you recall it, Tante Anna?

"Well," continued Stanford, "I remember he muttered 'dear child,' and let me go, with a pat on my head. Shortly after that he went to Rome, and when he returned, several years later, I was a big boy; but Tante Anna had me doff my hat to him, as to a member of the Grand Ducal family, when I passed him on the street."

"You should know him," said Muriel.

"It would, certainly, be a great pleasure."

"To him, also," she continued. "He would enjoy your singing."

"Oh!—do you think so?" said Stanford, with unaffected modesty.

"Of course," exclaimed Muriel, surprised into expressing, in her tone, a higher estimate of his vocal powers than she might have voluntarily conceded. "You will be glad to have sung for him. He is so appreciative of merit——"

"However crude."

"Exactly," responded Muriel, appreciatively. "Your art redeems you from such an imputation, however.

Now, seriously, would you like to meet him socially?"
"I should be delighted," exclaimed Stanford, with
undisguised pleasure.

"Then I will see him about it—to-morrow, if he is
receiving," she said, and she felt an impatient impulse
to go at once to the Royal Gardens to secure the assurance of his welcome there. The morrow seemed
so far off. Then, when Stanford expressed thanks for
the promised pleasure, her every nerve tingled with
delight that he should be, in any sense, dependent on
her.

"I assure you, Carl," observed Frau von Berwitz,
who was evidently much gratified, "it is the only possible way to meet him now. The old gentleman
rarely goes anywhere, save to Court and to the Fräu-
leins Stahr on Sunday afternoons for music; and as
for an invitation to his house—very few can obtain
even that for another."

"And for the best of reasons," interposed Muriel.
"So few really know him thoroughly. His greatness
is the obstacle to many who have the entrée to his
salon, and they hamper themselves so with affecta-
tions or silence that, personally, they never penetrate
the polished reserve of the courtier. You will note
how few have the courage to speak to him unbidden,
even in the lesson. Those who do are invariably the
older or the very young, naive first-year pupils, and it
is to them that he addresses all his remarks. Only
those whom he finds companionable, and who have
acquired ease of speech and movement in his presence,
ever come to know the true greatness of the man."

"And how about the old sophism that 'a man is a hero to everybody but his valet'?"

"Oh, I can assure you," continued Muriel, "Mischka is the most ardent hero-worshipper at the Royal Gardens. He seems to think his a sacred trust, and Pauline's regard for 'Herr Doctor' is positively touching. She has been with him these thirty years; first as housemaid at fourteen or fifteen years of age, when he went to live at the Altenburg in such grand style back in forty-seven; and, later, as housekeeper of the simple apartments at the Royal Gardens. I don't know what he would do without her. Were he a babe she could not care for him more tenderly.

"Yes," she added, "the loyalty and unaffected devotion of all those who come in close contact with the dear old Master speak the most eloquent praise of him as a man."

They still lingered on the terrace in rapt enjoyment of the still night, but at last Frau von Berwitz made a move to depart.

"Come, dear children; it's sacrilege to stir, I know, but the morrow is almost here, and—Muriel must recognize limitations to her endurance."

The moon had cleared the treetops in the adjacent garden, and revealed the vine-grown roof and upper windows of the old mansion in a picturesque radiance. With uplifted eyes Stanford began to sing under his breath the German lines of the 'Serenade':

> Leise flehen meine Lieder
> Durch die Nacht zu dir,

"That sounds natural," interjected Frau von Berwitz, tapping her approval against his arm, on which she leaned.

"Surely, Tante," he replied, interrupting his song, "you don't mean to insinuate that I would sing English to such a gable as that?"

"It wouldn't be fitting, would it?" she said, halting to note the typical points of the archaic dwelling. "Yet, why not?" she added, ingenuously, forgetful of the text to the "Serenade." "Your countrywoman occupies those rooms."

Muriel preceded them to the inner court, feigning not to have heard the dialogue, but listening with quickened heart-beats for his answer; and when he stopped to close and bolt the heavy iron door, she slackened her steps until they again followed.

She hoped, with a tendency to conviction, that some suggestion of herself, perhaps unacknowledged in thought, had unconsciously brought the music to his lips.

She lifted her face to the sky, and the glory of the starlight seemed to enter and expand her soul, and to guide her footsteps over the stairway, now in darkness.

"Happy Gretchen," she murmured, at this reminder of the maid's negligence, and with a new consideration for the pair of sweethearts down in the great arch of the façade.

The entry door was unlatched. She pushed it open, · and, catching up a lighted lamp, went back to meet the others. Stanford took it from her, and then lighting her own lamp, he handed it to her at the entrance to the cloister, as Frau von Berwitz went to summon Gretchen.

"I will watch you to the end," he said, his words conveying a caress. "It must be dreary to pass all those old portraits and mysterious doors."

"Good-night," she called over the threshold of her ante-room.

"Good-night," he answered in the shadowy distance, and she heard the far-away click of a lock after her door was closed. Muriel turned the lamp low, and, leaving it on the stand without, ascended the two steps before her bedchamber. The moonlight was shimmering through the open windows across the floor and the white pillows of her couch. Impulsively she threw herself on the soft silken counterpane to think it all over again and again, until blinded by happy tears, and she closed her eyes to hear the tender refrain of his last words, "good-night."

The sweet breath of roses stole into her dream and touched her face with dewy freshness. In luxurious indolence Muriel half-opened her eyes, only to close them again and spring suddenly upright with a startled gasp. The sun was shining full in her face. She looked down at the rumpled folds of her dress and turned to catch the gleam of the pale yellow light in the ante-room. A childish treble, rising in subdued monotone from the garden below, was abruptly silenced by seven reverberating strokes of the clock in the castle tower. Then the soft murmur went on, and the day was begun.

CHAPTER XVI.

The daily life at the Court Gardens moved in accordance with a special code which had been evolved by the necessities of a phenomenal career.

Mischka, therefore, experienced at first much difficulty in adjusting his own to Liszt's division of the hours of day and night. Although an eighteen months' apprenticeship served to insure his response to the alarm clock, he was, nevertheless, not always awake when its insistent whirr brought him, at half-past three, to his feet.

On such occasions his somnambulistic entrance into the bedchamber of so light a sleeper as Liszt served the original purpose, and frequently resulted, it is averred, in a very conscious exit.

As usual, after a protracted absence, the Master, upon returning from Aachen, had found himself burdened with the duty of attending to a voluminous correspondence, which the considerable assistance of his intimate friend, Herr Hofrath Gille (of Jena), and Mischka had but just enabled him to regulate. Also, his Leipzig music publisher had become clamorous for fresh copy. His ambitious spirit being indifferent, under this pressure, to the consideration due to infirm age, he had ordered Mischka to arouse him at three o'clock. Thus, with no other sustenance than the usual potations of brandy and water, he had almost completed a portion of his work, when Herr von Ilmstedt came, a half-hour early, as escort to six o'clock mass.

The Allee gate was locked. He lingered in the bright sunshine on the promenade to trace the faint silhouette of the Master's head which the artificial light in the salon cast against the drawn blind by the writing-desk, until Pauline, who lodged near at hand, came to open the house and rewake Mischka. Ilmstedt disposed himself on a trunk in the ante-room to conduct his habitual inquiry into the household affairs, whilst the valet polished Liszt's shoes and brushed his street garb. To gratify Ilmstedt's curiosity about the new composition, Mischka, when he went 'to assist the Master at his hasty toilet, sent the eager pupil into the salon.

Ilmstedt, quite overcome at this privilege, never knew how he crossed the room, but, as he gazed at the still wet notes, he was consumed with desire to possess this creation of Liszt's. His very soul seemed a fair price, until it occurred to him that the barter could be made for less.

Fearful of detection at the desk, he sauntered towards the piano, examining the contents of his purse and mentally scheduling some important points.

"6 a. m. Mass.

"7 a. m. Return. Meister breakfasts on coffee, rolls and eggs.

"7:30 a. m. Meister lies down to nap.

"9:30 a. m. Meister rises and tries over new piece at piano.

"9:45 a. m. Meister rewrites it for publisher.

"10:45 a. m. Meister throws my copy—the original!
—mine!—mine!—mine!—my own copy forevermore
—into the waste-basket."
Supplement.
"10:45 to 11 a. m. I—in ante-room. Servitor on
guard—gold in one hand; my manuscript in the
other."

* * *

A desultory fingering of the keyboard had just
ceased when Mischka, on the stroke of twelve, threw
open the door of the salon to announce "Fräulein
Holme."

Herr Arthur rose from the piano to take leave.
Three compositions which he had orchestrated during
the Master's absence in Aachen stood on the music-
rest. -

"Really masterful," cried Liszt, enthusiastically, calling Muriel's attention to them. "Indeed, I do not believe that Richard Wagner could have made them
more effective."

"Oh, yes," he concluded, "it is all deserved. Adieu,
dear Arthur."

"I fear I disturb you, Meister," began Muriel when
they were alone. "I hesitated about allowing Mischka
to request an audience for me, when he said you were
not at leisure before dinner; but I had a——"

"An important something to discuss with the old
Meister," he interposed. "Well, you need not have
done that, for, as Don Carlos said to the Marquis of
Posa, 'My doors are open to you. Enter freely at
all times.'"

"How generous, Meister. I hope, though, that I do not strain my welcome if I come now to beg a favor."

Liszt answered her anxious expression with a burst of genuine mirth. "Come," he said, proffering a chair, "be seated."

"Not to-day, thank you, dear Meister. Otherwise I should detain you too long. I only wished to ask permission to bring into the lesson to-morrow a countryman of mine who is here visiting Frau von Berwitz. It would give him unspeakable pleasure, and—make me very happy."

"Of course! Of course! Is that all?" he interjected continually, with the utmost indulgence in his voice. "Of course. Friends of yours will always be welcome at the Royal Gardens. I am happy to grant you any request," he continued, with a gentle deference which bespoke his true estimate of his pupil. "In fact, you yourself are always so thoughtful and considerate of others, that I am doubly happy to be able to do you a favor."

Muriel caught her breath. "Oh, Meister!" she gasped, curbing an impulse to embrace him and then rush madly from the room. Her crimson cheeks and bedewed eyes, however, proclaimed the thanks which she could not steady her voice to speak.

"He—my countryman—Mr. Stanford," she faltered at last, "has a very beautiful tenor voice, and sings Schubert most artistically."

"So?" exclaimed Liszt, employing a monosyllable of elastic functions in every-day German. "Perhaps he will favor us to-morrow. Ah! nein," he added hastily, with an eloquent gesture and a quick change of expression. "Better still. Come with him this afternoon at four. Kömpel's string quartette plays. Yet," he said reflectively, "I have bidden only the gentlemen of my class. Ah! Pray ask Frau von Berwitz to honor me by her presence. No; I will write her."

He had crossed the room and taken up his pen before Muriel could convince him that it was unnecessary.

"Very well, then, if you will kindly deliver my message."

"Now, dear master, I shall no longer keep you from your work," she said, indicating the fresh manuscript before him.

"Oh, no, no, no. That is ready for the publisher. One moment!" he exclaimed, with sudden thought, beginning to grope among sundry papers bearing, in his own hand, the symbols of his art; and he mused aloud: "A few alterations and it will be as good as the second. No?" Wheeling about he peered into the waste basket. It had been emptied a half-hour before. Again he scanned the papers. "That is strange! Humph!"

Muriel was too familiar with present conditions not to know the cause of his vexation when she saw his resigned glance towards the ante-room. Then she remembered having seen Ilmstedt leave the house as she came in through the rustic gate, joyously intent upon something which he buttoned in his coat before going out by the Allee.

"Never mind," said the Master, yielding to his love
of harmony in the household, "I will give you the
printed copy later. It will look better than my pen-
manship."

Muriel was glad that the latter thought amused
him, for, just because of his open-handed generosity,
she felt his disappointment more keenly than her
own. Furthermore, she believed the incident would
incite him shortly to the gift of a still more precious
manuscript. It never occurred to her to censure
Ilmstedt, were he the culprit, for aught than undue
haste in his transaction. Otherwise his method
of collecting souvenirs was a tradition of the Royal
Gardens.

Sunshine only found place in Muriel's heart on
the homeward way. The old park presented landscapes of hitherto unknown beauty in its gentle undulations to the singing waters of the Ilm. Even
the noisome cries of the peafowls on the lawns fell
as music on her ears, though sweeter still came, further on a human chorus of treble voices from a
leaf-embowered playground. Involuntarily she halted
to smile at the little urchins tumbling about in blissful disregard of soiled frocks and dirty faces; but
only an instant, for withal, the old mansion seemed
at that moment the one haven in the world most to be
desired. One little man, feeling a soft hand touch his
tangled locks, slowly turned in grave surprise to find
its owner vanishing in the shrubbery.

For the first time in her Weimar experience Muriel
passed lightly over the paving between the library

and the palace, unmindful of its furrowed edge. Nor did she observe the sentinel before the guard-house until, rounding his hands above his mouth, he concentrated his lung power in a prolonged yell and startled her out of her serenity.

Like so many Jacks-in-the-box a handful of soldiers sprang into sight and formed line. A succession of inarticulate energetic orders from the commanding sergeant caused them to move about as briskly as if they were controlled by electricity. A snare drum rattled forth a stirring salute as a royal carriage, dashing through the grand gateway from the palace court, rumbled across the oblong that Muriel had just quitted. However, the interior being unoccupied, the men smiled perceptibly at an order to disperse, and then Muriel noted their resemblance to animate beings. In fact, the sentinel and three others proved to be old acquaintances—young noblemen serving their twelvemonth as avantageurs before donning a lieutenant's epaulets. One had evidently been caught napping, for his comrades laughingly pointed to his reversed helmet as they made salutation and retreated to their lounging-place behind the columns of the portico.

The uniforms recalled Count von Hohenfels. How the past had receded before her new-born happiness! "It was only last night," she mused, "and yet—so long ago." Sorrow for the hopelessness of his affection filled her heart.

"What can I do?" she cried in despair; reverting then, quite naturally to thought of Stanford—"We must practice together from now until dinner, if he is to sing this afternoon," she exclaimed, with a surge of joy which obliterated memory. "To think of it! His glorious voice for one hour all to myself."

Pulsating with emotion, she entered the deep-cut street. As if in response to the first echoes of her tread, a shadow from the terrace fell suddenly across the way. Looking up she met Stanford's inquiring eyes. He smiled and disappeared, and she knew he would let her in at the street door.

CHAPTER XVII.

"I and Liszt," laboriously croaked an asthmatic voice, "have been acquainted for more than thirty years. We have travelled together several seasons and visited the whole of Europe. Ah! we did have some notable experiences—I and Liszt."

Rivington tarried a moment, an appreciative listener, behind the shrubbery, then, softly closing the Allee gate, he turned into the area before the house at the Royal Gardens. An adipose, beery-visaged septuagenarian was propped up on an end of the long settle under the windows. He winked sagely with one eye at Frau von Berwitz, Muriel and Stanford as he wheezed out: "Then he was tall, spare and straight as an arrow, and had an eye like an eagle's. Well, one night I and Liszt were in——" Muriel interrupted him to present Rivington. Then Professor Schmidt began anew:

"As I was saying, one night I and Liszt were in Si——"

"Good afternoon, ladies," cried a fresh, cheery voice, breaking into the impending anecdote, "Goodday, Schmidt." The celebrated leader of the quartette, followed by his associates, passed by with a friendly bow and went into the house.

"As I was saying," repeated the narrator, "one night I and Liszt were in a Silesian city, and the con-

cert was, as usual, crowded, and people turned away
from the doors. Of course it was an ovation from
A to Z, and I and Liszt——"

"Ladies and gentlemen," called Mischka from a
salon window, "Herr Doctor has risen."

There was a general movement towards the house.
Frau von Berwitz, preceding with Professor Schmidt,
was overheard saying, "You were about to relate
an anecdote of your tours with the Master, Herr
Professor."

"Yes—yes," he responded, punctuating each word
with file-like respirations. "To begin again, I and
Liszt——"

The three young people fell behind to vent their
mirth at this extraordinary individual, who prefaced
everything with "I and Liszt."

"He always does it," exclaimed Muriel. "Long
ago he was Liszt's business manager, or something
of the sort; but now he draws a pension as a superannuated member of the Grand Ducal orchestra.
He belonged to the wind instruments, I believe."

Their subdued laughter faintly mingled with the
sounds of a good-humored strife within. In the
open door to the cellar, an irrepressible German youth,
known to his colleagues as "Emil," was struggling
with the housekeeper for the possession of a quart
bottle of champagne.

"Ah, let me go, you bad boy."

"Now, Pauline—dear Pauline," he pleaded, his
eyes sparkling with mischief, as he tugged at the bottle, "let loose."

"To your health, Pauline," cried a gay comrade, coming from the kitchen with a glass of effervescing wine, which he impudently waved before her eyes and then sipped leisurely as she scolded him with a smile on her lips.

"Ach! du lieber Himmel! you have opened a second bottle! Let go, you wicked child." Freeing herself from Emil's clutches, she locked the cellar door and dropped the key into her pocket.

"Ach! Missy," she exclaimed, espying Muriel, as she wrapped the bottle securely in her apron on the way to the kitchen. "Only see, these unruly boys are teasing me, as usual. There is no getting rid of them."

"Rid of us? Now that is good," retorted Emil saucily. "You would not be rid of us, dearest Pauline, for anything in the world."

For reply she sprang across the kitchen threshold and, slamming the door behind her, turned the key in the lock.

"Herr Emil is right," said Muriel, as they continued their way up. "Those young fellows tease her continually, but having always had their kind to deal with when the Master is here, she has become quite attached to—or better said, accustomed to them."

The members of the quartette were grouping themselves in the centre of the dining-room as Frau von Berwitz entered in advance of those crowding into the ante-chamber. Instantly Liszt turned from the players to receive her.

"Madame, I am proud to see you here," he said,

offering both hands and touching her forehead lightly with his lips.

"Ah, America!" he ejaculated, with a similar greeting for Muriel. The latter, in recalling his undeviating tone of cordiality for all who entered his house as special guests, turned, no less nervously, however, because of her joyous premonition of a still heartier reception awaiting Stanford, to make the presentation.

The Master, extending his hand, said with an engaging smile: "You are very welcome." Then, addressing the trio, he continued with a gesture at the musicians: "I had the table removed. Stringed instruments sound better in here. Too many hangings—too much furniture in the music-room. Pray be seated; we shall begin at once."

Some pupils were already there. Others came in whilst the instruments were being tuned, and, lastly, two white-haired men, Herr Hofrath Gille, of Jena, and the Court organist Gottschalg. A few found chairs; the majority seemed to prefer standing along the walls.

Liszt took a seat between the two ladies before the salon door. "I trust the glare is not too strong?" he said, in apology for having drawn the curtains of the window facing them in order to give the musicians light. "My failing eyesight"—he raised his hand with an impatient movement to his brows— "has caused me considerable worry of late. I injured it some years since during a residence in Rome. I lived at the Villa d'Estes, Tivoli, and always drove to and from the city. As the return trip was gener-

ally begun after sundown I had a lamp placed in my
carriage that I might economize the interval by reading, for the way was long and had to be traversed
several times each week."

"Oh, well," he subjoined, with an expressive shrug,
"the mischief has been done."

In trying to conceive Stanford's impressions of
this first visit to the Royal Gardens, Muriel found
herself contrasting Liszt's elegant, guarded flow of
language with his oftentimes reckless, caustic epi-
grams when, untrammelled by a host's obligations,
he mingled with his pupils in the class.

However, the Master turned the channel of her
thoughts by opening the score of a Beethoven quartette, and handing it to her to follow. After signal-
ing the players to begin, he leaned back in his chair
and closed his eyes. If particularly pleased with
some passage of music, or the manner of reading it,
he would open them again and cry "Bravo!"

He feigned not to hear when the entrance of Emil
and two associates in his pranks caused a slight com-
motion. One of them found a chair. Two minutes
later his head was hanging heavily forward. Liszt
suddenly opened his eyes to gaze fixedly at him without moving a muscle.

A muffled explosion of laughter from Arthur very
nearly created a scene.

"What is the matter?" whispered Rivington.

"Meister looked at Hermann with so much re-
spect."

"Just you wait," said Emil, snapping his eyes, "he'll

get his head blown off to-morrow—if he is sober by that time."

After the Beethoven number, Pauline, bearing aloft an elaborately-decorated cake, entered to clear the way for Mischka, who followed with a huge bowl of champagne punch. The Master himself served the ladies, whereupon the young men devoted themselves to the punch.

By some inexplicable chance no one stood near when Liszt turned again towards the buffet.

"Do not spare the punch, gentlemen," he remarked, in evident surprise.

A significant smile passed over the assembly. Stanford picked up a glass and said: "Permit me, Meister, to drink to your very good health."

"That is very kind," he responded, with a look of pleasure. "Excuse me one moment. I never drink champagne—bad for me." Pouring some claret from a decanter he touched glasses with Stanford. Muriel observed that the latter only put the beverage to his lips.

"Miss Holme tells me you have been in Weimar before," said the Master.

"I attended school here from my sixth to my eighteenth year."

"In that case you should be called a son of Weimar."

"Indeed, it seems like home to me. It is impossible to stay away. This is my tenth visit since leaving Germany twelve years ago."

"Sapp'rrement! It is quite incomprehensible to me how you Americans can cross the Atlantic so often. I could never make up my mind to the trip. I have always had an aversion to long sea voyages. The journel across the English channel was as much as I could bear." Liszt shook his head ruefully. Raising his eyes he scanned Stanford's face.

"I hope we shall have the pleasure of hearing you sing to-day. You have brought your music?" he questioned, with penetrating directness. Instantly something of that expression with which he always unnerved his new pupils possessed him.

"Yes, Meister," replied Stanford, wincing as at an ordeal, "if an amateur may venture to sing before you?"

"Oh!" he interjected, with an expostulatory toss of the head, though by no means displeased at the traditional homage. "After another quartette we will adjourn to the salon."

He rested his hand on Stanford's arm, as if to confirm his good-will, and said to the musicians: "Well, gentlemen, how about the new quartette?"

Some one tendered the score, which he shared with Muriel, though he kept his eyes closed during the most of the performance, and she, in her agitation over Stanford's prospective début, followed the notes mechanically, without thought of the composer's name. Nor did she know that she was assisting at a first hearing, until everybody crowded round to view the score. She suspected it to be the Master's work, but having once relinquished her place, she was too abashed to ask the question.

In the midst of the general discussion the players

took their leave, and then Liszt soon bade his other guests enter the salon to hear Stanford. Escorting Frau von Berwitz to a place at the further end of the room, he took a seat beside her as a signal for general attention. In that moment a sense of responsibility vanquished Muriel's chronic timidity at playing within these four walls, which seemed ever echoing the inspirations of the great Master. Her sentiment and judgment combined in the choice of "Am Meer," because, for him, the least exacting of their favorites from Schubert. Happily, the first touch of her skilled fingers gave her countryman courage to combat that paralyzing, humiliating fear which, at the decisive moment, invariably assaulted candidates for Liszt's approval. Ere he had completed the lines:

> Das Meer erglintzte weit hinaus,
> Im letzten Abendscheine,"

Muriel knew that he would do himself justice, and hearing a surprised "bravo—bravissimo!" from the opposite end of the salon, she once more yielded herself to his enthralling power. Utter silence followed the dying strains, until the Master rose to cross the room and fold the singer to his breast without a word.

A succession of whispered "bravos" and light applause bespoke the mind of the lookers-on. Stanford had created a sensation.

Muriel's heart swelled with sweetest triumph. She had welded the first link in the chain which would bind him to her.

Liszt motioned her to rise. Sinking into her

place he searched the index of songs and turned to "Sei mir gegrüsst." "That is for you," he said, looking up at Stanford. "You have sung it, of course?" Without waiting for assent his fingers fell with velvety caress upon the keys. Liszt's touch seemed to fire Stanford's blood. His delivery of the invocation:

O du Entriss'ns mir und meinem Kusse
Sei mir gegrüsst sei mir geküsst.

revealed attributes both intensely human and divine.

Muriel leaned heavily against the sofa and drove her heels into the carpet in the effort to control her features. She was enraged at allowing herself to be shut in where every one could read her face. She looked out of the window and tried to think of other things, and all the time Stanford was singing with a passionate fervor, a perfection of phrasing, to which she had not yet been able to incite him. Every fibre of her being rebelled at this maddening realization. The primal motive of their coming was forgotten. She could have annihilated everything and everybody—but him—in the room. The loving, venerating pupil had suddenly, without the slightest warning even to herself, become a victim of the fiercest jealousy. She hated Liszt for his sway over Stanford, as she condemned the latter for his unsuspecting faithlessness.

"If I were but sure of him," cried her wounded heart, "they might all play his accompaniments at once, for aught I would care." Again all her resentment would melt away before the irresistible tenderness in that ever-recurring refrain:

"Sei mir gegrusst sei mir geküsst."

Then she fell to wondering, with a wild yearning to know the truth, if, at all, his marvellous power of expression were not art; if the tenderness and affection breathed forth in song did not leave his heart barren of such sentiments? Yet in recalling the increasing gentleness of his speech and manner in their simple home-life, she fell once more into happy confusion. In this emotional fever Muriel followed the song to the end.

Stanford waited with lowered eyes for the final note of the accompaniment. It did not come at once, for the Master again took up the theme, artfully reworking it during the next ten minutes into a marvellous harmonic texture of his own fancy. His eyes, reflecting each minute shade of expression which characterized his improvisation, were in themselves a study. The auditors leaned forward in spellbound attitudes, unwilling to lose one glimpse of that deeply-lined, transfigured face.

To Muriel each soft, stirring note of the music conveyed a gentle rebuke for her rebellious mood. Then and there she could have thrown herself on the Master's neck and implored forgiveness. She seemed never to have loved the dear old man so much as in the consciousness of having given him an ungrateful thought. Her face was hidden by her hand, and she had scarcely heeded her penitent tears until aroused by an abrupt silence in the room.

Liszt was powerfully moved by the music. His eyes had a thoughtful, far-away look, as if searching amongst tender memories of a dead past. His voice sounded low and thick when he pushed away from the piano and spoke to Stanford:

"Come to-morrow—to the lesson. Your welcome is assured for all time. Aufwiedersehen!" Grasping both hands he kissed him warmly on the cheeks.

Where the soul of music enters, human hearts are joining in wonderful accord; fleetingly, it may be, but firmly while it lasts.

"Good-byes" came reluctantly.

"Dear Meister," whispered Muriel, so softly that none overheard, "I thank you from my heart. You have made several people very—very happy to-day."

"So have you. You have my gratitude also, dear friend," he repeated, as if calling himself with effort to the present. With impulsive disregard of the conventions he took her in his arms, for the first time in their acquaintance, and affectionately kissed both cheeks.

"Remember it is the old Master who thanks you. God bless you, dear America. Aufwiedersehen! auf-wiedersehen!"

CHAPTER XVIII.

Pursuant to her desire to acquaint Stanford with the life of the Liszt clique, Muriel had proposed, at dinner, an evening at Werther's Garden, a popular open-air restaurant adjoining the Grand Ducal Theatre.

However, after her mental struggle in the musicale at the Royal Gardens, she wavered in her plan for lionizing him.

When an ingrate, humbled and penitent before Liszt, she was disposed to put a rational construction on Stanford's transgression in having, without her accompaniment, surpassed his previous vocal efforts; but upon leaving the house her heart chilled to his grateful speeches and renewed devotion. They seemed to her an admission of his thoughtlessly inflicted slight; to feel that she had been out of his thoughts for any period of time, however brief, gave her bitter pain.

In her overwrought, nervous state, she immediately began to cherish her grievance with a morbid tenacity which no amount of reasoning could weaken. She was disinclined to create other opportunities for him to upset her tranquillity; her selfish desire was to pursue life as they had begun it, in the seclusion of the von Berwitz abode; but she had gone too far to retreat. Her promise was given, and she had no choice but to face tortures inevitable, as the

afternoon had proven. Under present conditions
she felt it quite justifiable to plead a headache and
keep Stanford at home, but having once divined his
interest in the proposed entertainment, no personal
sacrifice seemed, in that moment, too great for her
to make—anything rather than cloud his most trivial
happiness.

"If I but knew," was the refrain of every query her
mood suggested; and yet, upon so short an acquaintance, Stanford could not have shocked her
sense of propriety more than by telling her that
which she most longed to know.

Her unconscious silence and listless air provoked
Frau von Berwitz's spirit of inquiry. With a painful
realization of her own dullness, Muriel said that she
was perfectly well and desirous of adhering to their
original plan for the evening. Nevertheless her
alternating fits of forced pleasantry and deep abstrac-
tion having depressed the other two, it was a very
bored-looking trio, which sought, towards eight
o'clock, the narrow short cuts over the rough-paved
town to the little square environing the bronze images of that immortal pair, Goethe and Schiller.

It was the weekly "band night" at Werther's Garden. The familiar strains of Weber's "Euryanthe"
overture were rising in tonal splendor from the superb regimental brass within the shaded enclosure,
as Stanford lingered at the gate to pay a trifling admission fee. The lights were not all turned on, but
here and there, in the deepening shadows of the trees,
family groups had assembled for the evening meal.

Muriel looked down the long avenue of tables, which held the promise of so much brilliancy later on, and shuddered at thought of the weary hours in store for her. She could not talk. Her brain refused to yield its one burning theme. Her head seemed bound with tightening steel. Involuntarily she put up her hand, and the shadow it cast made her think of the lonely bypaths in the shrubbery. The idea possessed her to dart into one of them and elude her companions. Frau von Berwitz, being ahead, would not see her and——. She pictured herself escaping from the garden, running through unfrequented side streets to the station, from which the train carried her, quick as thought, to the furthermost corner of Europe that she might be alone when her heart broke.

She was already sorrowfully contemplating her own lifeless body in the dreary wastes of Siberia, and thinking how Stanford, who would arrive in frenzied haste by troika, would fling himself remorsefully at her side and wildly protest against cruel fate, when, turning impulsively, with the image of his agonized face still before her mind's eye, she saw him tapping the tables and chairs with his cane—she fancied in secret annoyance—as he followed, looking indifferently to the right and left.

However, Muriel was not alert enough to evade Stanford's penerating glance.

"What is it?" he asked, stopping in tender solicitude before her.

"Nothing," she answered, with a short laugh, in

which there was the trace of a sob, as the absurdity of her mental attitude occurred to her. Afraid to trust her voice further, she turned and started towards Frau von Berwitz, uneasily aware of Stanford's puzzled scrutiny as he paced silently at her side.

Beyond the music stand, where they could command the main promenade, a body of young, gaily-uniformed officers faced each other above a long table. At sight of Frau von Berwitz, Lieutenant von Jahn rose hastily to his feet to lead the general salutation. Count von Hohenfels was not of the party, owing to the presence of his mother in the city. Seeing no other military coats about, Muriel's heart was lightened with the hope that she might be spared the necessity of mediating beween Hohenfels and Stanford, when they abruptly came upon the officer supping with the Countess and Fräulein Panzer in a roofed area at the extreme end of the garden. It was too late to avoid a meeting or the inevitable bidding to share their table.

Muriel and Hohenfels, at least, conformed, with secret thanksgivings, to the dominating hush which good-breeding exacts during music; she, indeed, was not in a mood to dissemble with success, especially after the occurrences of the past few hours, and Hohenfels' uneasy glances indicated his purpose to follow her initiative.

It depressed Fräulein Panzer, however, to see the two young people so ill at ease. Even Frau von Berwitz and Stanford too, she fancied a trifle out of sorts. Feeling it incumbent to create a more cheerful tone in her party, she filled the pause with droll stories of the local clowns discovered by her roving eye, until convinced of success by a spontaneous burst of laughter from all but the deaf Countess, who could only smile her approval. The music rose again, and with it came a hush so profound, from the throng now gathered, that the light footfalls of two advancing couples reached them from the further end of the gravelled walk.

A low murmur of voices followed their course, as the two ladies of the quartette bowed right and left, until they came upon the last vacant table in the enclosure.

"Everything that walks in Weimar knows them," remarked Fräulein Panzer, watching their friendly reception of some long-haired youths of marked national types, who had sprung up in various quarters of the garden at the close of the music.

"The Fräulein Stahr, with August and Ilmstedt," said Muriel, in response to Stanford's inquiring look. "They will come over to make your acquaintance when they see us, for they have already heard of your afternoon's success."

"Without question," observed Fräulein Panzer, with unusual acridity. "They know the daily happenings at the Royal Gardens ere the sun disappears behind the Ettersberg!"

"Do they employ carrier doves?" asked Stanford, with humorous appreciation of the "Little Canary Bird's" fit of spleen.

"No! Magpies!" She retorted, with a sharp chirp.

Like other Weimaraner, she regarded Anna and Helene Stahr with a curious mixture of tantalizing emotions, because of their lifelong devotion to Liszt and their disinterested absorption in his pupils. She invariably greeted any mention of the sisters with a sarcastic smile, a shrug or an elevation of the eyebrows, though by no means unwilling to acknowledge their really great influence on the advancement of musical art, whether as instigators of some enterprise, local or foreign, or in the better-known capacity of instructors to the musically inclined youth of the Grand Ducal capital.

"They will expect you to sing at their house tomorrow afternoon," she continued in her former tone.

Stanford smiled dubiously.

"Oh, they won't let you off."

"Sing for them, by all means, Carl," interposed Frau von Berwitz. "Their musicales are a matter of history. Their father, Adolph Stahr, the poet and historian, was Liszt's most intimate friend when they were children. It is now about thirty-five years since Liszt began going there on Sunday afternoons in summer. Formerly he played, now his pupils make the music while he sits in the front row and listens. Nearly all the great artists of the time have appeared there. One room is devoted to their pictures, autographs and souvenirs generally. It is probably one of the finest collections extant. Muriel has named it the 'Museum.'" They all looked at Muriel expectantly. She tried to speak, but could not; and laying her arm on the table, leaned over it to fill an awkward pause. She breathed with effort; the blood seemed to leave the region of her heart and surge remorselessly against the weary tissues of her brain. She felt anew the agony of the afternoon's ordeal. She could suffer no kind of interference with Stanford! Both Frau von Berwitz and Fräulein Panzer had preceded her in a once-cherished plan; innocently, she knew, but she could not forgive the act, for each new helping hand weakened her hold on him. The thought roused her craft; the moment gave inspiration.

"Annihilate feeling and lead," it said: "be not led!" The force of an invincible will animated her word and glance.

"Will you not go with me now to meet them?" she said with composure to Stanford; "it will please them."

The two Americans wended their way amongst the crowded tables to the Fräulein Stahr. The noisy welcome to Muriel put Stanford in touch with the spirit pervading the convivial board, as he edged his way into the circle of young celebrities, who had become, with the traditional self-satisfied bearing of the Lisztianer, totally oblivious of the curious attention of the townspeople. When he remarked on the Babel of tongues, Muriel counted off to him the representatives of eleven different nationalities. They were all talking at once, seeming never to expect replies; at least, that was the impression made on Stanford, for before he bade them good-night, the only words he had uttered were in promise to sing the following afternoon for the Fräulein Stahr.

"They were too many," observed Muriel, as they sauntered back to their party. "You must go with me some evening to the Russischer Hof, where chosen ones only meet with the Sisters Stahr for supper. There I can insure you reminiscences worth carrying to America."

Stanford darted an eloquent glance—one so entirely for her that she retarded her steps to turn her face to the crowded garden for one ecstatic moment before material thoughts obtruded on the precious memory.

But she would not yield to so brief a promise of divine happiness. She had been too often subjected to attentions of ephemeral import to readily trust men's eyes. Heaven was not for her—yet. She remembered the voice of warning: "Lead! Be not led!" and confronted him with unperturbed countenance.

He moved his lips to speak—hestitated as if unable to articulate, and—they had reached the table.

CHAPTER XIX.

Sunday afternoon, at four o'clock, Liszt's barouche drew up at a gate in Schwanseestrasse. August, who had driven with him, sprang down and helped him to alight. Anna and Helene Stahr, in white muslins with fluttering green ribbons, came flitting through the garden of a modern brick residence to meet them half way. From the music-room of their second-floor apartment the more favored pupils went to receive the Master at the head of the staircase, while the dubious ones hovered with faint hearts about the entrance, and a bevy of pretty girls, unknown to the Lisztianer, shrank into the remotest corner. Following the treble-crescendo, Liszt came to a halt on the threshold.

The long, closely-fitting coat of his ecclesiastical rank enhanced the dignity of his bearing, as he benignly grasped the first timorously extended hand. Encouraged thereby, the others now moved briskly forward to pay their respects, and Anna Stahr actually propelled the strangers along before the Master, to present them in turn ere he indulged in his well-known propensity for cutting off introductions by taking a seat in the front row of chairs.

The Fräulein Stahr settled themselves to the right and left of him, and gave the second places to Muriel and Stanford, whilst the rear end of the escorting procession, taking a roundabout course, poured in through the dining-room door and sought the nearest vacancies.

Silence fell like a curtain, and, as by magic, Arthur and Ivan, the latter a young Russian with a prodigious technique, appeared seated before two upright pianos.

During the flutter of expectancy over the first notes of a programme full of surprises, which they had prepared to welcome the Master home, Muriel noted the absence of the pretty strangers, and espied two pairs of bright eyes covertly inspecting Stanford's handsome face from the dark folds of the dining-room portière.

"The Master is nothing to them beside Carl," she reflected, in instantaneous rebellion.

The realization that she had called him "Carl" to herself, for the first time without forethought, sent the hot blood over her face like a flame. Often, in solitary musing, she had conjured up his magnetic presence, gazed into his fathomless eyes and heard his name linger fondly on the breath of all nature, until "Carl—Carl—Carl" had become the dearest refrain of her beloved music. Even though she hardly dared trust the promise of his eyes, still, in the memory of that last meaningful glance at Werther's Garden, peace of mind had descended like a blessing divine, bringing rest to her slumbers and sunshine to the new-born day.

Stanford's welcome had a ring of eager delight when, in obedience to intuition, she had made her first appearance for that day at dinner; not only in

order to obtain extra rest, but also to gain an expression of his desire for her companionship.

No woman, however much she may help a man in
his wooing, wishes to seem easily won. Muriel,
therefore gloried in the unmistakable devotion in
Stanford's word and glance, as they sauntered across
town to the Fräulein Stahr. Fears and resolves, in
fact, had no place in the all-sufficient present until
her notice of Stanford's admirers induced a telltale
color which caught Liszt's ever-ready eye.

With a perceptible start Muriel sank back in her
chair, and the Master, developing a precipitate interest in the music, exchanged his seat for one between
the two pianists where he could unobservedly advise
them, or play at either end of the keyboard to broaden
the harmonies. Soothed by this manoeuvre, Muriel
hearkened to the music as if every note were played
on the strings of her heart, for just beyond the semi-
circle sat Stanford, with half-turned face, clearly more
intent upon her than upon the performers.

They were playing from memory "Faust," the favorite symphonic poem of Liszt, who indulged in inter-
mittent bravos of delight. Then his face would settle, with a low droop of the upper lip which gave him
a stern, commanding expression, while his fixed eyes
seemed penetrating regions too distant for others to
follow. The music faded to a pianissimo, and the
Master began humming softly as he marked the time
with the forefinger of his right hand. He himself
was hearkening, in fancy, to angelic choirs, his countenance wearing a look of peaceful elevation. So far

had he wandered from earthly scenes that the swelling harmony of pure young voices in the adjoining room was soaring gloriously towards heaven ere he was roused to the sweet reality.

A moment he was motionless and.silent, listening to reassure himself, and then he turned a radiant face to the Sisters Stahr. Every heart mirrored its response to the happy, spontaneous smile that passed through the room; a portière glided noiselessly aside, and just over the threshold stood the singers— the pretty strangers—their bright young faces upturned to an invisible leader.

A soft happy light stirred the depths of the Master's gray eyes, and the heavy lines of his face relaxed under the stress of genuine emotion.

Although, as creator of a new form in musical art— the symphonic poem—none could dispute his claim to immortality, it was no secret that he was ofttimes grievously irritated in old age to have his maturer works ignored by neighboring musical autocrats. This modestly planned production, therefore, sounded not only the first notes of the crusade to overcome that prejudice, but told, also, of the love of his loyal and grateful disciples.

The final note of song floated heavenward. The portière glided into place. Arthur and Ivan played to the end. Then the Master, overcome by his gratifying surprise, could no more than shout "Bravissimo!" as he embraced successively the Fräulein Stahr and the performers, including Alfred, the hidden choir-master, and his winsome band.

Since Liszt's arrival the temperature in the room had risen to almost unbearable height. He had as 	deep-rooted a dislike for draughts as for conservatories of music. The rooms were, therefore, kept practically airtight. As poor Arthur and Ivan stood before him, patiently mopping their faces, he gave indication of the stifling heat by constantly running his fingers through his long, silky hair. "Mariechen" crept up behind, and, with forefinger and thumb, pilfered the loose strands littering his shoulders, twirling them, for safe keeping, about a button of her dress. Her pantomime was inimitable, and when she stealthily drew away, she confessed to her laughing colleagues to having collected, at odd intervals, almost enough for a locket.

A gesture from Liszt and a movement towards the door drew all eyes to a novice, a guilty window-opener, who drew back abashed as a half-dozen people sprang to close it.

Helene Stahr slipped away to hasten the programme by introducing another surprise.

The strident noise of a violin undergoing the process of tuning cut into the confused murmur of re-seating.

"Ah! · My little Paganini!" The Master's face glowed with delight, and he walked swiftly, with hands extended, towards the dining-room; but the portière moved back, and a fairylike young creature in white lace bounded forward to meet him.

"Who is 'Little Paganini'?" quizzed Stanford, amidst a furore of plaudits and bravos.

"A countrywoman of ours, who carried off both prizes at the National Conservatory in Paris, Arna Trebor," said Muriel. "Robert, really; for she reversed the spelling of her name to satisfy a whim of her manager."

"The Arna, also? The backward is odder than the forward spelling."

"Oh, no; that is a birthright. To settle a dispute for a name, her uncle threw some letters of the alphabet into a hat, and drew for the first combination that made sense. A-r-n-a was the result, according to her mother." And Muriel called attention to a tall, fashionably-attired woman, the centre of an admiring group.

"A handsome pair, and inseparable. They spend their summers here, and, through Liszt's championship, Arna has been showered with honors galore. They returned last night from a tournée. Her orders, her gifts from crowned heads and societies, and her mementoes generally, offset interest in the collection there." She finished by pointing to the "Museum" entrance.

Beyond the threshold stood a group of choristers, intent upon her and Stanford. "How miserable his wife would be," reflected Muriel, as a sickening paralysis crept into her arms. "How miserable his wife would be if he yielded to the sway of other women. Would he? Could he?"

"Really, you have the most penetrating eyes I have ever—felt," Stanford exclaimed, in a bantering tone. "What do you see?"

"Nothing," retorted Muriel impulsively, and forgot her mercurial mood.

"Oh, what a blow!"

They both laughed light-heartedly, and resumed their places, for Liszt had bowed Arna to her station with the deference due genius double her years.

The violinist raised the Stradivarius and sank her pretty head, with its curling brown locks, upon it. One stroke of the bow on the soulful strings, and the great, laughing gray eyes assumed a look of dreamland.

The violin spoke to them like the voice of a human heart; but a voice made beautiful by the knowledge of a refining and ennobling art. None would or could resist the spell of the graceful Arna. They listened and looked as though she were a creature divine. The very harmonies seemed born of her fingers and the vibrating of the strings of the old violin. Never were composer and interpreter more in accord.

"She feels his thoughts," observed Muriel softly to Stanford, who had placed his chair next to hers after the intermission.

"Whose?"

"The composer's—Bird's—Arthur Bird, who wrote that romance. He is a countryman, you know."

"Does a woman always feel her countryman's thoughts?" Stanford leaned slightly nearer, with a roguish twinkle of the eyes.

"Not if he be fickle," retorted Muriel, brightly. "They would be too inane."

Stanford laughed, and subsided at a cue for silence. As she raised her bow, Arna's countenance glowed with a coquettish light. A shower of crisp, scintillating notes sprang from the pulsating strings like a meteoric fire. .The rhythm, the grace, the warmth and playful abandon of the Sarasate "Spanish Dance" were irresistible; while the fearlessness of her extraordinary technique swept the emotions of the hearers to a stirring climax of wild applause.

"Inimitable! Unquestionably great!" cried Muriel, excitedly.

"Her personality is half of it," added Stanford, all aglow with interest.

"Of course," replied Muriel, calmed by his observation. "She suggests what a celebrated violinist recently said to me: 'I love my husband better than any man living, but I don't love him a quarter as much as I do my violin.'"

"Has a piano that same power over a woman?" inquired Stanford, with a return of his gay manner.

"It could have."

"Is it the rule?"

"A paradoxical rule, perhaps."

"How so?"

"Isn't a woman full of contradictions?"

"Delightful contradictions—yes." Stanford was oblivious of his surroundings, as he brought his laughing eyes nearer. "Now, seriously—no evasion."

Looking sharply about her, Muriel leaned discreetly back in her chair, but a less capricious tone marked her words, and she lowered her voice as Arna silenced applause by retuning her violin. "An artist is, first of all, a woman—the artist afterwards. She demands love for herself—admiration for her accomplishments."

"Isn't that a bit selfish, demanding a fourfold return—to judge by your violinist—for what she gives?"

"Ah! My violinist was nurtured on the homage of the public. It was her daily bread."

"Then would not the man in the question better take time—the artist—by the forelock, and prevent the début?"

They laughed like two innocent-hearted children, and Muriel continued, archly: "Why? To let her dream of what might have been?"

"But would she—if she loved her husband?"

"Even then," replied Muriel, with a sage expression, which changed as she added, "but she wouldn't regret it—if she truly loved." There was a warmth in her voice, a sympathetic thrill—almost a suggestion of happy, unconscious tears.

Stanford flushed slightly. "That," he interposed, "is the ideal wife."

"Yet, a practical one," she added, softly, for, in honor of Liszt, Arna had begun his "Elégie," a favorite composition, which he always accompanied in his own house.

With senses prepared by this play at hearts for the keenest enjoyment of music, they found it in watching the player's lovely face reflect the minutest shade of sentiment pouring from the soul of the old violin.

Her versatility fascinated—enthralled the more deeply with each new mood, until her mere presence bespoke inspiration.

Luxuriating in the mystic charm enfolding her, Muriel lazily turned to bask in the sunshine of Stanford's countenance. Transfixed by Arna's magic, he was lost in the snare of her dreamy eyes. Muriel watched and waited. There was no more music for her. Every stroke of the bow cut like a knife into her heart. Then came great jubilation, through which Stanford sat motionless, his eyes on the violinist, like one intoxicated.

Arna hugged her beloved instrument under one arm as an adoring circle formed to express their rapture.

Helene Stahr touched Stanford's arm and spoke quietly. He started as from a dream, answered inaudibly, and, looking at Muriel, gave an ecstatic sigh which she only heard. He shook his head, smiled as if unable to find words, and rose to open his folio of songs. Liszt saw the move and resumed his seat.

"What is it?" asked Muriel, who had not rehearsed for the occasion. Stanford handed her the Master's setting of Heine's lines:

> "Thou art like a beauteous flower,
> So pure, so lovely, so bright."

"An appropriate selection," she observed, with a nod and smile at Arna.

"Yes," said Stanford, indifferently, looking deep into her eyes.

Muriel caught blindly at the first group of notes,

and the song began. So simple, so tender, so unaffected was it, following the tense nerve-strain of
Arna's witchery, that it soothed like sunshine after an
electric storm. Ivan, avowedly the most appreciative
of the class, sprang up to say feelingly: "That will
be a green spot in my memory of the most exquisite——"

"Green, Ivanus?" exclaimed the Master, embracing
him and Stanford at once. "Green? The color the
song calls odious?" With characteristic sawlike respirations, Liszt fell to laughing.

"May I sing that song, Meister?" asked Stanford.

"Charming! Charming idea!" he answered in
French, in accordance with his preference, when sure
of being understood.

Observing the grand, seignorlike poise of his head
after he had dropped lightly into his chair, Mariechen, the complement of Emil, the jester of the class,
whispered prophetically: "Du lieber Himmel! His
vitality won't hold out over to-morrow's lesson—after
that! I'll pay for his dissipation."

"Do you play, Fraulein?" inquired von Ilmstedt,
solicitously.

Mariechen displayed the whites of her eyes and
raised her hands despairingly.

"And you?" she asked in return. "And you,
Vilma? And you? Humph!" Again tossing up her
hands, she brought them together with such a report
that the Master, thinking it meant for Stanford, began
to applaud. Mariechen hid her eighteen years of
self behind the Master's great chair and tried to swal-

low her handkerchief as her colleagues smothered their mirth.

Stanford followed Muriel's reckless attack of Schubert's spirited song with notes of such flaming tonal color that a vocal fibre of hitherto undisplayed beauty, roused by the dramatic insistence of his delivery, vibrated through the room like an electric current.

Impelled beyond the limitations of self to the realm of the infinite, heads and hearts greeted the inpouring echoes from abyss and aerial height until a boundless universe seemed to resound with joy and thanksgiving. Perhaps there was conscious command in the refrain—a command of which love made an appeal.

Ade, ade und reiche mir zum Abschied deine Hand.

To one heart, at least, were they words of both despair and hope. To the ravished sender only glory and endless ecstacy.

Victor of the day, beyond any they had ever seen proudly he stood, a god among men, waiting for the final note of accompaniment to acknowledge the ovation.

It was a scene of scenes for even Liszt's Weimar.

Arna impulsively caught up her violin, and with a word to Muriel they began the Schubert "Serenade." Stanford laughingly resumed his former station, and, with a complimentary bow for Arna, sang in English, to the passionate thread of obligato, phrases as exquisitely enunciated as when born in the poet-mind. All the resources of their wonderful art came at will to the gifted trio.

"Heart spoke to heart, touching again with poetry hearts as rich in music lore as their own. It was a fitting close to an ever-memorable day; a tribute to the memory of other days—dead, like the hands and voices which made their music. A spirit of the past hovered over their young heads—a past to which belonged the snow-white head of the aged Master whose still youthful spirit met the present in just as sweet accord.

Into the adjoining apartment where these eloquent years found record, came the guests, after he had gone, with grateful speech and fond farewell. A pensive humor guided conversation, for, where the depths of human hearts have been sounded, the frivolity of careless moments finds no entrance; and moments like these are sacred to the musician—doubly sacred to those whose efforts have inspired each other to perfect unity of thought and action.

After almost superhuman effort to be conventional, Muriel had left Stanford and the Fräulein Stahr. Her pride in his success made love, adoration, so holy that the mere vision of another became profanation.

But as she stood by an open window, Rivington approached. His refined, poetic expression appealed to her, and, surmising his loneliness from the eagerness of his greeting, her first thought was to enlist Stanford's interest in the youth. In gladsome anticipation of his voice and words, she turned to look for Stanford.

Beyond the threshold of the museum he stood with the Trebors, steeped in the witchery of Arna's upturned eyes as he bent over her with a devotion which Muriel had dreamed only hers.

Deaf to other sounds, she heard, in fancy, that self-same voice—now the voice of a man of middle age—saying "Muriel Holme? Muriel Holme? Ah, to be sure. What a flirtation I had with her back in Weimar, when old Meister Liszt was living, fifteen—twenty—humph!—never mind the years—ago."

Muriel turned again and looked out of the window. "He has never heard me play before others," she reflected; and the day grew brighter.

"Shall we go out there? It looks cooler," she said to Rivington. "Helene, dear, my countryman is absorbed in your collection. When he comes out, please tell him that I wish to practice, and have gone on. Good-by, Anna. Aufwiedersehen, dears: to-morrow evening at the 'Russian.'"

CHAPTER XX.

Frau von Berwitz carried a satisfactory excuse for Muriel when she and Stanford went, at Fräulein Panzer's invitation, to a quiet Sunday evening tea with the Countess and her son. When they returned the lights were out in the vine-grown gable.

Muriel was not again visible until summoned to dinner the next day. She was radiantly well; Stanford, a trifle subdued, with less assurance of manner and a shadow of reproach in his eyes. The interchange of attitudes flattered Muriel and increased her consciousness of reserve power stored for the test performance at Liszt's.

They had sauntered all too leisurely to the lesson, it seemed, upon reaching the park gate at the Royal Gardens. Snatches of music floated toward them, and as they drew nearer they were greeted by friendly gestures from an overheated group by the open window.

"I fear the Master is in a bad humor," said Muriel, noting a grotesque shower of treble tones from the piano. That Mariechen's prophecy was fulfilled she was assured at the entrance to the salon.

"Does it give you pleasure to do that?" he said, repeating the burlesque.

"No, Master," replied a familiar voice.

"Then what makes you do it?"

"I thought it right, Master."

"Well, it is not! I recommend you to do it so!"

The speakers were concealed by the crowd, which, including privileged visitors and newly arrived pupils, numbered thirty or more.

"Fie! fie! fie!" cried Liszt angrily. "Why stop with a dozen false notes, when twenty are just as easy? Halt! Try that again!"

The frightened youth grappled vainly and valiantly for the cue to the Master's lost favor, even when he saw him rise in silent disgust and repair to the remotest corner of the room.

Muriel and Stanford found him, scarlet-faced, bending over the writing-desk, in a fruitless quest, smacking and tasting his lips as usual when annoyed. With modified heartiness he extended his usual welcome, and said, smilingly, "See how they wilfully harass me." However, with unfailing perseverance, he started for the round table.

"Who plays this?" he asked, catching up a composition.

A dozen paling faces turned askance. "I do, dear Master, said poor "Norway," faintly.

The eleven fortunates smiled at each other and regained their normal hues. The first player had retired in disgrace to the leathern chair by the writing desk, the personification of abject misery. Ferreting him out, Liszt placed an arm round his shoulder. "Come," he said, leading him in that position to the piano, "turn the leaves for 'Norway.'"

The Master invariably sought means of prompt redress where his words, however just, caused pain.

Therefore "Norway" gained by her colleague's loss. While mildly impatient in his careful criticism, he relieved his pent-up cynicism when beyond her hearing in one of his excursions about the room.

"Marie," he said, demurely, to a renowned oratorio singer. "There is a small railway junction between Leipzig and Dresden, named——"

"Risa, Meister."

"Thanks!" he responded, with a sly return of her glance. "It boasts a Conservatory of Music. I recommend it—for some people."

Too self-conscious to join in the ripple of laughter passed down to the piano, "Norway" tremblingly gathered her music up and faded from sight in the dining-room.

"Now for a game of chance," said the Master, shuffling a deck of playing cards into fan shape. "It is too hot for sustained effort to-day. August, place that new composition of Zarembski's on the piano. They who draw a face card must read a page at sight."

A bomb could not have created greater consternation in the crowded salon. Timid ones slipped behind curtains, dropped upon ottomans, or glided into the dining-room. The sudden thinning-out, the gasping sighs and frightened glances, incited Liszt's most sardonic humor. The refugees were first sought, Mariechen being pulled from behind a portière, and Vilma from a soliloquy at the dining-room window. Then a successful débutante from Berlin stubbornly refused to draw.

Only the tense silence during the dialogue equalled the pitch of Liszt's fury.

"So! Humph! Very well! I shall not hear you play for a fortnight, if ever again!"

Naming the order of trial, Moritz, a phenomenal Polish virtuoso and extraordinary sight-reader, led off.

Then Mariechen flopped limply into place. Though an earnest, promising student, and already a concert pianist of modest renown in Thuringia, as a prima-vista bungler she was supreme.

Presaging fun from her serio-comic expression, Liszt stood opposite her with encouraging words. With a spasmodic facial contortion he signaled her to stop.

"Quick! quick!" Oh, Mariechen, Mariechen!" he groaned, "I didn't think it of you!" Mariechen's head sank lower, until it rested on the piano in hopeless chagrin. "Oh! oh! oh! Here, August, extricate this lady from her dilemma."

Mariechen bounced up, overjoyed to escape the oft-recurring duty of butt for Liszt's ridicule. Yet his was not aimless jesting. Therefore, Mariechen was heard to plan daily sight-reading , for at each chance meeting he cried, "Oh, Mariechen!" adding, "I wouldn't have believed it!"—while, in pantomime, he appeared to fly from her.

Other successes and failures, rousing praise or imprecations, ended the trial.

A beardless novice from Great Britain, however, captivated every one in a rigorous début. Mollified by this worthy acquisition to his class, Liszt, in moving about, happened to catch a first glimpse of the performer, grimacing in rhythm. With the short puffs of laughter peculiar to him, the Master stopped before a listening group. "How like a monkey," he whispered. "He recalls the story of an unsuccessful photographer who took up dentistry. A patient came one day moaning and tremulously pressing his hand to his jaw. 'Now try to look natural!' exclaimed the dentist, cheerily grasping his forceps. 'Put on a pleasant expression!'"

The laughter quickly spread from one group to another, in traditional fashion, until it reached the one behind the player, just as he left the instrument.

"It is nothing," said Ivan, his sponsor, kindly looking into his frightened eyes. "The Master has been telling a funny story."

"Oh!" said the boy, and smiled too, for Liszt generously applauded and came to advise him.

"Now, Miss Muriel," he said, gallantly offering his arm.

"I hope it won't bore you to hear it again, dear Master," she said, her heart thumping painfully as they walked to the piano.

"Certainly not, dear colleague! Certainly not! We will see if it can be improved!" And he moved his chair to the side of the room, the crowd opening for him a vista to the keyboard.

Aware of Stanford's surprised look, Muriel turned with apparent calm to her work, though none knew better than she the secret condescension felt by the average Lisztianer for his sisters-in-art—as a class.

Few of them, indeed, combined the temperamental impulses of the artist virtuoso with the unfailing dignity of a gentlewoman.

"The tip of 'Norway's' tongue, held lightly between her teeth, always protruded from the left corner of her mouth.

Round-shouldered Fräulein L. dove incessantly at the extremities of the keyboard.

Fräulein H.'s head nodded like a Chinese idol's.

Mlle. P. put her cuffs in her pocket and loosened her collar.

Fräulein R. might have executed the famous piece in which Mozart struck one note with his nose—or, for that matter, any number required, to judge by Liszt's ceaseless admonition, "Don't stick your nose in the keys."

Among those who displayed gentle breeding and played like scholarly artists, Muriel was pre-eminent. Her attitude never suggested athletics, nor offended by its incongruity. Neither did any love of display lead her into shallow or degrading artifices. Like Arna, her appearance won half the victory ere she sent a thrill through the hearer by the force of her interpretative genius. But Muriel's position at Liszt's had been rather equivocal, owing to the influence of Adèle aus der Ohe's musicianly virtuosity.

Ivan had said: "There is much in descent. Adèle is German; Muriel, American. The latter can, therefore, never be her sister-artist's equal."

But a surprise was in store for Ivan.

Adèle had not yet arrived. Therefore Muriel feared no rival, though she recalled Ivan's statement that no woman—excepting, possibly, Sophie Menter —could play Liszt's "Don Juan Fantaisie." To this she had retorted, "There should be no sex in art." A manifold purpose now ruled her determination for a crowning success, despite the length of the composition. Liszt had made some cuts in it the previous season, and a winter's hard practice had made it her most eloquent medium for expression and virtuosity.

The start was like the plunge from a precipice into space—the dividing-line between safety and the awesome unknown. Muriel caught her breath, and, before she realized it, the familiar notes were secure in her grasp and the spirit of mastery hers as certainly as in her own work-room. The inspiration lacking there, was here the air she breathed. To Stanford's presence she owed the power of endurance; to love of him, the tender grace, the deep, noble sentiment, and passionate abandon in delivery. On theme and variation she touched in ever-excelling gradation, until, soaring to the heights of revelation and immortal glory, the crown of greatness was in her grasp. Now of the elect in art, she felt her mission accomplished, and she waited with bowed head for the dying wave of inspired tone.

There was great demonstration, led by Liszt. Yet Adèle, Arthur, Ivan, and a half-dozen others had roused similar scenes. The walls echoed and re-echoed the great achievements of many years.

Muriel listened in a half-hearted way to Liszt's

earnest review of her work .and to Ivan's comp'i-
ment, "A credit to such a Master, Fräulein": and she
waited vainly for some expression of approval from
Stanford.

All but the circle of intimates were dismissed; Liszt
accompanied Stanford in some songs; and then, in the
cool of the evening, he and Arna played Beethoven's
"Kreutzer Sonata" in a way to send them all home
with hearts full of nobler emotions.

Muriel and Stanford were neither of that age ready
to fly asunder, wounded to the death by some trifle,
or to forgive, forget, and join hearts in eternal bliss.
A barrier, indefinable yet real, had come between
them. Muriel read it in his non-committal manner
as they returned through the park, and was irritated
at the failure of her brilliantly conceived triumph.
Still under the influence of her daring technical feat,
she was emboldened to employ Liszt's habit of simile
and enforce a response.

"There is a famous picture," she said: "'Il Pen-
seroso.'"

"I have seen it," remarked Stanford.

"Why do you reflect its sentiment?" she asked,
according him a brilliant smile.

"For having learned to think of you as human,"
answered Stanford quickly, with a penetrating glance,
"only to find you a goddess!"

"Don't you like goddesses?" said Muriel, her eyes
snapping mischievously.

"No! That is, not in the way I know you. Don't
you know," he said impulsively, "don't you know that

men hate to meet women in the arena for any sort of contest but one?"

"What is that?"

"Hearts!"

"Ah!" Muriel caught her breath and looked out toward the Ilm. "I thought you believed in the equality of rights!"

"I do—in theory." Stanford was compelled to laugh at this admission. "But circumstances—certain conditions—don't you know—can make the practice —peculiarly undesirable."

"What has that to do with my having a little music in an amateurish way?" inquired Muriel, suddenly jumping at conclusions.

"Everything; for you are no amateur."

"Then, what is an amateur?"

"One who cultivates an art for love of it only, I suppose."

"Strictly speaking, then, I am an amateur, and will never be anything more—unless in adversity," she added firmly.

Stanford's face brightened. "Absolutely?"

"Absolutely," said Muriel, with decision—"though it rob me of the godlike," she added, with a gay laugh.

"On the contrary," said Stanford warmly, in spite of a sudden return of roguish humor as their foot-. falls drew Frau von Berwitz to the terrace rail, "it deifies the art you possess."

CHAPTER XXI.

Ivan once called the frequenters of the historic alcove in the public-room at the "Russischer Hof" "The Lisztianer behind the scenes." When he tired of hearing himself quoted, he spoke of "The Oracle of Music," and was lauded—prodigy of intellect as of digital skill.

Even a faintly original or witty saying found uproarious favor with the mercurial spirits who were elected annually from the choicest stratum of Lisztianer by Anna and Helene Stahr, the founders of the "Corner Table." The cry, "Ladies and gentlemen! Listen to this!" was enough to win the attention of all—artists within as well as townspeople without the alcove.

The narration aroused a shrill chorus of Lisztianer, reanimated grinning waiters, and sent the citizens with pursed mouths and quizzical glances, back to gossiping. Voices whirred and soared from early until rational bedtime.

Eleven o'clock at the "Corner Table" was dissipation for the Fräulein Stahr. Even ten o'clock brought languid "good-nights" from wily youths, lured to unseemlier revels at the "Hotel zum Elephanten."

The circle was complete, when Muriel and Stanford entered the public- room between eight and nine o'clock.

"A revised and fingered edition of Herr and Frau Jack Spratt," Ivan's genial voice was declaring be-

hind the screen which formed the alcove. "August
orders one supper; Anna eats the meat, and he, the
vegetables." At this there were gasps of feminine
laughter followed by general mirth, through which
a hoarse treble rose brokenly: "Your health, my
friends; your health."

"Anna never raises a glass but to propose a toast,"
observed Muriel, during a series of clicks and disjointed "Prosits!"

"O-o-o-o-oh! My dear! my dear! Mr. Stanford!
Mr. Stanford! Come right here, Miss Muriel!
Waiter! waiter! Beer! beer! Quick! quick! Here, you
fellow; two beers! Hurry up, or you don't get a penny!"

The boy reeled off, choking with laughter, and reappeared with two dripping mugs, in time for the
established first toast.

"Meister! Meister! Meister! Meister!" rang along
the circle.

Anna Stahr reached for her mug, and found three.
Muriel and Stanford had passed theirs to her, unnoticed. Unabashed, Anna caught them up gleefully
and sipped at each. This inspired Emil to tell of the
newly made widower who, stopping for refreshment
on his way from the cemetery, sighed as he paused
with glass in hand: "Ah! how poor, dear Louise did
enjoy a good swallow of beer with the foam on it, like
that!"

Ivan repeated Rubinstein's reply when asked if he
would again make the dreaded voyage to America:
"Why should I? That my son may drink more
champagne?"

Moritz thereupon recalled a story of Rubinstein's early colleague at Weimar, Hans von Bülow, who greeted a newly presented musical critic of renown at Copenhagen, in this wise: "An impossible nose!" and turned on his heel.

His insolence reminded Muriel of old Professor R., in Berlin, who heard his neighbor, the United States Minister, whisper to his wife during a performance of a Schubert Symphony, "I don't care for that." "It was not written for red-skins, anyway," retorted the Herr Professor fiercely.

Fresh supplies of beer floated them into personal and duller reminiscences of concert tours. Somewhat after this fashion: "Great furore—almost a panic! Awfully bad beer! Press ran into ecstatic riot— thought of getting out extras—but reconsidered when receipts were declared."

Arthur, who had foregone the afternoon lesson in order to practice, spoke of his mother's assertion that he had, according to strict count, played Chopin's G major prelude just seven hundred times that day.

"Practice!" the word dispersed the party. No lesson to-morrow implied slavery to the piano.

August and Ilmstedt escorted the Fräulein Stahr.

"Aufwiedersehen, to-morrow night!" resounded through the darkened street; and the two Americans sauntered off under the trees in Karl Platz.

. Frau von Berwitz had not yet come in, Gretchen told them, between simpers, in her pretty Thuringian dialect, when they surprised her in the black archway seated beside the outline of a man.

"Let us go to meet her," exclaimed Stanford in English.

When they reached the terrace steps he said: "It is pleasant here. She will come this way. Let us promenade."

A pale soft light, forerunner of the rising moon, glanced on the tree-tops and slipped down the rose-tangled gable. "Moonlight o'er the earth is stealing," sang Stanford and he fell to humming the "Serenade."

They turned to retrace their steps—gently, not to mar the glory of the night. Muriel's upturned eyes reflected the glittering firmament. Stanford averted his face, singing again softly,

> All the stars in heav'n keep watch, love,
> While I sing to thee!

The witchery of the words—the voice, the night—of love, pure-hearted and ideal, held them in speechless bondage. Alone—the world asleep—soul joined to soul in celestial union, oblivious of time—place—and the muffled tone of their own unhalting tread.

A footfall on the terrace—the dream was over!

Before them bending boughs of exquisite cream roses filled the air with fragrance. Stanford culled a half-blown bud.

"Will you take it?" he said, with his heart in his eyes.

Muriel half glanced up, put out her hand, then—Frau von Berwitz stopped before them.

CHAPTER XXII.

"London" was the postmark on a letter which Stanford fingered nervously while sipping coffee with the two ladies next morning under the plum trees.

"You have lost appetite, Carl!" said Frau von Berwitz, noticing that he barely touched substantials.

"More than that," he replied, after a fourth reading of his letter. "I cannot escape it. I must go by the one o'clock train."

"Which way?" inquired Tante Anna, in alarm.

"To London."

"London!" gasped Frau von Berwitz.

"A suit involving a large sum of money for a client brought me over," said Stanford, avoiding their eyes. "I am wanted in London at once. I may be able to return here. I do not know," he added, after a thoughtful pause. "I will try, anyway," he continued, banishing gloom in a sanguine smile and a renewal of devotion to both.

* * *

Yet—he was gone—gone without a parting word or glance which Muriel might cherish.

"Aufwiedersehen?" she asked herself, as Frau von Berwitz drove with him to the station. "Aufwiedersehen? Every one says that here!" A taunting voice whispered: "Muriel Holme! Muriel Holme! Ah! to be sure! What a flirtation we had during old Meister Liszt's time—back in the eighties. She must be an old woman now—if she is living!"

"They say it is bad luck to watch people out of sight," said Gretchen, looking up at her from the middle of the street. "I am going in."

Muriel drew back, blinded by tears. Entering the Cloister unseen, she groped the way to her door and turned the key in the lock.

The balm of tears restored her faith in Stanford. Love leaped forth to protect him from her own doubts—to save her from guilt when bidden—if ever —to return trust for trust. Moreover, Muriel was too enamored of love itself to relinquish one degree of its ethereal consciousness. "He will come again," she promised herself, "if a steadfast heart can draw him here! Until then—I believe in him. Yet," she reflected, knowing that sore trials were inevitable, "one victory over self leads to another."

Resolutely crossing the court, she faltered at the threshold of the room where he had sung his way into her heart. Its desolation chilled her. Bravely she tried her piano. The music was gone—a profanation in its discordant responses drove her to the garden. The very flowers there seemed hanging their heads in sorrow. The sweetness of life was only slumbering—not dead. Work was impossible.

"I will go everywhere now," said Muriel, reviewing the scene once hallowed by his presence: and a sob caught her breath. "It will be easier to come here next time, perhaps."

Returning from the station, Frau von Berwitz found her apparently sleeping in an easy chair in the summer house.

"I was waiting for coffee," exclaimed Muriel, . brightening spasmodically to hide her feelings from Tante Anna, never suspecting the dear woman of having read her secret, through that instinct for romantic sentiment characteristic of her nation.

"Let us take coffee at Belvedere," subjoined Muriel, in quick thought of a place not associated with her countryman. "Anything to kill time until I know that he is safe in London," she reflected.

"We can ask Fräulein Panzer and Countess von Hohenfels to drive out with us, and"—Muriel acknowledged a second twinge of conscience—"and invite the Count, Bernsdorf—Rivington—and—and—yes, Rivington," she repeated with homesick longing to hear her mother tongue and look upon a compatriot. "The gentlemen can join us later—for supper. We will pass the evening there."

The drive to Belvedere changed happily the current of Muriel's thoughts. Beyond the villa district the leaf-arched way took an easy ascent to the royal estate crowning the eminence. Edging a compact low-roofed hamlet, a stone's throw from the castle, a shaded refreshment plateau looked far down the meadows to the roofs and tree-tops of Weimar clustering about the terminus of the serpentine Allee. In the background the giant Eltersberg, sentinel of the encircling hills, reared its verdant head.

Weather-wrinkled peasants were rollicking indoors, while recreating city folks enjoyed the salubrious air and the wide stretch of Thuringian landscape. Here coffee was served to them under the trees, Frau von

Berwitz providing homemade cakes from her convenient reticule.

Urged by wily Fräulein Panzer to walk home by moonlight, Muriel unwittingly dismissed the carriage before starting to stroll—after the gentlemen had arrived—through the beautifully ordered private grounds at the rear of the residence. The façade was purple in the mellow glow as they halted again at the opening on the terrace to watch the sun's posthumous glory fade slowly above the Eltersberg.

Though excursionists had monopolized the garden in their absence, a supper-table had been reserved for them on the verge of the declivity.

The odor of new-mown hay floated upward from the meadows in the gloaming, reflecting lamps brightened under the mantle of night, and a male chorus clicked glasses to the rhythm of spirited drinking songs. Far below the outlined union of black hill and starry sky, the lights of Weimar glimmered through a canopy of fine silver haze like marshalled will o' the wisps.

The carousers drove off in wagons with cheer and song; isolated groups silently vanished, and the moon rose over straggling worshippers of the night. Last of all, Muriel's party turned reluctantly from their beloved Thuringian hills to the shadows of the Allee.

Fräulein Panzer scrambled ahead with Rivington, and Bernsdorf walked off with the two matrons in almost unseemly haste.

After sacrificing every other consideration for the afternoon and evening to restore their normal relations, Muriel felt herself grow white with annoyance at this concerted opposition to her will. To think that they could so take advantage of his absence! It outraged the fondest dream of her life.

Hohenfels' opportunity to offer himself was, also, hers to settle the question for all time. Almost eagerly she joined his lingering pace.

She felt as if acting in personal defense of Stanford. Alert to shield him in every sense, her heart surrounded him with an armor of affection—that sort of affection which finds best expression in a caress without words. Looking up almost defiantly, she perceived the honest, gentle question in Hohenfels' gaze.

"What has he promised?" she asked herself in thought of Stanford, "that I should fight his battles?" "Nothing," was the sorrowful response. "But I love him!" her heart cried out in anguish, and once more blind passion steeled her for the coming trial.

In the half-light the tremulous appeal in her luminous eyes stole over him like a spell, and brought her name involuntarily to Hohenfels' lips.

"Muriel! Muriel!" he whispered, with a new softness in his voice.

"Don't! Don't!" she cried, putting out a hand in protest, suddenly conscious of desire to spare her old friend pain.

"Why not?" he continued, tenderly. "Can't you see that I love you? I have loved you so long and so devotedly, but I could not—I dared not tell you of it until I had something more than a heart and name to offer you. Now I can honestly come to you and ask the question, Will you be my wife?"

Grasping her hand tightly in his own, he leaned low to read the answer in her eyes.

The right word would not come. She could not wound him by anything stilted or commonplace. The ticking of her watch rose above the receding foot-steps. She tried to speak and looked helplessly into his eyes.

Misinterpreting her hesitation, he cried passionately: "Do you love me, Muriel? Say that you do? Really? Yes?"

"I am so—so sorry," she repeated, with an effort, gently freeing her hand.

"No—no! You shall not!" he said, drawing her nearer. "You are all the world to me. I cannot think of life without you. You must love me! Say that you do—be it ever so little!"

He was so unlike other suitors she had known in Germany, in his manly sincerity and purity. The passionate vibration in his voice made her tremble and forget self-imposed obligations. It ravished her senses to feel his burning glance and weigh the fervor of his appeal. Unconsciously she played with emotion as if it were a toy.

Stanford's face was before her; and they two once more alone in the old rose-garden.

"Muriel!" Hohenfels was now speaking for himself. The vision was gone. Muriel recollected herself with a moral shudder.

"You have no stauncher friend than I," she said

quietly, pressing his hand warmly and letting it go. "If, by word or look, I have led you to think of me in any other relation, I humbly ask your pardon. I could not consciously wrong you so much."

"You have done nothing. You have merely been your own sweet self. I love you for what you are! Oh, Muriel! tell me now—do you care for me?"

"As a friend—after the manner of friendship—yes."

"No more? No more?" he pleaded, with all the gentle, subtle tenderness of his nature. "Could you not learn to love me? I would be so patient—so true. Try it. Decide at leisure. I will wait—if you will only try."

"I wish I could—since you wish it!" exclaimed Muriel, impulsively, with all the frankness and sincerity of belief in her firm tones. "It pains a true woman to reject the honest, undivided love of a noble, generous-hearted man—but it never can be—so."

"Why not? A little of your love will suffice me. If you will only be my wife, I will be so devoted, so faithful, so fond that you will some day give me your love."

"It is wrong of me to argue," said Muriel, more to herself than to him. "No, my friend; with all my regard for you, it is impossible. It was not meant to be. Something here tells me so," she added, placing a hand over her heart. "We have been friends—let us remain so. You have done me an honor which falls to few women. No woman could be more deeply touched by it. I cannot say more. It hurts me to speak of that which is sacred to our hearts. Let this pass, as if nothing had been said, and—and—when it is right that it should be so—let us resume our friendship." .

Muriel put out her hand. "Shall it be so?" she said, in a firm, yet sympathetic voice. Hohenfels was silent and as pale as the moonlight touching the fragrant meadows bordering the Allee.

"Listen," he said at last, and, as he spoke, the color crept back to his face and eyes, and his words glowed with the eloquence of strong feeling. "This is not a mere passing fancy, but the one great, enduring love of my manhood. Since knowing you it has grown and strengthened, till now it rules my entire being. Your image is before me night and day. In the midst of active duty on the parade ground, your dear voice rings in my ears; its music lulls me to sleep and welcomes the return to consciousness. You are my heaven—my all—of this life and that to come. Think what you are doing. I love—I worship you! Consider what that means. Take time. Do not answer me now! I will wait. You will see how patient I can be if you will only give me one chance of hope. Think well," he exclaimed, passionately. "It is the eternal happiness of a man which you have the power to make or destroy by a word."

"I know," replied Muriel, deeply agitated by his manly appeal, "but—it hurts me to make you suffer by saying it, for you will always be the same dear friend to me—I can never become your wife! Try to forget that you have wished it. Think of me kindly— do not make us both unhappy by referring to it

again. Some day it will be easier for you, and then—
it will be all for the best, dear friend."

As she was speaking, the possibility of a similar de-
velopment in her own case weighed her heart down
to breaking. The desolation—the agony of living in
such a state—appalled her. Pity that another human
being—an old, tried friend—should suffer so, through
knowing her, overcame her. She looked at him with
all the compassion in her nature roused to expression.
Words failed her, and with an uncontrollable sob, Muriel covered her face with her hands. They were both
so utterly miserable—the world beyond the shadow
of the lindens, so sad, and yet so sweet. She had not
realized until then—until she saw his bared head
bowed in mute grief before her—how strong the bond
of friendship had grown—and how was it possible to
heal the wound she herself had made?

Muriel composed herself and silently offered her
hand. Hohenfels took it without lifting his eyes.

"Is there no hope?" he said, with an effort.

Muriel shook her head sorrowfully.

"Good-by! Good-by!" he said brokenly. "Try to
think of me always as being that which I would like
to be. Don't let thought of me make you unhappy.
I love you so well that I could not bear to have my
memory bring one pang of regret, or the slightest
shadow over your life. Let it always be sunshine; and
when—when—you are happy in your own land, know
that the prayers of a faithful friend in Germany watch
over and protect you!"

He was quiet, very quiet, for a moment, and all the

earth seemed listening in deathlike stillness. "Good-by," he murmured, with the agony of parting in his eyes, sinking reverently on one knee and clasping her hand to his heart as he uplifted his face in benediction. "God always guard and keep her!" A stifled sob in which there was no relief of tears shook him from head to foot. He pressed her hand passionately to his cheek, to his forehead, his eyes, and covered it with burning kisses.

Muriel turned away her head, and then. he rose quietly, and, without a word, they started down the Allee. Near the Royal Gardens they came in sight of their companions.

"Remember," said Muriel, under her breath, "we are friends,—for eternity!"

They clasped hands in one long pressure, and then they came upon Bernsdorf and the two matrons.

"See, Muriel," observed Tante Anna, pointing to the side window of Liszt's music-room. A student-lamp and a familiar head threw a faint silhouette against the drawn blind.

"The dear Master," responded Muriel, with the trace of recent emotion in her voice; "he is still working."

CHAPTER XXIII.

Knowing Muriel's unhappiness, Tante Anna, with feminine art, strove vainly to obtain a definite expression of Stanford's designs. But their letters were infrequent, and soon Muriel was bereft of even the small degree of comfort gained by remembering his former constancy, for although his hastily penned lines bespoke sincerity and hearty regard, it was, maybe, only the same regard, Muriel was prompted to think oftener than her sense of justice to him approved, which he vouchsafed an ever-growing throng of adherents. Though devoting, with unfailing courtesy, several clauses to her in each letter to Tante Anna, once only had he written to her, and then after the frank, unaffected manner of his verbal intercourse.

After fitting intermission she had responded, and then came an unbroken, heart-wearying lull.

Latterly the influx of old pupils and privileged guests from abroad had enlarged Liszt's class to its maximum. Muriel, therefore, won temporary immunity from active participation. Frau von Berwitz promptly arranged for a brief vacation at Friedrichsruhe in the pine forests, to which Muriel demurred, in the unexpressed belief that Stanford might return as abruptly as he had departed. With this in view, she carefully instructed Gretchen of her whereabouts, did she leave home for only an hour.

Under such nerve-tension Muriel existed, planning diversions for each day, binding herself to nothing which restricted freedom. The ever-hopeful present was her support. The future——?

"The fourth Thursday since he went," she mused, early one morning, at breakfast in the old rose-garden. "Three weeks and two days since he said "Aufwieder-sehen!""

"Still no word from our American," remarked Gretchen for the fourth successive morning, unconsciously employing her own appellation for Stanford —revised for outside gossip—as she came with the first mail.

"What is the day of the month?" inquired Tante Anna, looking up from her paper.

"The second," answered Muriel, quickly. "Why, Tante Anna," she continued, brightening as if grateful for the reminder, "Saturday, 'July the Fourth,' will be our great American national holiday. Let us celebrate it—here—no—in the house—for the Meister must come, and he would take cold here—and we must have music, too—the pianos."

Muriel developed her plans with feverish intensity. Had it been a wise precedent to establish she would gladly have made her colleagues her daily guests at the suburban pleasure resorts during the past weeks; but equality of being and doing was a tradition of these summer gatherings at Weimar, and Muriel conformed silently, though impatiently, to the routine amusements of her circle.

She had not seen Hohenfels since the eventful night at Belvedere. He was popularly supposed to frequent Bad Berka, an adjacent resort, where his mother and Fräulein Panzer were staying for a short time.

Rivington, however, had become so devoted in his friendship, that Tante Anna jocosely referred to them as "the Holme-Rivingtons." Undaunted thereby, Muriel felt a new independence in accepting the escort of her youthful countryman to the "Corner Table," and to every haunt of the clique centered by Anna and Helene Stahr, who, if conspicuous at times, were, nevertheless, interesting, instructive, and always kindly disposed. Consequently, Rivington being the only other American then with Liszt, Muriel sent him a note proposing that invitations to the national cele-bration go out jointly in their names. Following this, Liszt's verbal promise to postpone the regular lesson in order to attend the fête, decided Muriel on the final arrangements.

"Meister dislikes a crowd," she said to Tante Anna. "I shall ask only the pupils and, of course, the Fräu-lein Stahr. Why can't I invite Alvary? One out-sider will make no difference, and then he goes so soon to America, it would be a sort of——"

"Beginning with the people," suggested Frau von Berwitz.

During the midday dinner, a messenger from the Royal Gardens came with a note for Muriel in the Master's unique hand.

"My honored colleague:

"Be not too extravagant in your feast. Have—punch—cake—sandwiches? No—that is too much. Otherwise I really cannot come. Remember, then—punch—cake—and perhaps a glass of red wine or a little cognac for the old Master. No more. Your devoted   F. LISZT."

Muriel's tardy arrival at the lesson next day confirmed the Master's belief in her contemplated extravagance.

"To-morrow is the grand fête! Cake—punch! Remember—no more! And yet—a little music. Yes! Before all things we must have 'Yankee Doodle'! Nah. Play it for us—now!"

Though somewhat disconcerted, Muriel accepted the words in the friendly spirit of their utterance, and dashed off the giddy measures at a rattling pace.

"Yan-kee—Doo-dle!" sang the Master under his breath, at each recurrence of the name; then mouthed the ensuing words, as he swung his head from side to side in rhythm with the music, his features alive with glee, and his right hand beating time as for a grand orchestra. "Brava—brava! Famous!"

"Ah! An idea!"

Levelling his index finger at Arthur, he shook it with a sober expression.

"A task—for you! Yes—Arthur must do it. Take the theme 'Yan-kee—Doodle,' and make of it a festival piece for to-morrow! Much can be done in twenty-four hours," he added, at signs of a demurrer. "Two pianos! Something—grand! And—ah, yes— A-me-ri-ka—must play it with you." Turning a searching glance, his eye fastened on Rivington.

"Yes, Master," was the happy response.

"Further," and the Master turned to Muriel. "Do you chance to know Rubinstein's variations on 'Yankee Doodle'? No? They are dedicated to your William Mason, too. Capital things—capital! Only one fault—a trifle long."

"Something like fifty-three pages, I believe," observed Rivington.

"Just so," said the Master, laughing with him. "I believe they are published in Leipzig. Have them to-morrow—and—each one shall play a variation at sight.

A wave of general consternation swept over every face.

"They are beastly things to play—let alone read at sight," growled Emil, to be overheard by all excepting the Master, who was saying, "Have a little more music. You play something," he indicated Muriel, "and Arthur—and—not you, Mariechen. Oh, no— you haven't retrieved yourself yet," and the patriarch paused to have the laugh on his offending pupil. "But—Alfred shall play, instead. And now, to work!"

Listening with unusual indulgence to the automatic precision of "Old Counterpoint," whom he had rechristened upon first acquaintance, Liszt suddenly changed countenance, tapping his forehead with evident satisfaction.

"Where is my little Baedecker?" he inquired, rising and leaving the piano.

"Here, Meister," laughingly answered Muriel, who, as bureau of general information to the Master, had long borne the soubriquet.

"We must commemorate the festival with a picture—a group," softly said Liszt, moving aside.

"I will have the photographer at the house on Saturday," responded Muriel.

The Master puckered his mouth and stroked his chin in dissent.

"Better not," he murmured, with a significant smile. "We don't want any—any other ladies in it, do we? Just you, Rivington, and—my poor self. Let it be an —American group."

Muriel could scarcely credit her senses for a moment. The honor which he had volunteered was one accorded, to the best of her knowledge, to scarcely more than a half dozen of his most celebrated pupils.

Leaving her gasping for a fitting word of thanks, the Master shuffled back to his place at the piano, laughing immoderately at his final remark, "Let it be an—American group."

As Muriel and Rivington lingered a moment after the lesson, Ilmstedt, who was passing slowly out, overheard the Master say to them: "To-morrow, you see—your fête day—is just the time. Meet me at Held's at eleven; and—you, Amerika—will perhaps come and walk down with me?"

"Indeed, Master, I can't permit you to walk. I will have a carriage here."

"No, no! Remember—no extravagance! Without a carriage. We walk to Held's."

CHAPTER XXIV.

Saturday dawned behind clouds as far as little Weimar was concerned. As he came up Marien Strasse, at ten o'clock, to fetch the Master, Rivington stopped in at the hostler's to order a carriage at the Royal Gardens a half-hour later.

"Yes," drawled Menke, as he stood, hat in hand, running his fingers through his hair, "but Herr Doctor sent Mischka down early to say I was not to let you have a carriage, in case you came for one."

"Ah—leave that, Menke, I'll bear the blame. See, it's beginning to sprinkle now. He can't walk in the rain."

"Very well, Herr Rivington, if you will give that to him as an excuse, why I'll hitch up at once."

The Master had not yet risen from the early nap which always followed his breakfast when Rivington reached the Royal Gardens.

Mischka, quite refreshed in appearance and good-natured, was writing at his square table facing the great open window.

"Well?" said Rivington, questioningly.

"All goes well," said the servant. "I don't believe any one has heard of it; and Herr Doctor got up well disposed this morning."

"God be praised!" said Rivington, with a sigh of relief. "Mischka! Mischka! Look!" Ilmstedt had just appeared in the distance, coming up Marien Strasse.

"Ya—Ya!" said the Hungarian, with a wise nod. "But he won't get in. I'll tell Pauline." With that he dashed down the stairway. "She's on the watch," said he, reappearing. "Nobody will get past her. Donnerwetter!"

Mischka had heard a sound from the salon. Tearing open the dining-room door he vanished in his usual headlong way to answer the Master's call.

A moment later a murmur of voices preceded their entrance to the dining-room. With his right hand the Master was brushing his long. snowy hair back from his face, and Mischka was supporting him by his left arm, as Rivington came forward with his morning greetings.

"Amerika!" articulated the Master, with much deliberation, extending his hand with a sleepy smile. "Nah," he interrupted his walk to conceal a huge yawn. "Suppose you get the last 'Musikalisches Wochenblatt' from the table, in there," he said, indicating the salon, "and read me the news while I am being shaved.

Sinking into an ordinary straight-backed chair by the dining-table, the Master stretched out his feet, interlaced his fingers across his waistcoat front, threw back his head, and closed his eyes.

Mischka had all the appliances ready, and went rapidly to work.

"Well, what is there new?"

"Not much, Master."

"That is old."

"Well," said Rivington, with a short laugh; and,

bracing himself against the arm of an easy chair, he began to read to the scraping monotone of Mischka's razor:

"Musical Jottings"—"Johann Schmidt, an excellent pianist, gave a concert of modern and classical compositions last Monday evening before a numerous audience in the grand hall of the Hotel de Rome. The young man—for he has not yet attained his nineteenth year—is the possessor of unusual natural endowments, and displayed, especially in the Rigoletto Fantasie from Liszt, remarkable digital facility, coupled with——"

"That is original!" interrupted the Master; and Mischka had to suspend work to allow a chuckle of amusement.

Rivington ran his eye down the column. "Ah, yes! The venerable Meister Liszt attended a concert given by one of his pupils, Fräulein Marie——"

"Mariechen!" interposed the Master.

"Fräulein Mariechen Bilbach," said Rivington gravely, noting the correction to the interruption of Mischka's task. When the Master had recovered from the spasm of laughter, Rivington continued, "in Sulza. Of course the great man's presence insured the young artist a crowded house, and she returned to Weimer the richer by several hundred marks."

"So! Well—something different," observed the generous spirit who scorned reminiscences of his beneficence.

"John Bull and 'God Save the Queen,'" read the pupil from the other page."

"Bull—Bull—'John' Bull. A good substantial name!" observed the Master, with dry humor. "Bull!"

"An English writer has undertaken to prove Dr. John Bull, an eminent organist, born in 1563 (d. 1628 in Anvers), the composer of 'God Save the Queen.'"

"Ah—let us have that!" exclaimed the Master.

Whilst Rivington was in the midst of the long story the wheels of a vehicle grated on the gravel before the house door.

"What! Didn't you give Menke my order?"

"Certainly, Herr Doctor," replied the valet.

"My fault, Meister," said Rivington.

"I shall walk," was the firm retort.

"But, Meister, it rains."

"Not much," he replied, with a show of relenting, and he rose to look at the weather. "Well, I'll join you in a few moments."

Ilmstedt was not discouraged by Pauline's refusal to admit him to Liszt's apartments. As his sole purpose was to throw himself in the way, and thus connive for an invitation to join the group and be photographed, he resolved to be at the atelier, as if by chance, when the trio arrived. He had jealously guarded their secret; perchance a fifth might swell the party and injure his own opportunity. Yet, in retracing his steps, by happy accident he thought of Ivan, who disapproved of every new-comer, regardless of his musical status. He had been photographed with the Master the previous year, and might, therefore, render valuable aid of some sort— as yet undefined in Ilmstedt's mind—especially as Ivan illy concealed his jealousy of Rivington's favor with the Master.

"To think of that upstart being immortalized in such a way!" he answered Ilmstedt in a rage. "An honor which but few of Franz Liszt's greatest pupils have won! Come! I will be there with you!"

"Held," said Ivan, finding the photographer alone, "you have a group on to-day?"

The man elevated his shoulders and eyebrows questioningly.

"Oh, come. I know all, about it!"

"Herr Ivan!" responded Held, who had been sworn to secrecy.

"I will give you one hundred marks in advance," said Ivan, coming nearer and lowering his voice, "if you will smash the plates after they are taken."

"Never, Herr Ivan!"

"But, Ivan, not if I am on them!" gasped Ilmstedt.

"Shut up, you fool."

"Two hundred, Held, two hundred marks!"

"Not in eternity, Herr Ivan; one act against the wishes of the good old Master, who has done so much for me!"

"Then you admit it is the Master?"

The alarm-bell rang as Muriel and Frau von Berwitz stepped into the atelier.

"Most excellent!" exclaimed Ivan, eyeing a large new photograph of Liszt, which had that day been hung up.

Before the greetings were ended, the carriage from the Royal Gardens had halted without.

Held rushed bareheaded to the curb, and returned, supporting the Master on his arm.

"Everything is ready," he said; "I shall detain you but a moment."

After some little dispute as to position, they were taken—Liszt seated before an upright pianó, with Muriel at his side a trifle to the rear, watching his fingers wander idly over the keys, and Rivington, with one arm resting upon the instrument, stood looking down at the Master.

"Capital!" shouted Held, in glee. "Have patience just a moment longer, Master," cried Held anxiously, as he shifted the sides. "Now! Ready?—There! Ah!"

At that moment, as if to catch a glimpse of the group ere broken, Ivan, who, with Frau von Berwitz and Ilmstedt, had been asked to stand behind a portière, appeared in the archway dividing the two rooms.

An awkward step—a frightful crash—and Ivan, with flaming cheeks, stood facing Held across the prostrate form of the camera. Together they raised it into place, and Held tremblingly inspected the apparatus.

"Ivanus!" ejaculated Liszt, recognizing the miscreant with paternal indulgence; and, did he surmise design on the part of his fiery pupil—as the Americans believed—he never revealed it by word or glance. A sunbeam abruptly pierced the gray light of the atelier and silvered the whitened locks of the old Master. "Ah!" he exclaimed, with a movement to shade his eyes, "the day is yours, Amerika!"

"The day—but I fear not the picture, dear Meister," responded Muriel, with a disappointed glance at the photographer's unhappy face.

"Both," he calmly replied.   "We will sit again!"

"Meister," exclaimed Muriel," with fresh interest, "I was thinking as I came from your house yesterday what an ideal scene that daisy-flecked lawn, up by the hedge, behind the Allee gate, would make for a photograph.   It has sprinkled lightly; I don't believe the grass would be wet."

"Charming idea! Charming idea!" And rising hastily Liszt said sotto voce to Rivington: "See that Held and his apparatus come with you in a droschke."

Whenever Rivington, in after years, recalled this famous celebration of the American "Fourth" on the historic soil of Saxon Weimar, two incidents led the procession of crowding memories.

The first came before his mind's eye as a memorable picture:—

Frau von Berwitz stood in the small drawing-room listening to a desultory conversation between Arthur and Liszt.

"Yes," said the Master, "I heard that you played the Chopin Preludes and the entire set of Paganini Studies in your first recital in Berlin.   A feat—not for the masses—but for you, and I honor you for it!"

Frau von Berwitz was a smiling witness of the young man's joy at such rare praise from Liszt, who had been to him a most exacting disciplinarian for a decade.   Her spontaneous pleasure gave an abrupt though graceful turn to the drift of thought.

"Dear Meister," she said, "let me kiss the hand

which has made so much beautiful music for the world;" and with a quick movement she raised it to her lips.

The Master with courtly ease grasped both her hands warmly and, in his accustomed way, imprinted an acknowledgment upon her forehead.

But the music—all combined, in fact—was secondary to Rivington's solicitation about his speech. He was toast-master and had to say it all in German. It wasn't much, to be sure, for little Fritz—who was on a visit to his grandmother from Berlin—had been able to memorize it, though apparently absorbed in a story book, as the household worked to compose it the night before in the drawing-room.

"Ladies and gentlemen," the youth had heard a piping voice proclaim outside the great open door of Muriel's music-room, where he sat alone in reverie, after Held's triumph with his camera, at the Royal Gardens. "Ladies and gentlemen, in my country's name I thank our greatly-honored and dearly-beloved Master for the honor which——"

"Fritz—Fritz! How dare you!" shouted Frau von Berwitz from an upper window. Then he heard hers and Muriel's muffled laughter as four pair of small boots rattled the gravel in their scampering flight down the garden walk.

"Dearly beloved Master" rang in his ears. "Geliebter" was the German of it, and it was very like "verliebter," which means that one is very much in love. "What should I do," he had said at rehearsal, "were I to be confused and say verliebter Meister?"

"Herr Rivington—Herr Rivington, you must not even think of such a thing," said Frau von Berwitz, trying to keep a sober face, "as sure as you•do, you will say it to-morrow."

But he didn't, and the Master was highly complimentary and responded with "Amerika!"

The floral decorations and feast were not in accordance with Liszt's admonition of economy, but he yielded without a dissenting word, possibly forgetting his threat in the diversion which Arthur's arrangement of "Yankee Doodle" had created.

"Suppose you repeat that!" he said to Arthur and Rivington, from his place between them at the two pianos. The introduction, without a trace of "Yankee Doodle" in it, had been a most majestic, Olympus-scaling mass of harmonies. After its repetition, which Liszt followed with a serious countenance and an occasional nod of approval, one of the pianos trolled out the familiar breakdown. "Yan-kee-Doodle," repeated the Master, but he soon had to stop it, for the changes grew wilder and more startling. He exclaimed with delight at the climax and led the assembly—the two pianists included—in a crescendo of laughter, as the closing chorus from Beethoven's Ninth Symphony sprang up against "Yankee Doodle" —above a reverberating bass—the "Bell Theme" from Wagner's sacred music-drama, "Parsifal."

It was a clever hodge-podge, with merits on which the Master descanted in detail.

After all, the greatest sport of the day came with reading at sight Rubinstein's Variations, and not the

least of it was furnished by Mariechen—Mariechen
Bilbach, who had hidden herself behind one of the
heavy curtains in the library.   Here the Master found
her in his search for deserters.

"I would much better have left you there, Mariechen," said Liszt with a comical sigh, as she ceased
mincing the variation allotted her.

"Here! Moritz," he said to the young Viennese,
who surpassed them all as a sight reader, "this lady is
in trouble.   Be gallant."

There was other music.   Muriel, Arthur and Alfred played, and then Liszt drove home.

It was a pretty sight, as his open carriage wound
its way through the narrow, crooked street, to witness
the homage of the common folk.   The laborer in
coarse blue homespun stood aside with his burden
and doffed his hat; the schoolboy ceased his antics to
uncover his tumbled curls, and to each the aged Master touched his hat and returned a smile.

Music still floated from the open windows of the
old mansion.   Arthur was playing Liszt's Rhapsody
No. 2.   The composer was seen to turn his head
slightly and say something to the three boys who
were accompanying him home.

"Why is it never played in the lesson?" asked Rivington of Muriel.

"Meister is tired of it."

"Nevertheless," interrupted Alfred, "it is the best
of his rhapsodies."

Faithful to the custom of exclusive circles, the
guests fell off after the order of recedence, until Mu-

riel was left combating the insistent wiles of the "Inner Circle" to drag her to the "Russian" for the evening. She felt like a traitor in neglecting the memory of Stanford for an entire day, but consented reluctantly to join her comrades for an hour.

The house was quiet, and Tante Anna was dozing in an easy chair in the dimly-lighted drawing-room when Muriel returned.

"Is that you, Muriel?" .

For answer Muriel sank down on an ottoman at her feet and laid her head in Tante Anna's lap.

"What! Crying? Dear child, you are quite exhausted;" and the matron stroked her hair tenderly.

Muriel shook her head without speaking.

"Well, what has happened to you, dear?"

"Rivington—he—" said Muriel, with a muffled sob.

"Oh, I see," exclaimed Tante Anna. "Rivington has declared himself! I have seen it coming. Silly boy! He ought to have known better."

"It was bad taste, I know," sobbed Muriel.

"I referred to the difference in your ages, my child."

"I am really very advanced," retorted Muriel, laughing with Tante Anna in spite of her tears.

"Arna said, too," she continued brokenly, "that Ivan is jealous of every man who looks at me, and is only waiting for an opportunity to insult poor—Rivington, in order to give him a good pummelling. He would kill him with those great fists of his. You know he can strike four notes over an octave."

Tante Anna became almost hysterical, but Muriel talked on with the tears in her eyes.

"That—other one—had to first spoil our delightful friendship by his—his indiscretion," said Muriel, seeking a suitable phrase in compassionate thought of the man who loved her best of all. His last words haunted her night and day: "God forever guard and keep her!" Once more they were alone in the dim shade of the lindens; his sad upturned eyes seemed penetrating her deepest consciousness; his passionate kisses thrilled every nerve-fibre. Muriel threw her arms about Tante Anna to save herself from the memory. Had she not said to him: "It can never be." What folly to indulge such thoughts. But he loved her and was true, and her life was blank without love. Where was Carl? Had he no tenderness in his heart for her?"

Tante Anna smothered her laugh to find Muriel so desperately serious; but a mirthful outbreak was inevitable as Muriel added: "All the men I like are handicapping my freedom. If they keep on like that I sha'n't have a friend left!"

"There is Carl, my dear!"

"No danger from him!" replied Muriel promptly. Then her heart began to beat so violently that she was embarrassed for words.

"There—there—don't cry any more, dear!" said Tante Anna soothingly, sobered by the fear that she had gone too far in her last statement.

"True patriotism caused it," observed Muriel, smiling through her tears. "The sky didn't do it's duty to-night;" and she pointed to the starry light without. "It always rains the Fourth of July in our country."

CHAPTER XXV.

Muriel had such a dislike for hysterical women that she was greatly disturbed by her own lately developed tendencies. Sunday morning she awoke with a determination to make every effort to regain her own self-respect, and she resolved, moreover, that the rest of her stay in Weimar should be a silent apology to Tante Anna for all the anxiety she had given her.

Being naturally introspective, however, Muriel could not help becoming more or less absorbed in what she considered the complications of her present life. They interested her this morning like the intricate features of a difficult piano piece.

Must she, indeed, pay a lifelong penalty for one brief week of bliss? She tried to look at Stanford's attitude philosophically. In either case, might not disappointment be inevitable?

Did not ardent love matches end, as a rule, in conjugal misery? "Romanticists," some one had written, "should begin a novel with marriage." "Could that ever become my romance?" she asked, turning from the piano in the direction of Hohenfels' miniature field of action.

"God forever bless and keep her!" sobbed the voice of her friend. The scene changed. At her feet, in the dim shadows of the lindens, he knelt, a figure of dignified, if abjectest despair, and beyond them stretched the silent moonlit meadows. The breath of new-

mown hay touched her cheeks. In measured chime
the palace clock announced the hour.

Muriel recovered herself with a nervous tremor.

"I may be compelled to sail without revisiting Weimar." A simple clause in the letter, but just received
by Tante Anna, recurred with stinging force. Muriel
sprang to her feet, proudly erect, as if to face an in-
tentional affront. At that moment mild-eyed Gretchen, bareheaded, and in an ancient bedraggled military great coat, paused, with muddy palms, outside
the open doorway.

"Even the skies weep over his long absence," she
said, in her musical dialect, placing her arms akimbo
to turn her face to the warm, soft rain. The incongruity of her poetic thought and grotesque appearance brought an involuntary smile to Muriel's flashing eyes.

"Has Hans gone again?"

"Ach, Fräulein, Ach!" Gretchen collapsed with a
spasmodic giggle, and headed for the exit.

With a sense of suffocation Muriel stepped upon
the threshold, extended her palms to the rain and
pressed them to her flushed face. Each cool touch
seemed helping her to still reviving memories; she
saw that the whole place was redolent of a morbid
past; she longed to exchange the walled garden for
the freedom of the hills. They, at least, looked off
somewhere—out into the world, away from heart-
breaking sorrow. Yet, gazing. in fancy from the
heights, upon the little city, she could have gathered
it all tenderly in her arms to implore forgiveness for
that one moment of infidelity.

Wo mein Herz und mein Lied sind,
Da bin ich zu Haus'.

Abt's song rang in her ears.

Hastily equipping herself for a walk, she was down the long path and at the street door ere she noted the muffled thunder of the troops marching from church. The sound appealed to her. It belonged to the happy, visionary period of her life. An echo of its former inspiration prompted Muriel to watch for familiar faces.

"Not one," she mused, with an overpowering sense of desolation.

The street was deserted. The rain trickled a mournful monotone from jutting eaves. "Anything but midsummer in town," she continued. "One day like another—and each like the day after the funeral!"

The palace loomed up like a sepulchre in the mist. The sentry gloomily measured his solitary paces before the guard-house.

"God forever bless and keep her!"

The stirring refrain greeted every uniform. Muriel stopped, perplexed. She did not actually wish to see Hohenfels. He was in Bad Berka to-day, but the knowledge of his absence made the town lonelier. To avoid the military quarter, she turned into the mediaeval streets, where the presence of homely groups in deep doorways and beflowered windows brightened her course to the Belvedere Allee.

As she ascended from the park lowlands, an hour later, near the historic "Tea House"—a Goethean creation in Greek architecture—a great-coated officer

coming out from a shrub-hidden path suddenly inter-
cepted the way.

"I beg pardon," he cried, with an apologetic salute,
springing aside for her to pass.

"Oh!" exclaimed Muriel, with a slight gasp, timidly
offering her hand. "Good-morning!"

"I—I was going your way," stammered Count von
Hohenfels irrelevantly, grasping her hand in evident
confusion.

"Oh!"

"I was only walking for—companionship," he said,
catching desperately at the last word.

"Oh!"

This final reiteration brought Muriel to herself.
"Can I say nothing but 'Oh'? He'll think me de-
mented because—because of Carl"

As they came opposite the Royal Gardens they saw
the Master leaning from an open window and conversing with two women before the house.

"Ah, yes! I forgot to say," mumbled Muriel, imi-
tating his diction—"Arna and Mrs. Trebor!" she exclaimed, retarding her steps for a careful look; nor
did she hasten after acquiring this bit of news—even
the freshest of news from the Royal Gardens. For
Time had raised her estimate of Hohenfels' worth.

His refined, handsome features and distinguished
bearing impressed her singularly in her half-shy
glances.

"Will you come in?" she asked, at the street door,
looking him at last frankly in the face. "I know that
Tante Anna will be pleased to see you."

"Thank you; not now. I dine with comrades at the 'Erbprinzen' in five minutes. As an officer I must be punctual. My greetings to Frau von Berwitz. Adieu!"

Grace remarked the happy light in his eyes. "Aufwiederschen!" she said, quickly.

"Aufwiedersehen!" he responded, with still brightening countenance, waiting to close the door.

"Aufwiederschen! Aufwiederschen! Aufwieder-sehen!" sang unseen voices with every stride towards the old Market Square. The day grew brighter. "The sun?" he said, and glanced upward. The fine warm rain moistened his face and fell in spray on his weather coat. There was something friendly to him even in that damp touch of the heavens. Were they offering congratulations? Happy illusion!

"What has come over you, old fellow?" asked his neighbor, von Jahn, at dinner. "Up at the barracks you looked as if you had lost your last friend. An hour later you emanate beams of light that would turn the sun green with envy, should that curtain of mist suddenly lift."

"Aufwiederschen!" pealed the unspoken response. "Aufwiedersehen! Aufwiedersehen!" sang invisible choirs. "Aufwiedersehen!" flamed in giant letters against the festive walls. "Aufwiederschen!" branded cloth and plate, and sparkled in the amber depths of his glass.

Futurity smiled at him through "Aufwiedersehen!" and every thought melted into the sweetest of cadences, "Aufwiedersehen!"

CHAPTER XXVI.

A rubber at whist with Liszt, Arna and Ivan, after the lesson on Tuesday afternoon, caused Muriel to miss a call from Hohenfels.

Surmising her disappointment, Tante Anna said that he purposed attending, the next afternoon, the weekly band concert at the Erholungsgarten—an exclusive open-air resort controlled by a union of the best social elements of the city.

Muriel said that she would go, too. Then she wouldn't—she would—she wouldn't—and finally decided to go, after recalling a saying that a woman never knew her own mind, because she had, at first, impulsively accepted Tante Anna's invitation.

In a moment of inspiration she posted a note to Rivington (who, after his ill-fated proposal, had gone to Eisenach), half-commanding him to be of their party, adding that he had been too silly to be humored, that he must come home and behave like a rational boy of nineteen, unless he wished to be reported to Liszt.

Foreseeing no quicker cure for his malady, she was not surprised to have him ushered, with abashed countenance, into the music-room, just as she was completing her after-dinner hour at the piano on Wednesday.

"Forgive me," he said. "I shall prove my gallantry by telling you that it was all your fault!"

"There," Muriel raised a hand in protest, "that was worthy the palmy days of the Altenburg. I don't believe that anything more than pianistic excellence is required to make you a worthy Lisztianer of this generation!"

An irresistible laugh put Rivington at his ease, and Muriel had gained another friend.

"Listen!" And gliding across the room, Muriel stopped under the rose-canopy at the threshold.

Music from the Erholungsgarten on the hilltop floated sweetly distinct across the Ilm. A single cornet was playing Schubert's "Serenade." Day faded into night; a shaded lamp filled the room with a rosy glow, and the listeners bowed their heads in silent rapture.

"And my heart for thee is yearning; bid it, love, be still!" A tremor broke into Muriel's sober expression as the voice sighed its last tender appeal.

"Bid it, love, be still!"

Neither Muriel nor Rivington seemed to breathe through the soundless pause.

Sweet mignonette and heliotrope mingled with the scent of roses; a bee hummed unnoticed dangerously near Muriel's head. The portentous outline of a creeping shadow startled her to consciousness. Her heart leaped as if to rend its bonds. She dared not look up and betray her joy. A decided footfall on the gravel demanded recognition. Catching her breath, she turned expectantly.

Arna Trebor bounded, with a peal of silvery laughter, upon the step before her. Muriel's face was a curious study, and Arna remarked it. "I was over there," said Muriel, recollecting herself and indicating the Erholungsgarten. Arna knew better, but said nothing, and, presently, with her mother and Tante Anna, they all went to the concert.

A never-ending stream of promenaders was already in possession of the labyrinthian ways of the garden, and infringing upon the territory allotted to coffee-drinkers. Tante Anna's party surrounded a capacious table in a latticed summer-house, in full view of the animated scene, as Mrs. Trebor feared the slightest exposure to cold for her daughter. "Arna must be careful," she said, "being subject to rheumatism in her arms, which is fatal to her playing."

Four dapper young officers, followed by the admiring gaze of all the women folk, left the promenade to join Tante Anna's group. They were Count von Hohenfels, and three footlight worshippers of the fascinating violinist, who eagerly bunched their stools in her vicinity, ready to absorb her enthralling smiles and chuckle over her sparkling witticisms.

With consummate tact the Count gave Muriel that tender, non-committal deference which some women love.

Rivington showed a disposition to make the best of the new order of things in his devotion to the two matrons.

In this friendly harmony Muriel began to experience that same subtle thrill of ecstacy which sublime music gave her after a period of deprivation. The strains of the band spoke directly to her soul; she even removed her gloves to enjoy the sympathy of her clasped hands. Life's joys were once more hers; the horizon of the future receded to the infinite.

The convivial glass at length replaced coffee-cups, and Tante Anna embroidered industriously to the time of tuneful measure.

A mellow warmth lay in the sun's dying rays; the incense of flowers stole in through vistas of this fair Saxon land, so rich in its music and wit. The souls of Goethe, of Schiller, of Herder, of Wieland, and of Liszt seemed to animate the scene and enhance those salient characteristics which had given little Weimar an international renown.

Muriel reflected with divided affection upon a choice of homes. Here, brain and heart throbs met unfailing response; over there—his home! Disturbed by the sad reminder of sweet days gone, she turned to the diversions of a side vista in the arbor, where promenaders came up from the valley.

Suddenly Muriel became deadly pale.

Hohenfels, with eyes for her face only, said softly: "What is the matter?"

Feigning not to hear, Muriel carelessly studied her programme.

Hohenfels watched the color sweep over her face.

"How warm, to-day," she observed indifferently, pressing her handkerchief to her brow.

Hohenfels saw her glance furtively at Frau von Berwitz, who hearkened with half-bowed head to the music.

Looking up as a foot scattered the gravel, the

matron's eyes rounded in astonishment. Without lowering her glance, she deftly shifted the embroidery onto the table and left the arbor.

For some inexplicable reason Hohenfels found himself watching her with uneasy interest. He saw a procession of boarding-school misses, arm in arm, leisurely ascending the promenade. Then a distinguished-looking stranger in fashionable London attire entered the open space, scrutinizing the gathering opposite the arbor.

"Mr. Stanford!" exclaimed Arna and Mrs. Trebor, in a breath, as Tante Anna stopped him.

Hohenfels observed the happiness fade from his rival's face when, after a well-tempered reception, Muriel gave strict attention to the music, for the slight noise of Stanford's reception had raised a series of hisses from without. Even in the ensuing pause she delayed only long enough to make some careless inquiries about his unexpected arrival, before resuming conversation with Hohenfels.

After more music a general scurrying of young people towards the assembly-rooms indicated the evening programme. Nevertheless, other groups than Tante Anna's lingered at the tables, when the commanding rhythm of the dance and the dull tread of feet announced the opening polonaise. A waiter came to take orders for supper, and then they all went for a stroll about the grounds.

Stanford naturally remained at Tante Anna's side; but, upon their return, he laid hold of the chair next to the one he had chosen, and offered it to Muriel.

"Thank you," she said graciously, moving up to the table. Noticing that there was no vacancy for the Count near them, she slipped the chairs closer together and made a place for him on her left.

Balmy twilight merged into as balmy night, and a delicate silver crescent rose in the calm blue sky. Distant music, descending feet, glasses clinking in tuneful unrhythm, sepulchral "prosits" and soft feminine laughter, rose, died and fitfully resounded above the ceaseless murmur of many voices.

When Tante Anna gave the signal to disperse, Hohenfels naturally started off at Muriel's side. She had never once left him out of the conversation, even when Stanford attempted to monopolize her. In truth, in spite of his direst misgivings about Stanford's renewed visit at the old mansion, Hohenfels found himself thinking with involuntary pride of Muriel's unwavering partisanship.

After bidding the Trebors good-night in the shadow of the darkened palace, he accompanied her to their door. At their approach Gretchen's Hans sped out of the black arch and hobbled away over the rough paving.

"Thuringia was created for lovers," observed Stanford, looking after him as they came to a halt, and Muriel, glancing up at Hohenfels with a happy "Gute Nacht," added "Aufwiedersehen!"

Then a wing of the great door suddenly fanned Tante Anna's face as Gretchen's musical giggle and light, tripping step receded towards the inner court. Stanford tarried to turn the great key and bar the

door, but Muriel went on to help the maid light the
lamps in the vestibule.

"Oh, no! Not yet!" exclaimed Stanford, coming in
with a vexed expression, to find her, lamp in hand.

"You need rest."

"I assure you, I do not," he insisted, earnestly.

"You are too polite to admit it," retorted Muriel,
with a gay laugh and a shake of the head. "Good-
night! Good-night, Tante Anna!"

CHAPTER XXVII.

"Of course you are glad!" said Gretchen in an anxious whisper. "Haven't you told the whole neighborhood by this time? Go 'way! Go 'way! Sh! Sh!" With a vicious flap of her apron at the sparrows circling above her head, the maid ran for a mop.

"To the fountain! Over there—by the church. You'll get enough to drown you there—and I hope you will, too!" Rubbing vigorously at the droppings from the pump, Gretchen gave a final "Sh!" and, lifting the watering pot, she crossed the court muttering: "Of course you are glad; we are all glad he has come;·but this is no time to serenade him! Why, it's a half-hour early for even me, you stupids!"

"Mariechen," toddling eagerly from the round apron to smother her cries, and, closely followed by the mother, rebounded into the garden.

Gretchen, springing back, rolled the baby into her apron to smother her cries, and rebounded into the garden, closely followed by the mother.

"Ach! Mein Gott! Mein Gott! You—miserable— Oh, Frau Schulze, Frau Schulze," gasped poor Gretchen, with tears in her eyes, that—that——"

"Here, take her away!" the mother said placidly to Elsa.

"It all comes of my getting up before-times to have everything nice for him, too!" mourned Gretchen.

"How is he?" inquired the neighbor, fumbling in a capacious pocket for her knitting.

"Just beautiful!" exclaimed Gretchen, suddenly forgetting her sorrows; and placing her arms akimbo, she looked her readiness for a chat.

"Ach! it is so lovely to have him here again! A household of women—no men—it is not life, Frau Schulze.".

"You are evidently not cut out for an old maid," observed the neighbor.

"God forbid!" ejaculated the girl fervently. "Why, when he went away my ladies became so melancholy that there was no staying in the house with them."

"So I heard."

"Heard?" repeated Gretchen, sweetly. "Heard?"

"Say, Frau Schulze," she said, suddenly transformed by curiosity, "who told you that Hans was back?"

A ringing laugh was the response.

"Ach!" whispered Gretchen tremulously. "Our Fräulein! Our Fräulein!"

Grasping the watering pot in one hand and Frau Schulze's sleeve in the other, she tiptoed in long strides to the remotest corner of the garden.

"You see," said the maid resignedly, beginning her work, "she hasn't been very well since he went away, and Frau von Berwitz cautioned me about disturbing her of a morning."

"Now, say, Frau Schulze," she continued impatiently, "who told you about Hans?"

"Frau Schwartz."

"There! I thought it! The old vixen! She is

always watching us from behind her window curtains!"

Muttering a popular threat, the maid gave the direction of the obnoxious matron's residence as black a look as her comely features would express, and proceeded, with a softened expression at mention of Hans, to tell her story:

"I thought that Hans—I thought Hans never would return. He had been working for Herr Müller ever since finishing his military term, and was offered more salary if he would remain another year, ·but he had not seen the old folks in four years and said that he would first go home for a week's visit. That was in June. The night before he left we had a quarrel, a little quarrel—our first—and parted in anger. ·

"'Never mind, Fräulein Gretchen,' said he, 'you will repent this!' and turned on his heel without even a 'good-bye.'

"'Ach Gott!' thought I, 'he is just stubborn enough to make it hard for me,' and he did.

"Two weeks passed without my seeing or hearing a word of him.

"'Ach Gott! Ach Gott!' thought I, 'that is what he meant about my repenting,' for I knew that his father had been coaxing him to work in their town.

"Well, I had made up my mind that I should never again see him, when Frau von Berwitz sent me to the Rathhaus Restaurant on an errand last Monday night a week ago, and—we ran face to face in the doorway. He made out not to see me, and looked straight over my head.

" 'Herr Je!' thought I, 'two can do that!'

"The next night I was sitting out in the big door-way watching the children romping in the street, when he came walking by, smoking his pipe. I turned my face away, but out of the corners of my eyes I could see him look at me.

"Pretty soon he came back, and quite near, too, but I kept on looking up the street like I hadn't heard him. When he got to the beer hall he turned round and walked straight back to me. Then I looked away again and saw Frau Schwartz hiding behind the curtains.

" 'Good evening,' he said.

" 'Good evening,' said I, and I looked up surprised, and not a bit glad, either.

" 'Will you not shake hands?' said he, for you see I had taken no notice of his hand when he put it out.

" 'Have you been away?' said I, as if I had not noticed his absence, and I gave him my hand.'"

"Well?" inquired Frau Schulze.

"Oh, that old Frau Schwartz was watching and spoiled it all," said Gretchen vexedly, "for he wouldn't let it go, and——"

"And what?"

"What? Why—nothing."

"Nothing? Aren't you going to marry him, now?"

"Marry him? Marry him, Frau Schulze? Why, of course! You don't think that I would flirt with a

man, do you? But of course it won't be until after
our American and the young Fräulein are married.
Frau von Berwitz couldn't break another girl in by
that time, and I wouldn't leave her in the lurch when
so much is doing."

"Married?" gasped Frau Schulze meanwhile. "Married? When was their engagement announced?"

"Not yet," answered Gretchen, simply.

"Then how do you know it?"

"Frau Schulze," said Gretchen, dropping the watering-pot to resume her favorite attitude, "if I had had
only a quarter of an eye instead of two good whole
ones, I could have told you that a month ago."

"Then you think they will be married right off?"

"Of course!" said Gretchen in surprise; "what's to
hinder? They are both rich; not poor like Hans
and me, who have got to lay by a bit first."

"Well," observed the neighbor, resuming her knitting with an incredulous look, "the first thing they
will have to do will be to get engaged."

"Leave that to either one of them!" retorted Gretchen wisely.

"Gretchen Stemmler! Do you mean to say that
your Fräulein would propose to him?"

"No! certainly not, Frau Schulze!" replied Gretchen
indignantly, "but a girl can sort of—of—help a
man toward saying it, can't she? Don't I know?
Ach!"

"Don't we all know?" said Frau Schulze, who was
more interested in the prospective nuptials than in
her companion's chagrin.

"But say, aren't they going to give an entertainment to announce the betrothal?"

"Of course!" exclaimed Gretchen, clapping her hands in glee. "Of course! I had quite forgotten that. What a grand· affair it will be, too, with our Fräulein to do the ordering? And Frau von Berwitz will have to wear her black satin, with the long train and low neck, which she wears at court, and all the family jewels. Mein Gott! it'll be beautiful!"

"And the Fräulein?"

"Oh, she'll have a new dress from Berlin—all white—and she has such wonderful things, too! You remember the new dress she brought me in June? It is heavenly! And she paid for the making of it, too. Ach! the Fräulein is stone rich!"

"All Americans are," said Frau Schulze.

"So they say," remarked Gretchen absently.

"Depend upon it," she continued, with understanding, "everything will be of the finest. I don't see but the Rammans will have to take full charge of the refreshments after all, for we'll have enough to do, Frau Schulze, in looking after the floral decorations and the guests."

"Mary and Joseph!" ejaculated the elder of the two, lapsing into her southern dialect,·"what a crowd there will be!"   .

"No, there won't," said Gretchen emphatically. "Meister Liszt hates a crowd, and he'll be the first invited; and he'll kiss them both and bless them! It will be worth something, too, you know, for he is an Abbé!"

"Then we will have all the Lisztianer, the Fräulein Stahr, Herr Hofrath Gille, from Jena, Her Hoforganist Gottschalg, Fräulein Panzer, Count von——"

"Whew! Nay, Frau Schulze, that won't do. He's in love with our Fräulein himself. Now, how are we to manage that? Poor man! How he will feel! But we can't leave him out. He's a friend of the family, and the Countess, his mother, is a school friend of Frau von Berwitz."

"Well," continued Gretchen, with a sigh, "I suppose it'll have to be. Then, there are the young officers who visit our Fräulein sometimes, the von Ilsensteins, the von——"

"Mariechen!" called Stanford's voice, not ten paces away.

Gretchen's knees almost gave way in her fright. "Herr Je!" cried she and Frau Schulze in a breath, and, grasping the watering-pot, the maid hid her face at work.

"The black man! The black man!" articulated Mariechen between terrified shrieks, for Stanford had caught her bending over a pansy bed in disobedience to Elsa's warning of her fate, and was tossing her above his head.

Roused by his voice from the most restful sleep of weeks, Muriel stole to her vine-sheltered window in time to see him pacify the little one on his shoulder, and to hear the mother say: "Ach! dear sir, she has done nothing but prattle about you and wish for your return."

Yielding to a delicious languor, Muriel closed her eyes to the scene without. Her thoughts were with Stanford, and soon she, too, was with him, by the Ilm, crossing the stone bridge and passing on through the Park. He did not seem to see her, but she lost sight of no fleeting change of expression as she glided by his side past the broad lawns before Goethe's cottage. The birds were singing, the flowers, the shrubs, the long grass and trees were nodding him welcome.

The rapture of Nature's joy shone in his face—an involuntary response, but to her—to her alone—she knew that he dedicated consciousness and each warm heartbeat. At Ober-Weimar she heard him say, "No, the other way, it is shorter to her," and, taking another direction, he came to a rustic bridge over the Ilm in the upper park.

Above him, great trees, intertwining their branches, arched the length of the stream; below, escaping sunbeams danced on the silent waters; and, as he looked, a grey-bearded boatman, gliding noiselessly from beneath the bridge, found mooring at the foot of a giant oak and stepped upon the mossy bank. Descending the knoll, Stanford accosted the stranger.

"Is your boat to let?" he repeated, having received no response.

The man stood like a statue. Passing him a coin, Stanford stepped into the boat and pushed into mid-stream. Silently the weird boatman watched him round the bend in the river. -

Still gliding along the river path, Muriel saw Stanford lay down his oars to watch the gold-fish dart affrightedly from their shallow pools near shore, as his boat troubled the placid surface. Serenely he floated on through alternating sunlight and shadow, past the familiar haunts of his childhood.

The stream broadened beneath a clear sky, and from either bank weeping willows dipped in the rippling tide. Absorbed in thought, he failed to notice the landscape flit more and more rapidly by.

"Will he not see?" Muriel held her breath in an agony of suspense. "Is there no one else to warn him?" She tried to call, but her voice died in her throat. Wringing her hands in frenzy she sped madly along the low bank; but faster still and stronger flowed the current.

The distant thunder of mighty waters now rose and swelled until the earth trembled beneath her feet.

"Save him! Save him!" shouted a familiar voice from the high bridge concealing the fall before the palace. A military form sprang down the steep bank as Stanford struggled for the oars. They snapped at the first touch of the resistless current. In wild alarm he half rose and turned toward the shore. He lifted his arms in mute appeal to her—to her who

was powerless to save him! The fragile bark rose on
the last billow, and, with a look of unutterable love, he
disappeared in the mist overhanging the yawning gulf.

Muriel fell forward towards the flood. Strong
arms caught her; the same familiar voice sounded in
her ear; then darkness came on, and the scent of new-
mown hay filled the air.

"God always guard and keep her!" whispered an
echo of the past. "God save her now," was the low-
spoken word, and she recognized Hohenfels' face
dimly in the moonlight.

A shadow fell on the meadows. Muriel trembled
as if an icy hand had touched her; tears blinded her
eyes; a cold perspiration bedewed her forehead, and the
crown of her head seemed scorched by a burning sun.

*   *   *   *   *

Half-dazed and startled, Muriel knew not where
she was. Yawning gulf—resistless current! How
vivid the vision seemed! Slowly the familiar surroundings came again before her. She thought of
the gentle Ilm as it falls before the old bridge at the
palace. Would not the Weimeraner laugh if they
knew its dream-transformation. But alas! What
could it mean? Was it a warning? And, overcome
by her old fear of the water, she shuddered as if
chilled by an icy wave.

"Am I unnerved from over-practice," she thought.
"Must I then leave Weimar and its ideal musical life?
Oh, no! Not yet, not yet!" And the song rose in-
voluntarily to her lips:

Wo mein Herz und mein Lied sind,
Da bin ich zu Haus'.

CHAPTER XXVIII.

Wo mein Herz und mein Lied sind,
Da bin ich zu Haus',

sang Muriel, adapting the rhythm to her steps as she came through the Cloister.

"'Wo mein Herz und mein Lied sind.' Humph!" observed Gretchen, looking up with sparkling eyes as she bore her cumbersome tray across the court. "It's the first time the Fräulein has sung since he left us for London. Frau Schulze will believe me straight off the next time I tell her anything."

"Leave Weimar now?" mused Muriel, as they tarried long after breakfast under the old plum-trees. "Leave Meister and these memorable reunions? Miss one of them? Ah, no! 'Wo mein Herz und mein Lied sind, Da bin ich zu Haus'" and she lapsed into placid enjoyment of Stanford's voice as he read from the morning paper words which she did not heed. Indeed, the day passed like a dream. She felt as lazy as Mime habitually looked when Frau von Berwitz reminded her at coffee in the summer-house that she and Carl were, even then, due at the Royal Gardens.

The season there had attained its zenith. Distinguished musicians from abroad, newly initiated Lisztianer, courtiers and literary celebrities filled the rooms to suffocation. Though Meister presided with the utmost grace and suavity, Muriel detected a fleeting expression of annoyance at the overwhelming

253

numbers when he was finally left alone with his whist
party. A quieting rubber relaxed the tense muscles
of his face; and when, at his request, Stanford sang
Schubert's Serenade, Muriel felt that some of her own
happiness repaid the dear old man for his long,
weary day.

Then, while the garden lay in shadow, and cooling
breezes stirred through the rooms they told him
good night and passed out into another dream-
world.

At the Allee gate, Muriel looked at the sky and then
at her watch. "I think," she said, "that Tante Anna
will be waiting tea for us. Mr. Stanford and I would
better take the short cut home. Good night, all.
Remember, Arna, at nine o'clock."

Muriel's spirits rose as they entered the romantic
gloom of the park. Stanford became moody, almost silent. Instinctively she knew the burden of
his mind, and with a woman's last vanishing instinct
of self-protection she plied him between hope and despair, between ecstasy and misery, and between decision and afterthought, until she saw this master
singer, this leader of men, trembling, all but suppliant
before her.

"Why do you not speak?" said her eyes.

"How can you think of such a thing?" contra-
dicted her eyes, and all the while the tenderness of
her nature seemed to envelope him like a magic charm
to ward off any pain or evil which others might in-
flict.

So, held in check by Muriel's subtle counterplay,

Stanford reached the old mansion with the dream of his heart unspoken.

Rivington came with Arna and Mrs. Trebor before they rose from supper; and following them Count von Hohenfels and his three comrades of the Erholung's party. Arna, with her violin, received the homage due to a goddess; when, at last, she lowered her bow after playing an obligato for Schubert's Serenade, eleven strokes from the castle tower floated in from the garden door to call the end of another Weimar day.

Historic Weimar! What music—what great works have been your heritage since Goethe and Schiller first gave you immortality! What is your future? Where the genius to perpetuate traditional glory? Is it even now at your threshold, or will generations unborn still ask—where? Glory like yours is not for barter. Fate alone controls it.

Stanford was left talking with the young officers at the street door.

Muriel could hear the voices as she waited for him at the drawing-room window. With her chin on her folded arms she was studying the stars and humming softly, "Du meine Seele, du mein Herzen," unmindful of the conversation. "Words are sacrilege in such a silence," she mused again, as the clank of sword and spur grew faint in the street and ascending steps came nearer; "only not his—they are music—like his song."

"Where is Tante Anna?" Muriel leaned back in her chair.

"Coming!" responded a voice without, and footsteps died in the gallery. Stanford entered lightly, and pushing an ottoman towards the window, placed himself at her feet. "What a glorious sky," he whispered.

"Yes," said Muriel, following the direction of his gaze.

Tante Anna did not return, the city had gone to sleep, and they were alone in the intoxicating silence of the night.

"How divinely Arna plays," murmured Muriel at last, with an echo of bewitching melody in her voice.

Stanford turned quickly. Though both were deep in shadow, Muriel felt the intensity of his eyes. "No more so than you," he remarked gently.

"That," she said impulsively, "that is the first compliment you have ever paid my music."

"Don't you know why?"

"No."

"It is because I care so much more for you—for you yourself," he repeated, with a passionate throb in his voice, "That—that—the music—is quite another thing! You don't mind my telling you, do you?" he asked eagerly, seeing that she had drawn back in her chair.

"No," said Muriel, in an easy tone, prolonging the word as if under consideration. "No, why should I?"

"I hoped you would not," he said, rather gravely, "for I am going to ask still more of you—that—you will never send me away from you—never—so long as we, both of us, live!"

"I never have done that," she said, very gently. "Would you?"

Muriel listened to the distant rumble of wheels. Her watch seemed racing with her heart. She noticed that a moth fluttering to death in the lamp sent shadows flickering on the patch of light from the corridor. "I don't know," she said with effort, and took hold of the arms of her chair.

"Could you, knowing that I am miserably unhappy away from you—that you are life itself to me?"

Muriel could not withstand the loving entreaty of that voice; his eyes seemed piercing her heart; she felt as if she should suffocate unless she escaped the spell of his influence.

"We have known each other so short a time," she answered evasively.

"And I have waited a lifetime for you. Will you keep me waiting now?"   ·

"Waiting?"

"To be my wife—my better self."

"And my heart for thee is yearning," sang the stars. "Bid it, love, be still. Bid it, love, be still." Why did the night, the stars, and the sapphire sky waft back those inspired words? Why did all Nature lend him aid, but to fulfill the decree of the inevitable? How, then, could she resist his pleading? How withhold the love which was his by divine right and hallowed by every throb of her heart. "I know, I know," cried her Mentor, "but not quite yet. That which is lightly won is lightly valued. Raise objections. There are none," reflected Muriel in consternation. "It was meant to be from the beginning." "Remember your ardor, then, in planning his diversions." "Certainly!"

Muriel straightened up with maidenly modesty.

He saw the movement, and he brought his eyes nearer that she might read there the love which his lips expressed in words so tender that she dared not longer look and listen.

"Remember!" spoke her Mentor.

"You haven't a better friend living," she said gently at last, when all thought of argument failed her. "But —again she looked to the night for strength; a breath of new-mown hay touched her face; the meadows were white in the moonlight, and a voice was whispering: "God forever bless and keep her!"

The horror of her dream suddenly chilled her.

"Let me think about it," she said at last, calmly. "Marriage is too serious to arrange hastily. When I give my hand I give my life and all that it holds."

"I know it," interposed Stanford in such worshipful tones that Muriel faltered and turned away.

"I cannot say Yes," she said, "and leaving every other consideration out of the question I have too high a regard for you to say No without reflection. Give me time to think."

Again he interrupted with gentle pleading.

"Give me time to think," said Muriel, with unswerving decision, but so gently that Tante Anna, coming through the vestibule, could not hear voices. "I will tell you on Saturday night. Let us not refer to it in the mean time."

CHAPTER XXIX.

During his two days' probation, Tante Anna took no apparent notice of Stanford's altered manner. Gretchen was not supposed to see it, but to Muriel there was a touching appeal in the atmosphere of indefinable tenderness which seemed to hover about him.

The security of his promise to not renew his suit before the following evening was Muriel's sole strength in the intoxication of that idyllic first day. The clock in the castle tower chimed the echoes of her heart's song, and only the waning light told of fleeting time as they lingered in the summer-house, after coffee, while Tante Anna slumbered over her embroidery.

"Dear Helene!" exclaimed Muriel, with new sweetness in her voice. "It's her birthday, C——!"

"Almost—but not quite!" Tante Anna's eyes, sparkling, responded to her frightened glance.

"It would have ruined everything had I said Carl then!" reflected Muriel, her cheeks flaming. Stanford looked supremely happy and suggested verbal congratulations at once.

"And I haven't ordered even a flower!" she said, thinking of the gifts forgotten in her room.

"We will get some at the widow's on our way," observed Stanford, "for I did not mean to forget Helene, either."

"Nor Anna, dear Carl," interposed Frau von Ber-witz, as Muriel turned self-consciously towards the garden in memory of the cause of their forgetfulness. "You will find all Helene's presents duplicated, for no one thinks of giving to one and not the other. If an ornament, it would never be worn; for they dress alike, talk alike, and do everything alike."

"Two birthdays a year," remarked Stanford, with an amused expression. "That is racing with history."

"Arna's birthday falls on St. Valentine's day," said Frau von Berwitz, rising to go with them to the house.

"That keeps them young. Anna and Helene will never grow old if they each live to be a hundred," observed Muriel. "It's the way their hearts are made." "Why should I mention hearts," she reflected, going in advance to escape Stanford's eyes. "I shall be wearing mine on my sleeve next thing!" And Muriel fancied she had donned her mask.

At the artistic home in Schwannseestrasse, gifts from two continents were exhibited; one gift having special prominence, for it was accompanied by con-gratulations in the Master's characteristic hand. His disciples indeed crowded the music-room where Anna and Ivan were playing his Fourteenth Hun-garian Rhapsody. Flowers galore freighted the air with perfume, and, in the front row of chairs, the sisters Stahr, like Saint Cecilias, gazed devoutly upon the faces of the two artists.

Pressed to end the impromptu programme, Stan-ford sang Beethoven's "Adelaide" in a way to make

Muriel's fingers tremble on the keyboard. Then, as Ivan was declaring it a "revelation," Stanford lent his glorious voice to the chorus "Hoch soll sie leben," sung to a final clicking of glasses with "Das Geburtstagskind."

"You missed the afternoon," said Ivan to Muriel and Stanford, when only the comrades of the Russischer Hof remained with the Fräulein Stahr. "You must spend the evening with us. We'll sup somewhere."

"Tiefurt!" cried the chorus.

"Not the castle," remonstrated Ivan. "Nothing but clabber and eggs. I prefer beer and something to eat."

"The Rosenkranz," cried one, with a romantic preference for the verdant terrace and the ceaseless roar of the mill-dam.

"Better beer at the Felsenkeller," observed Ivan, with authority.

They stopped at the old mansion for Frau von Berwitz. Again "Das Geburtstagkind" was toasted, and then they sauntered, pairwise, out the grand old Chaussee to the vineclad hillside, where the arbored garden of the Felsenkeller gave vistas of lowland and park. Another birthday party, overflowing the house, taxed the resources of the modest hostelry.

"Hunger makes the best soldiers," observed Ivan, leading a raid on the kitchen.

Hands destined to command by their magic the homage of an entire musical world ere another anniversary of Helene's birth, prepared the feast. Then

"Das Geburtstagkind" rose into prominence as night closed round the illuminated board.   During a series of toasts Moritz digressed to extol Ivan's generalship and to predict an equally brilliant future for him as "head waiter," did he choose to end his planetary career in the art-world.   Later the infectious pleasure of Terpsichorean revellers indoors drew straggling devotees from the table to the confines of the ball-room, and, eventually, there came an invitation from the host for the Lisztianer to join the party.

In and out of the circle of waltzers flew Anna's and Helene's many ribbons, and the flowing locks, loose neckerchiefs and velvet jackets of the ultra artists; but just as the recruits were breathing the inspiration of the dance, the pianist succumbed to fatigue.

"Sapprement!" ejaculated Ilmstedt in annoyance. "Is our fun to be spoiled by that woman?"

"Not in the least," said Moritz good-naturedly, replacing her at the rickety instrument.

Again the ribbons, artistic locks and velvet jackets floated in mazy grace; now faster, now slower; then whirling till onlookers grew dizzy watching the crowd spin by.

"It is called 'rubato' in music," observed Muriel, as she and Stanford halted for breath.   "Inability to keep time," growled Ilmstedt, as his compatriot, a disciple of Brahms, whom he opposed, took such liberties with the tempo that the bravest dancer left the floor.

"There never was one of a genuinely artistic temperament who could play for dancing," said Muriel in defence of her colleague.

"Indeed, Fräulein!" exclaimed Ivan in mock 'indignation. "See you, now, what a machine I can be." Waving Moritz to the dancers he began a wild galop.

"The Tartar blood in him," remarked Moritz, as he and Helene gave up a breathless flight. "He fancies himself on the Steppes—taking a new one at each bound."

Hearing the laughter, the Russian glanced at the empty floor. With a fascinating obeisance to the pianist, he acknowledged his defeat by offering his arm and returning her to the office in which her sense of rhythm was more effective than his superior art.

The dance, the long, happy return over the hard, white Chaussee, the last tender good-nights were ended, and Muriel was once more alone with the night—her night, which she loved more than day in Weimar, where it spoke in poetic measure to heart and mind. Life, indeed, had become nothing less than a poem—a caress of the senses.

Only one sad minor strain varied the calm music of her thoughts. Again the heavy scent of flowers, the moonlight silvering the tree-tops and whitening the meadows; again pale in the gloom beyond the lindens, a maiden standing before a kneeling figure. "Farewell; God forever bless and keep her," sounded through the night-silences. And the clock that chimed the midnight tolled the knell of a heart as fond as her own.

CHAPTER XXX.

Another day in dreamland. Another lesson at the Royal Gardens, and Muriel was in the longest twilight of her life.

Meister had asked her to remain with Arna and Stanford for a rubber at whist.

Whist! Music was fit accompaniment for her reveries, but whist! Whist meant concentration of mind.

Impossible!

Meister selected card players as he did pianists. Heaven protect the one who made a false play!

Muriel assorted her cards with infinite pains. "Dry, stupid game," she reflected, as she spread them fanshaped. "Why didn't he ask Carl to sing?"

> Oh, du entrissne mir und meinem Kusse
> Sei mir gegrüsst, sei mir geküsst.

Ah, that divine voice, that heavenly strain! He had first sung it for her here—in this room, and how jealous she had become of Meister!

Muriel smiled absently at her cards.

"Your lead, Miss Träumerei," said Ivan, looking over her shoulder at the Master's, her partner's, face. The latter laughed spasmodically, for he loved the boy's genial, if fiery, nature.

Muriel begged pardon and threw down a club. Meister played the ace, and Stanford, casting the deuce of hearts, put out his hand to claim the cards.

"No—No!" said Muriel, stopping him. "Meister took that trick."

"Hearts are trumps, Fräulein Muriel," said Stanford quietly. "I shuffled for this game."

Divining the double import of the retort, the Meister laid down his cards and removed his spectacles in order to laugh with abandon.

"Second hand low; third hand high," Muriel constantly admonished herself in fear of a misstep, and then it came again her time to lead. "Hearts are trumps, Fräulein Muriel; I shuffled for this game," was all she could recall. "What did he trump?" she reflected in confusion. Meister looked at her across the board. Down went the king of clubs at a venture. Arna and Meister smiled faintly as they played, and then Stanford laid down a trump.

"Hearts are trumps, Fräulein Muriel; I shuffled for this game," flashed through her mind. "Ah! she gasped, and put out her hand as if to recall the cards.

"Too late," said Stanford, sweeping them in.

"A desired opponent," observed the Master, looking helplessly at her. "Really, a desired opponent!" and he delayed them long enough to hear a fitting anecdote.

"Now we resume with equal chances, 'Desired Opponent'; I have confused everybody," he said, taking up his cards and adjusting his spectacles.

Arna insisted upon his telling anecdotes after the last trick was decided, adding that he was taking unfair advantage of his opponents by this digression, which bit of pleasantry amused the Master to the ex-

tent of another five minutes, and they played their
hands out as best they could.

Meister's capital spirits were further improved by a
few puffs at his favorite cigar, which Mrs. Trebor had
kept lighted on a broad, flat shell of historic renown.

"Meister," said Ivan, "Fräulein Bittergrass——"

"The celebrated bas bleu!" interposed the Master
impressively.

"——and sister were below as I came in for the lesson."

"Mischka did his duty, I presume?" said the Master
grimly.

"Their faces indicated as much," observed Ivan
drily. In fact, I fear that their disappointment lay
mainly in losing the opportunity of illustrating to you
their dress reform."

The Master elevated his eyebrows.

"They shimmered in black alpaca and a sort of
enameled armor—a travesty in collars and cuffs."

The Master gave a prolonged laugh. "They are,
nevertheless, worthy women—worthy women," he as-
serted, with a will to be just, "but——" An eloquent
gesture supplied the idea. "Some years ago I attended the National Musical Festival at ————.
One evening a choral work of mine occupied the first
half of the programme. During the ensuing pause
a number of acquaintances came to my box to exchange a word with me, and amongst them Fräulein
Bittergrass and sister and the great Pumpernickel!"
Giving a mock reverence at this mention of an unloved pupil, whose nickname had outlived his patro-

nymic in Weimar, he continued: "Every one left but this picturesque trio. I hadn't asked them to stay. I didn't want to ask them to go. However, they made themselves comfortable in the front chairs. Instantly every lorgnette in the house was levelled at them. They leaned their elbows on the cushioned railing and faced the audience without flinching. The worst of it was they wore their red Garibaldis. Some misguided person brought them as presents from Rome twenty-five years before, and the sisters had never discarded them."

"Nah! 'Desired Opponent,' it is our chance," said Meister, glancing at his cards.

How the music coursed through her memory as she half listened to their badinage:

Das Meer erglänzte weit hinaus
Im letzten Abendscheine,
Wir sassen am einsamen Fischerhaus,
Wir sassen stumm und alleine.

It was her heart singing—singing because it could not keep still. They could not hear it. No! it sang in her own world—her own dear world of the ideal—the songs he had made her love! None could see; none could know; and her heart went singing:

Der Nebel stieg, das Wasser schwoll,
Die Möwe flog hin und wieder,
Ausdeinen Augen liebevoll
Fielen die Thränen nieder.

Something like a mist came between her eyes and the cards. The trump on the table before her was blurred red, she observed, as Arna led off. "I shuffled for this game," occurred to her. "Hearts are again trumps, Herr Carl!" The reflection interrupted the song, but the music floated on softly with her thoughts.

"Oh dear," said Muriel, leaning over the table to see the cards. "What are they?"

Meister has another pair of spectacles on the writing desk," remarked Ivan in his mellow voice. "Shall I fetch them for you?"

"No, thanks," responded Muriel, "but you may lower that blind a trifle, if you will. The light is right in my eyes." "Dear Ivan," she reflected, "What a good, big-hearted boy he is—if he did kick over the camera on Rivington's account; but we baffled him after all." She was thinking of the group as they appeared out on the carpet of daisies. "I would try my fortune with one of them, if I had one."

"But why? Don't I know already that he loves me?"

"Ich möchte ziehen in die Welt hinaus: hinaus in die weite Welt, wenn all so grün——" The music and the cards mingled in hopeless confusion.

Leise flehen meine Lieder
Durch die Nacht zu dir,

hummed Ivan softly.

Muriel turned in surprise.

"What is it?" said the Master, thinking he had missed something.

"I was serenading the Fräulein," said the boy good-naturedly.

"Did you think me asleep?" said Muriel.

"No," replied Ivan; "I simply wished to see if I had caught the theme of your latest rhapsody."

"Meditation," interposed Arna, by way of correction.

"No—rhapsody," maintained Ivan. "I never say 'meditation' since hearing what a price Gounod paid for his. The Master laid down his cards in anticipation of a droll story.

"Heinrich Urban told me about it last spring in Berlin," continued Ivan. "A compatriot, a piano student, who occupied a room above Gounod's apartment in Paris, was given to practice one day the first prelude from Bach's 'Well-Tempered Clavichord.' He began at nine in the morning, and was still playing it at five o'clock in the afternoon, when Gounod, who was in a creative mood, and had gone vainly from room to room in trying to write, snatched up his hat in a rage and rushed from the house. The faster Gounod walked the more the prelude haunted him. Suddenly above its droning rose a melody of such divine beauty that as it developed in his brain it sounded like a voice from Heaven. Hastening home he recorded it above its accompaniment, the prelude, and to-day singers know it as the 'Ave Maria' and violinists as the 'Meditation' of Gounod."

"And now, Miss Träumerei," said the Russian, with an engaging obeisance, "will you give us your rhapsody?"

"Ivan! Ivan!" observed the Master, with smiling reproof. "Leave Miss Muriel alone, or I shall come to her defence."

"I think, Meister, the severest penalty would be to make him play out my hand," and Muriel insisted that Ivan should take her place. "I am too dull to play to-day," she whispered to Meister, as she came around to sit by Mrs. Trebor. "I'll retrieve my reputation as a card player next time. I don't wish to deprive Mr. Rivington of his pet pseudonym."

"Oh, he is no longer the 'Desired Opponent,'" exclaimed the Master, turning to tap the shoulder of her compatriot, who was watching his play from the other side. "He has become an artist—under tuition!"

It came the Master's turn to deal. Then the first hand round disclosed the ace, deuce, trey and four of diamonds on the table.

"Wait!" cried Ivan, pointing at the cards. "Tradition says: 'Kiss the dealer!' Is it true, Meister, that Beethoven came upon the platform at your first concert in Vienna and kissed you upon the forehead?"

"Certainly," said the Master, in surprise. "I remember it well."

"Which was the spot?" inquired the Russian, moving as if to rise.

"Please don't tell, Meister," interposed Muriel, with sudden animation, "unless you wish it to become as celebrated an osculatory Mecca as St. Peter's toe at Rome!"

It had been a typical midsummer day, but it was very pleasant in the street as they came through town together at eight o'clock. The groups on the corners and in doorways eyed admiringly the "Lisztianer," and especially the idol of the public, sweet Arna Trebor. Since the day that Liszt's presence had made Weimar the home of pianists, the inhabitants, in according that guild their curious attention, paid also to the Master their richest homage for maintaining the reputation for great learning which Goethe and Schiller had first given the old capital.

For once in her life Muriel was glad to part with the Lisztianer. Just now they were superfluous, and as for the townspeople, their curiosity always offended her.

It seemed an interminable time since she and Stanford left Tante Anna in the summer-house, for each delay postponed the hour for which they both waited with beating hearts. The clock in the castle tower chimed eight as they crossed the silent court and entered the garden.

"Guests!" exclaimed Stanford with a shadow of displeasure in his voice as they neared the summer-house. "Women and a uniform!"

"Count von Hohenfels," said Muriel, "and—and— Fräulein Panzer!"

"Yes, my dear, 'tis I," exclaimed the little Canary Bird, springing forward to meet them. I have run over from Berka for the night, and Anna insisted that Fritz and I should remain for tea."

There was music after supper. Hohenfels played —though he carefully avoided improvisations—and Stanford sang as if his life hung upon the art of song.

With what different emotions Muriel listened to the last tender appeal of the serenade:

And my heart for thee is yearning,
Bid it, love, be still ; bid it, love, be still!

He had sung it; he had spoken it, and again sung it before claiming his answer. Now he only waited the departure of the guests. They were gone. Tante Anna stood with them on the lower terrace—and, then, she too was gone.

The night was all their own for a brief moment. Music floated in from the distance. The garden was all moonlight and shadow—shadow and moonlight, from the summer-house to where the vine-grown gable cut the deep-toned sky. The perfume of flowers bore enchantment in its breath. Words would not come in that intoxicating silence.

Muriel turned her face to the stars. The earth had vanished in darkness, and heaven was theirs! No! not "theirs"—her's—for he was waiting silently at her side until she bade him follow. Muriel's heart beat madly. What should she say? How should she say it? Why did he not help her? Yet how? Had he not asked the question? Was it not for her to answer?—that night—now—in that moment? Where were the finely-wrought phrases to make difficult his way? Where the courage to argue a point which her heart had long since yielded? Where the thought to foster speech?

This was their world—life suspended and silence between them? What was he thinking? Why did he not stir? Was it really he, or was it a dream? A dream? "No!" cried her bounding heart. "He is waiting for me! Look!"

Ah, that look! It held his life! Resolutions were forgotten! Their world—the garden—was moonlight and shadow; the air, the perfume of flowers; and time had gone to sleep.

CHAPTER XXXI.

Frau von Berwitz, in her best morning cap, was as non-committal as Hans in a fit of stubbornness. Gretchen watched her dress the breakfast table in the "parade" silver and china and the choicest flowers from the garden, with a white boutonnière on one plate and a big white bouquet on another. Eight chimes from the castle tower pealed out like wedding bells as Muriel and Stanford, returning from their walk over the hills, came into the central aisle.

Frau von Berwitz hastened forward to embrace and kiss them both. Gretchen wrung her hands in transport, and made a dash for the court.

"Frau Schulze—Frau Schulze!" she gasped with each bound up the spiral stairway. "It's done! It's done! Just take a peep into the garden, and don't tell a soul!"

The ceiling and floor of the old gallery danced congratulation as she bounced toward the kitchen where the tea-kettle sang and rocked, and even her heavy soles struck music from the paving-stone when she started back with her bounteous tray.

Gretchen stopped nervously at the garden threshold. Enter? Meet their eyes? Never! She would surely laugh—or cry! Which—which? The china on the tray began to rattle; she leaned against the wall for support; the precious burden seemed going from her grasp—followed by all her savings—and retarding the union with her beloved Hans.

Gretchen recovered herself and entered the garden with the utmost intrepidity, just in time to hear the Fräulein call the American "Carl." The Fräulein blushed rosy red and looked so pretty that Gretchen thought the American quite right to look his happiness. After breakfast her mistress told her that they would be married in September, but that she must not tell even Hans for the present. Only Herr Doctor Liszt should know it, and the young couple were going to the Royal Gardens for his blessing at noon.

This secrecy, she suspected, had something to do with Count von Hohenfels, for he came and made music with the others of an evening as heretofore, and then she would lead Hans to the garden door to hear their American sing with all his heart in his grand voice.

"It went on up—and up," she said one morning to the Fräulein, "until it seemed that it must reach Heaven itself."

Tears filled the Fräulein's eyes as she said: "You are right, Gretchen. I am sure that it has been heard there."

"With the angels' voices," said Gretchen solemnly. "That is why it is so sweet."

To her great astonishment the Fräulein threw her arms about her while she laughed away the tears; and then Gretchen could scarcely credit her senses when the Fräulein told her that she would give her a dower of five hundred marks if she would stay with

Frau von Berwitz until she had fully recovered from the fatigue of the grand wedding in September.

The days passed like a dream. No task seemed labor. The old mansion contained all of heaven that they desired, until one morning—over a week after the betrothal—the postman brought letters while they breakfasted in the garden. Gretchen will never forget the look which came into the American's face, nor the look which came into all their faces when he told them that his return by the next steamer for New York was imperative; that it concerned the business which had brought him over, and that he would have to take the one o'clock train in order to catch the Bremen boat next day.

The Fräulein was the quietest of them all. She only grew white and said: "It is your duty, Carl. Go—and return as quickly as possible, or—Tante Anna and I will come to you."

"Indeed we will, my child," said the mistress gravely. "But I hope it may not be necessary."

Then they all became cheerful, but in such a way that Gretchen had to slip into the court to cry, out of sorrow for them. After an early dinner she packed them safely into a carriage and returned to the house to avoid seeing him drive away, for it was such bad luck!

The Fräulein meant to be very brave. She resumed her practicing; she took long walks alone, and returned to her gay circle of an evening. But Gretchen saw her growing paler and more nervous every day. What long, weary days they were, too, waiting—waiting—waiting for the cable to announce his safe arrival.

"In seven days we'll hear from him—in six days— in five days—in four days,"the Fräulein continued to say each morning at breakfast; and once Gretchen heard her refer to a dreadful dream she had had, and to her terror of the ocean. But when she began to cry softly Frau von Berwitz pretended to be angry with her for courting such a foolish superstition, and the Fräulein dried her eyes.

"They must have been sighted off Fire Island last night," she said another morning at breakfast. "If they catch the tide and get over the bar, they will be landing about our dinner hour."

"In event of a good voyage," said Frau von Berwitz; "you must allow for delay."

"Even then we ought to get word by midnight, at latest," replied the Fräulein.

Midnight came—one o'clock—and then Frau von Berwitz said that waiting wouldn't work the cable for them. But the Fräulein did not sleep all night, and after breakfast she went to the railway station to investigate the delay.

Another night of sleepless waiting, and the Fräulein wired the steamship company at Bremen for news. The boat had not been reported from New York.

A third night—none in the house slept. Morning was as dark as the shadow over their hearts. Rain began to fall before daylight and continued throughout the early morning. The Fräulein did not even go to her music-room, but sat in a drawing-room window with her big, sad eyes fixed upon the street, watching for the messenger who did not come.

Frau von Berwitz had left her alone a few moments as Gretchen came into the dining-room to tend the geraniums. In bending over the sill Gretchen noticed Frau Schwartz cross the street and stop under the window where the Fräulein sat. The rain had ceased. In her hand Frau Schwartz held an open paper.

"Ach, Fräulein," said the woman, looking up, "everybody is so sorry to hear it, for he was such a handsome, grand young man."

"What do you mean?" said the Fräulein in a frightened voice.

"The young American."

"Which young American?"

"The one who just went away from here—from Frau von Berwitz's."

"What are you talking about?" said the Fräulein slowly and in a hard voice which had lost all its sweetness. "What do you know about the young American who has been here?"

"Only what the morning paper says," answered the woman, shrinking back.

Then as the Fräulein went on, Gretchen remembered having seen the daily paper lying untouched in the entry.

"Well, what does it say?" Her tone was so dull and so cold that Gretchen fairly shivered with fright.

"Why, it says," whined Frau Schwartz, evidently

enchanted to be the bearer of the news "how his boat was run into by another boat, and how he was drowned, with everybody else on board."

There was a terrible silence. Gretchen stood an instant as if petrified, and then the horror of it all swept over her. She never knew what prompted it, but a mighty force lifted her arm and sent the bucket of water which she was holding straight at Frau Schwartz's head. There was a frightful scream from the street, and then Gretchen heard a heavy fall in the next room.

"Ach, the poor Fräulein!"

She and her mistress, who had been in the entry, saw her at the same moment, as she lay like one dead upon the floor.

"Oh, Gretchen," moaned Frau von Berwitz, "her head has struck the chair."

"Gretchen's heart stood still. She knew that something terrible had happened, and what were they to do?

"Run," she called to the unhappy woman in the street, "run for the doctor, for you have killed her, too!"

They placed her on the sofa and tried vainly to restore her to consciousness. Neither spoke of the awful fate of their beloved American, but Frau von Berwitz was as white as the poor young Fräulein herself.

Gretchen felt a sob rising in her throat as the minutes dragged by like hours and the doctor did not come.

"I'll go too," she said to her mistress, and darted out of the room.

The doctor was on the stairway, and behind him a messenger with a telegram. Gretchen motioned the doctor to open the door, and then, with a boldness which it makes her blush now to recall, she opened the Fräulein's telegram. Fortunately it was in German:

"Arrived—well. Delayed by accident to machinery. Carl."

When she whispered the message to her mistress, she looked down at the Fräulein and began to cry. But smiles quickly broke through her tears, for the Fräulein moved and opened her eyes.

"Safe! Safe! " exclaimed Frau von Berwitz, fearing to say more, but holding aloft the telegram.

The Fräulein didn't seem to understand at first, and then she smiled a very little before closing her eyes again.

After a while, when she could speak a few words, she asked what had happened to her, and Frau von Berwitz, seeing that she had forgotten, said: "A little dizziness; nothing more. Carl is safe on land, so now don't talk any more, for the doctor wishes you to keep still until you are stronger."

Seeing that the Fräulein was in no danger, though the doctor said that the shock, when she was already so unnerved by over-practice, would probably confine . her to the house for a time, Frau von Berwitz began to grow very angry with Frau Schwartz, for the morning paper had simply repeated the arrival of a Liverpool boat which, during a fog, had collided near mid-ocean, with a smaller vessel, which was supposed to have gone down with all on board, as no traces of it could be found when they reversed the engines.

The florist's widow had said to a customer: "I hope it was not the boat by which the young American sailed."

The customer told a friend that the young American was supposed to have been on the lost boat; the friend told Frau Schwartz that the young American had foundered with the vessel, and Frau Schwartz had spent the morning carrying the news to the neighbors.

This information was returned by Frau Schulze who had been sent out to investigate the false report.

For one week it seemed to Gretchen that she did little else than answer the jangle of the old bell in the court. Count von Hohenfels and Mr. Rivington came twice a day, and Herr Doctor Liszt sent each morning to inquire about the Fräulein, until she was able to drive out with Frau von Berwitz. Then, one afternoon, the Meister himself and everybody else came to say good-bye to the Fräulein, who was so much affected thereby that Frau von Berwitz said that all she could do now was to get her out of Weimar—that Swiss mountain air would do the rest.

The Fräulein felt so sad at leaving that she would let no one but Gretchen see them off the next morning; and when the train began to move Gretchen turned about and ran into the station, for she remembered that it was "such bad luck to watch any one out of sight."

How lonely the old mansion seemed, with its music, its gay young life, and its mistress gone!

"I feel as if I could water the flowers with my tears," she had said to Frau Schulze, after closing the house for its long sleep—but then, Hans came in the evening.

Ah, Gretchen, what a fickle-hearted girl you were, laughing with the children and singing to yourself all next morning in the garden, as if you had never known the pangs of regret! And the flowers went on blooming, and the fruit ripened, and the days grew shorter, and then Gretchen heard that Herr Doctor Liszt and the last of the Lisztianer had departed for the season.

"Our Fräulein will not return now," she said sadly, to Frau Schulze; "and after you and I had planned everything for such a grand wedding, too!"

Even then, had Gretchen known it, wedding bells were ringing for the Fräulein and her handsome young countryman in the distant city of Geneva.

It was a quiet wedding, Frau von Berwitz wrote her; but such a happy one that she would start north next day with a light heart, especially as the young couple would pass a week with her in Weimar after a honeymoon trip in Italy; "and," she added, "Mrs. Stanford bids me say that she will hand you your dower then, so that you may arrange for your marriage with Hans as soon after as I can fill your place."

"Heigho, Gretchen!" sang her heart, and "Heigho, Gretchen and Hans!" sang the stars that night as they winked at the shadows in the great archway.

CHAPTER XXXII.

Have you seen Lucerne by night? Have you leaned on the parapet of the handsome modern quay and counted pebbles in the clear depths of the emerald lake—then cast your eye over a placid surface reflecting countless stars of the firmament, to that distant and awful shadow thrown by the black, forbidding wall of solid rock beyond, on whose stupendous heights twinkle, like a royal diadem, the far-away lights of a great hotel; and still higher, above an intervening width of dark vegetation, to where the rising moon imparts a silvery hue to broad fields, rivulets, islands, and peaks of snow amidst vast rocky plateaus and sky-piercing crags? And have you finally turned to those two mighty sentinels on the near right and distant left—Pilatus flaming from its towering summit a powerful crimson light like the beacon of a universe, and Rigi bearing aloft a brilliant solitaire, the composite gleam from the windows of the enormous caravansary on the Kulm?

It is such a night at Lucerne. The band on the piazza of the Schweizerhof has just gone; promenaders quickly leave the Allee on the quay as the lights of the hotel wink out one by one, until scattered groups only remain, softly conversing in the tongues of every civilized country, or awed to silence by the sublimity of the scene.

From an incoming excursion steamer float distant peals of laughter and music.

The great throbbing, glittering mass sweeps majestically on to the wharf below, out of sight, out of hearing, whilst a shimmering silver trail ruffles the peaceful waters and sends them lapping against the stone quay.

Out on the lake a single voice trolls out a gay boating song, faintly at first, but quite distinctly as the bark nears the shore. A lady and gentleman in the shadow of a tree rise in silence from a settle on the promenade, and cross, arm in arm, to the stone wall.

She is rather below medium height, a trim, well-dressed figure, as far as we can see. She lifts her face in the moonlight. It is that of a stranger—a sweet face, indeed, and just now full of passionate love as she turns a pair of dark, intense eyes upon him. Their heads are near, and he suddenly looks around as she says softly in German: "He has stopped. It was so beautiful!"

"Why—is it possible! Let us look more sharply. Yes, it is he; but in citizen's dress, for officers, you know, always doff regimentals when on a furlough. Listen," he whispers, turning his head to the lake.

The strumming of a guitar rises from the float of gondolas which dot the mirror-like waters, and, save for the low music of the oars, move silently and mysteriously about like great white swans in the moonlight. .

"It is Schubert's 'Serenade,'" he whispers, intent upon the final chords of a brief prelude.

Why does he start and peer curiously out over the waters as the tenor voice we have just heard sings:

Leise flehen meine Lieder
Durch die Nacht zu dir,
In den stillen Hain hernieder
Liebchen komm zu mir.

The eloquent eyes at his side look up questioningly, but no word of his interrupts the song. Dark forms emerge noiselessly from the leafy shadows of the promenade and assume individuality in the pale light of the quay. The parapet has become peopled as by magic.

A hundred heads bend low to catch the clearly-articulated words rising in sweetest melody from the waters. Now the boatmen, too, rest on their oars. Not a ripple is heard. Even the mountains seem listening to that marvellous voice as it soars and falls in divinest cadence, then floats softly, reluctantly into space.

A boat glides out and makes for the landing-steps near which the young lovers are standing.

The Count eyes it sharply.

"Come, Ottilie," he said; "here are some old friends of mine. We will assist them ashore."

He leaves her on the level and descends to meet the approaching gondola. The occupants look up inquiringly as he bends to steady their boat.

"Count von Hohenfels!" they exclaim in chorus, as Stanford extends one hand and drags his guitar after him with the other. Muriel, vivacious and girlish in her dainty summer apparel, follows, looking the personification of health and happiness; and then good Frau von Berwitz, apparently not a day older than when we last saw her in Weimar, steps ashore and adds her voice to the general hum.

The little lady on the quay eyes them with interest as they ascend, oblivious to her presence. Then the · Count introduces her as "My wife,.' and explains: "We were married just a fortnight ago in Silesia."

"Your cousin?" inquires Frau von Berwitz, with a sudden look of understanding.

"Yes," responds Hohenfels, as they overwhelm him and his bride with congratulations.

"Do you know," begins Frau von Berwitz, while they move towards the hotel, "I had quite lost account of you since your transfer to Eisenach."

"I sent you announcements of our betrothal and marriage," exclaims the Count, in quick apology.

"Which, probably, we shall receive here," interposes Frau von Berwitz, taking his arm. "Our letters have gone touring, for we left New York two weeks earlier than originally planned, and omitted Weimar altogether in coming here."

"You have been away long—a long time."

"Fourteen months," exclaims Frau von Berwitz. "And it is three years since Muriel and Stanford have seen Weimar."

"Have you taken out naturalization papers?" asks the Count jestingly.

"Not yet," laughs the matron; "but I am becoming very American in following Carl's interests in legal and public affairs generally; and now that he has been nominated for Congress, I shall probably be waving the American flag until election day."

"Oh, he. is sure to win," she continues, seeing his look of inquiry. "The nomination was forced upon him. But Muriel and I insisted upon a run over here for a change and a breath of Swiss air before opening the campaign. She makes him an ideal wife," she adds, with a satisfied nod at Muriel. "She has become indispensable to his public career, and they are so happy in their home life and social circle. They fairly idolize each other, and—— You must forgive me," said Frau von Berwitz, abruptly changing her tone, "but you know I brought him up almost from infancy, and they are like own children to me. Now tell me about your mother. I only know that Clara Panzer is passing the summer with her. She was, of course, rejoiced at your marriage?"

"Decidedly!"

"And you, too?"

He returns smile for smile ,and she asks: "Is she musical?"

"Sings like an angel."

"I am heartily glad for you. What—the hotel so soon? Well, good-night. We shall have a gay reunion in Lucerne," added Frau von Berwitz, extending her hand.

A keen observer would have noted a change in his face. Were there still regrets? Was not the fire even yet extinguished?

"A short one, I fear," he says, with hesitation, "for we leave for Interlaken to-morrow afternoon."

The Countess glances at him in surprise, but she only smiles response to the tender, almost appealing, expression of his eyes.

"Oh, too bad!" exclaims Frau von Berwitz. "We have just arrived from there. Ah, well; you will both visit me in Weimar in the autumn. But, in the morning, you must see our little one. He calls me 'Gra'-mama.'"

"With an English accent, too," remarked Stanford.

"I sometimes think," observes Muriel to the Countess, "that he loves Tante Anna better than he does me." And taking Carl's arm, she says: "I only fear that she will spoil him, as she has his father."

"I shall certainly try it," affirms Frau von Berwitz. "Now, good-night, my dears. We will let young Francis speak for himself in the morning."

"You see," adds Muriel, her eyes gleaming with unshed tears, "we have named him for the dear Meister."

Come with me again to the Royal Gardens. Pardon me if I accompany you to the door only. I will ring, and place you in charge of my kind old friend Pauline. She will conduct you through the upper rooms, which you know so well, and explain the interesting collection on exhibition there.

One moment, while I whisper: "Give her a good fee if this short and truthful excerpt from the term of her long service here have proven acceptable to you, for many is the favor she has done me in the dear old times. So, now, don't let me detain you. Look well after my friends, Pauline."

Wait! I forgot to say—and this sotto voce—don't ask her about any of our old acquaintances, for she knew them by other names. And I have told you this in confidence, you know! So, I will be here when you come down. Aufwiedersehen!

Listen! The echo of another more distant farewell floats out through vanished years from a rare morning in early autumn when the dear Meister called to me for the last time from the head of the worn stairway: "Aufwiedersehen!"

"Aufwiedersehen!" Ah! that echo has passed into eternity, too, and with it hopes never to be fulfilled. Now, as then, I seat myself on the settle before the house, and the tender memories of happy days crowd on me until I see the old rustic gate through blurred vision, and am glad that no one is near, for sentiment is for solitude only. The heaviest heart should wear a smiling face—it is so often the only comfort we can give to those whose burdens are heavier than our own.

See! This confession has effected its own cure, and I think now with dry eyes of the silent gardens before me.

Where are they of whose going and coming the Allee gate clicked record in the old student days?

The press of two continents gives daily answer.

I myself have seen one, a foreigner, winning ovations in America; another writes of triumphs in Russia; a third is astonishing the entire musical world with his transcendental virtuosity; a fourth is coming to the front in Vienna; a fifth is playing his way to popularity and greatness in Germany; I run face to face with a sixth in the streets of a great city; and, from time to time, kindly New Year's greetings, a few hasty lines, or the marked copy of a journal, sent from an American or foreign capital, bespeak the whereabouts or prosperous careers of others.

Why have they all separated forever? Why this unbroken silence where once the soul of music, living, gave succor and everlasting life to worlds without.

For answer, go to Bayreuth.

From an inscription on a laurel-strewn tomb in the old city cemetery you will glean the following:

Franz Liszt.
Died July 31, 1886.

The dear Meister! Generous to a fault, lovable and loving. His works live in history—his memory in the innermost hearts of his grateful pupils.

Out of all the alluring life which his presence in Weimar fostered, the musicales at the artistic home in Schwanseestrasse alone survive. Yet they too are changed, as the vacant chair before the piano gives mournful evidence, and, with few exceptions, the guests are strange to us.

Were the sisters Stahr not now at the seashore, I would beg permission to introduce you at one of their charming afternoons that you might inspect their rare and growing collection, and hear, possibly, a friend of the Liszt period play. Nor could I wish for better than fascinating Arna Trebor; for it would be, as Bülow once wrote of her, "a feast for the eye as well as the ear."

Ah, it is hard to sever dear old associations, especially such as have made Weimar, for almost four decades, the Mecca of every aspiring young pianist. When the warm days come, and the park and Allee once more don their verdant beauty, you will surely find there acquaintances made in this faithful, if modest sketch, revisiting the scene of treasured memories.

Like them, we will not say "good-bye." I cannot, when I look down upon the little city which contains the happiest reminiscences of my life. See it nestling confidingly in its midsummer sleep, close under the protecting heights of the encircling hills! In that eternal watch we leave it. Therefore, dear Weimar— it is not for long—Aufwiedersehen!